A MARRIAGE TO MURDER FOR

A HOPGOOD HALL MYSTERY

E.V. HUNTER

Boldwood

First published in Great Britain in 2023 by Boldwood Books Ltd.

Copyright © E.V. Hunter, 2023

Cover Photography: Shutterstock, Deposit Photos, iStock and Dreamstime

The moral right of E.V. Hunter to be identified as the author of this work has been asserted in accordance with the Copyright, Designs and Patents Act 1988.

Every effort has been made to obtain the necessary permissions with reference to copyright material, both illustrative and quoted. We apologise for any omissions in this respect and will be pleased to make the appropriate acknowledgements in any future edition.

A CIP catalogue record for this book is available from the British Library.

Paperback ISBN 978-1-80483-585-2

Large Print ISBN 978-1-80483-586-9

Hardback ISBN 978-1-80483-587-6

Ebook ISBN 978-1-80483-583-8

Kindle ISBN 978-1-80483-584-5

Audio CD ISBN 978-1-80483-592-0

MP3 CD ISBN 978-1-80483-591-3

Digital audio download ISBN 978-1-80483-590-6

Boldwood Books Ltd
23 Bowerdean Street
London SW6 3TN
www.boldwoodbooks.com

1

'Another scorching summer. What is going on with the weather? It's not at all British.' Alexi Ellis fanned her face with her hand and retreated further beneath the enveloping parasol on the terrace of Hopgood Hall, the boutique hotel in which she was a minority shareholder. A torpid breeze agitated the hot air like a rampaging hairdryer, sapping her energy. 'Perhaps we should consider installing a swimming pool if this is the way it's going to be in future, what with global warming and all.'

Alexi's friend and co-owner of the hotel, Cheryl Hopgood, held her baby daughter Verity on her knee, jiggling her up and down and making her giggle. 'We are only just about in profit,' she said, striking a note of caution. 'I enjoy not having to juggle the bills, deciding which ones to pay and which ones to ignore, so let's not get too ambitious. Summers as hot as this one may not endure. It's never safe to predict the English weather. Anyway, punters don't come to Lambourn to swim.'

Alexi conceded the point with a nod. 'True enough.'

'Just enjoy the peace and quiet while it lasts, which won't be for long.'

Alexi grinned, aware that the stag party they were preparing to host would indeed be raucous as the groom enjoyed his final few hours of freedom. 'That child will be walking soon.' Alexi grinned at her goddaughter as she tried to wiggle off Cheryl's lap. 'She's as impatient to embrace life as her father.'

'Give her a chance. She's only seven months old.' Cheryl paused. 'You're not serious about the swimming pool, are you?'

Alexi smiled at her feral cat Cosmo, who'd positioned himself beneath the fountain in the courtyard so that water splashed onto his upturned belly. A black cat with piercing hazel eyes flecked with silver, he clearly felt the heat as much as the rest of them. Toby, Cheryl's little terrier, who was half Cosmo's size, was devoted to the cat and had flopped down beside him in the partial shade.

'No, I guess not,' Alexi replied, responding to Cheryl's question. 'But you must admit, we've done well.'

Cheryl nodded with apparent reluctance. 'It's hard for me to think that way when our popularity is partly due to the ghouls who want to visit murder central.'

Cheryl was referring to the murder of a contestant in a celebrity cooking contest that had been held at the hotel during the winter. The show had topped the TV ratings, ensuring a steady flow of clients for Hopgood Hall. Well, that and the fact that Alexi and her partner, private detective Jack Maddox, had been instrumental in solving that crime as well as the murder of a woman in Lambourn a few months prior to that. Since no one could recall the last time that anyone had been murdered in a village dominated by racehorses, it wasn't surprising that the curious were drawn to the area, bursting with conspiracy theories.

Alexi was an investigative journalist, or had been until her position on the *Sentinel* was terminated. In retrospect, it was the best thing that could have happened to her, although at the time, it had seemed like the ultimate betrayal. Her editor in chief and former lover, Patrick Vaughan, had known that redundancies were in the offing but hadn't given her the heads-up. Instead, he'd tried to make her take a lower position. She'd refused and forced a generous settlement out of the paper.

Patrick had continued to pursue her, attempting to lure her back to London. He and Jack hated one another on sight but it was Jack whom Alexi now lived with. Although living with was an exaggeration, she reasoned. Jack's private investigation service had been enhanced by the publicity that the TV murder had created. He seemed to be working away from Lambourn more and more and was often gone for an entire week at a time. Alexi was cool with that. She'd gotten badly burned with Patrick and wasn't about to give her entire heart to another man. Not now.

Perhaps not ever.

Besides, she was busy with her literary commitments: a book on the inside view of the TV murder and various articles that she'd offered to the press. One such article, completed whilst she'd still been in London, was about homeless people. She'd visited a group of them beneath the arches several times, which is where she'd encountered Cosmo. For reasons that Alexi hadn't understood at the time and still didn't, the anti-social cat who disliked and mistrusted people in general had made an exception in her case and decided to adopt her. He was proving to be a very good judge of character. Although he'd mellowed, if he took against someone then Alexi had learned to trust his instincts. He had been banned from the TV set because he tended to attack people's ankles for his own amusement but had also become a star of the show and was another reason why people flocked to the hotel.

'Don't talk of murder in front of my daughter.' Drew Hopgood came up to them, moving silently for such a large man, and kissed both his wife and his little girl.

'It's all anyone around here does talk about,' Cheryl replied. 'But if it keeps the wolf from the door then who am I to complain?'

'This weather is just what we need for the celebrity wedding of the year,' Drew added, flopping down on the chair beside his wife, staring up at a crystal-clear sky and scooping Verity into his arms. He dangled her above his head, making the baby gurgle with laughter. 'Thank you weather gods. Nothing will go wrong this time.'

Drew nodded in the direction of the organised

action coming from the annex where the wedding of Crystabel Hennessey, minor television celebrity, beautiful socialite, online influencer and bridezilla extraordinaire was to be married in a few days' time to Giles Preston-Smythe, son of the most prominent trainer in the valley of the racehorse.

'It had better not!' Cheryl grinned. 'Although even I have been close to strangling Crystabel once or twice. How hard can it be for one woman to make up her mind and stick to it?'

'Fortunately, Marcel doesn't take any of her nonsense,' Alexi replied, referring to the hotel's celebrity chef, a natural on the small screen, who had been originally suspected of murdering the unfortunate contestant who'd met an untimely end. His innocence had only served to increase his popularity, which was another reason why the hotel was doing so well. Marcel's tantrums were usually public and almost always contrived to enhance his reputation as the ultimate temperamental chef. The punters lapped it up. 'She's met her match there.'

'Oh, here's Isobel.' Alexi raised a hand half-heartedly as the wedding planner approached their group. 'What's up this time?'

'Isn't it hot?' Isobel sat on a stool and removed her jacket. Why she was wearing one when the temperature had to be in the high eighties, Alexi was at a loss to understand. 'I've been watching the weather forecast like a hawk. A week to go before the big one and there's talk of the weather breaking: storms in the offing.'

'It wouldn't dare,' Alexi replied.

'You'd think not but I guess the elements aren't afraid of Crystabel.'

'Then they're braver than me,' Drew said with a theatrical shudder.

'We have a massive marquee,' Cheryl pointed out, indicating the structure with a wave of one hand. It was an extension leading off from the annexe, home to a flamboyant floral bower beneath which the couple would exchange their vows. 'No one will get wet and have their hats ruined.'

'Actually, that's what I came to talk to you about.' Isobel paused, looking fraught. 'Crystabel would like the marque to be set up facing the other way. She thinks the photographs will be better with that orientation.'

Drew laughed. 'Impossible. We've already explained that to her, several times. If the weather remains fine and the sides are rolled up, people will want to stroll into the courtyard not walk into the bloody fountain.'

Isobel rolled her eyes. 'I realise that but Crystabel really is a nightmare. She enjoys throwing her weight around and is quite the most demanding, self-centred bride I've worked with, which is saying something.'

'Why do you do this job if it creates so much stress?' Alexi asked.

'Why does anyone do anything?' Isobel shrugged. 'I kind of fell into it by accident and despite everything, it's a good living. For the record, not all brides are so demanding.' She smiled. 'Just most of them, but I can handle the odd tantrum.'

'I do wonder if Giles knows what he's letting himself in for,' Cheryl said. 'Unless he exerts himself, and he's done precious little of that over the wedding preparations as far as I've seen, then Crystabel will run rings around him once they're married.'

'I heard him and Simon Morton, his best man, in the bar the other night,' Drew said. 'They didn't realise I was behind the partition, sorting the wine delivery. No one else was anywhere near them and Simon was having a real go at Giles, telling him it wasn't too late to back out.'

'Hardly the role of a best man,' Alexi said.

'They go back years, I think,' Isobel said. 'Did

Simon say why he thought Giles was making a mistake?'

'Well.' Drew rolled his eyes dramatically. 'As you know, I'm not one to gossip, but...'

'Come on, don't keep us in suspense,' Alexi urged, laughing at his theatrics.

'Why am I only just hearing this?' Cheryl asked at the same time.

'It seems that Simon and Crystabel were an item for a while.'

'No!' Alexi and Cheryl cried in unison.

'I rather like Simon. You'd think he'd have more sense,' Alexi remarked.

'Clearly he does if he dumped her,' Cheryl replied.

'I gather they went on holiday somewhere exotic. Something happened, Simon didn't say what, but that was the beginning of the end.'

'Presumably Crystabel and Giles knew one another through Simon,' Cheryl said.

'And if Simon dumped her then Crystabel would have been hurt so targeted Giles in an effort to invoke Simon's jealousy,' Isobel added, putting her professionalism aside and joining in the wild speculation.

'Well anyway, there'll be trouble in paradise before too long,' Alexi said. 'If I was a betting person, I'd give it two years max.'

'Good for repeat business,' Cheryl remarked to Isobel.

'You joke but you'd be surprised how often that situation arises,' Isobel replied.

'Just emphasise to your client that even if we could change the orientation of the marque, it's too late,' Drew said. 'The people responsible for putting it up have been and gone. No one else can touch it. Health and safety, insurance and all that.'

'Ah, that's a good way out for me.' Isobel nodded her thanks. 'I don't think Crystabel was serious. She just likes to be dramatic.'

'She'll be here later with her retinue,' Drew reminded them all. The bride and her four bridesmaids were due to move into the hotel a few days ahead of the wedding and effectively take it over. Hairdressers, make-up people, dressers and so forth were all booked to do a trial run ahead of the big day.

'But the guys have first dibs. They'll be here for their stag night tomorrow,' Cheryl added. 'Our barman has ordered in extra supplies.'

'They're at Salisbury races before they come here,' Alexi said. 'I gather Giles's father has one of his best horses running. If it wins then it'll be one hell of a party.'

'It will be either way.' Drew waggled his brows. 'Boys will be boys. It'll be Giles's last opportunity to go wild before he settles down to a life of domestic disharmony.'

'You are such a cynic,' Cheryl chided.

'Well darling, I'm only saying what the rest of you're thinking.'

'I'll take them over a bunch of women on a hen night any time,' Cheryl said with feeling.

'I can't see Crystabel getting legless and losing control no matter what they do,' Alexi said. 'She's always aware of the camera lens. She has cameras following her around, as we all know, preserving the build-up to the big day for the edification of the viewing public and her loyal fans lap it up, if the viewing figures are anything to go by.'

'The coverage is as fake as her tan,' Cheryl said dismissively. 'She gets to say what's shown and what isn't and surprise, surprise, none of her tantrums make the small screen.'

'Which doesn't leave much else,' Isobel added.

'Where is the hen night taking place?' Alexi asked, curious to know what Crystabel had planned.

Probably something sophisticated. Definitely not the ubiquitous pub crawl.

Isobel shrugged. 'Some posh restaurant in Newbury, I think. Thankfully, organising hen nights isn't part of my remit. I gather the ladies are having a spa day followed by a slap-up meal.'

'Sounds as predictable as hell and not a lot of fun,' Alexi replied.

Cosmo stirred himself and trotted across the courtyard mewing, tail aloft and swishing from side to side.

'What on earth...' Alexi turned her head, curious to know what had made her anti-social cat stir himself and look so animated. 'Ah, I might have known.' A spontaneous smile sprang to her lips when Cosmo wound himself around Jack's legs, rubbing his big head against Jack's shin. 'He cares more about Jack than he does about me.' But her complaint sounded half-hearted, even to her own ears.

'You've said it often enough yourself,' Drew replied, grinning. 'He's a good judge of character.'

'What are you doing here?' Alexi asked, turning her face towards Jack as he bent to kiss her. 'I thought you were entangled in an embezzlement case in Swindon and couldn't get away.'

'Solved it,' he said, flopping down on the chair

beside Alexi. 'God, it's hot! No!' he added, when Cosmo leapt athletically from the ground and landed on Jack's lap with a surprisingly soft thud. 'Have a heart, big guy. I'm already overheating and you're the equivalent of a furry electric blanket.'

Alexi laughed. 'You two need to get a room.'

'We were just discussing the wisdom of hosting a society wedding and trying to decide if the rewards are worth all the drama,' Drew said. 'Poor Isobel is considering a career change.'

'Just so long as we get paid and they don't do any damage,' Cheryl said. 'The publicity will make it all worthwhile.' She grimaced. 'Probably.'

'Ah, there you are. I've been looking for you everywhere.'

Isobel groaned at the sound of Crystabel's voice. 'Hasn't she heard of that modern contraption called a telephone?' she muttered to no one in particular, standing and plastering on a smile as Crystabel strode across the terrace to join them, her four-inch heels tapping on the flagstones. 'Crystabel, what a lovely surprise.'

Alexi and Jack shared a smile when they noticed Isobel's fingers crossed behind her back. Cosmo leapt from Jack's lap and stalked up to Crystabel, teeth barred in a hiss.

'Yew! Get that creature away from me!' She flapped her hands at Cosmo. Alexi took her time calling him off.

'He's showing his affection,' Drew said, clearly struggling not to laugh.

'It's you I came to see.' Crystabel pushed past Isobel and homed in on Drew, sending wary glances in Cosmo's direction. 'You will have to keep that creature under lock and key on the wedding day,' she said, clearly struggling to regain both her poise and the upper hand. 'I won't have him terrorising my guests.'

'It's just you he appears to have taken against for some inexplicable reason, Crystabel,' Alexi replied sweetly, taking her turn to cross her fingers to negate the lie. 'But don't worry, he won't be on the prowl on the big day.'

Still with the baby in his arms, Drew remained seated and kept his gaze focused on his daughter.

'Something I can do for you?' he asked with the minimum of civility when Crystabel pouted and returned her attention to him. Much as Drew appreciated the business that the wedding would bring in, Alexi knew that he'd taken a dislike to Crystabel's autocratic behaviour – they all had – and refused to pander to her whims.

'Indeed. A change of plan. We've decided to come back here tomorrow evening after our day at the spa.'

'Your fiancé is having his stag party here,' Drew replied. 'It's all arranged. Surely, you're not intending to crash it?'

'They can have the bar.' Crystal waved a dismissive hand. 'We'll have the upstairs lounge and your nice chef can prepare a champagne buffet for us.'

Alexi and Cheryl looked at one another, at a loss for words. Drew passed Verity to Cheryl and slowly stood up, towering over the bride-to-be.

'We have a full sitting in the restaurant tomorrow,' he said calmly, 'so the buffet might not be possible. We don't have enough rooms to accommodate your party either. Your future husband has booked them all.'

'I happen to know that isn't true.' The diminutive blonde glowered at Drew. 'Giles only has half a dozen in his party. If they double up then there will be enough rooms for the rest of us.'

'Have you asked him if he's willing to do that?'

'That isn't necessary. Giles won't mind.' She huffed, clearly not appreciating being challenged by the hired help. No cameras were around and the butter-wouldn't-melt attitude that she saved for the small screen was replaced with the fiery determination of a spoiled woman accustomed to getting what she wanted. 'I had hoped for more cooperation from you than this.'

'Just as a matter of interest,' Alexi remarked, 'why do you want to merge your hen party with your fiancé's stag? The boys won't be able to let their hair down if there are ladies around.'

'I want the cameras to feature both,' she replied shortly. 'It will be nice for viewers to make the comparison.'

Seriously!

Drew reluctantly agreed to her demands but quoted an outrageous price for the buffet. Crystabel agreed to it without batting an eyelid. Drew, Alexi knew, would confirm the price in an email to her that would also be sent to Isobel.

'What was all that about?' Cheryl asked as Crystabel tottered off again, mobile phone pressed to her ear as she loudly berated someone about some hitch or other that was probably a product of her imagination.

'She wants to control the boys,' Jack said. 'If I was a betting man, I'd wager that she and her entourage won't stay upstairs for long. They'll venture down and mingle with the stag party, curtailing their wild activities and ensuring that Crystabel remains the centre of attention.'

Cheryl sighed. 'Poor Giles.'

'Poor Giles nothing,' Alexi replied briskly. 'If he doesn't man up then he's only got himself to blame for a life of being dictated to.'

'He doesn't strike me as the type to put up with being told what to do,' Jack remarked. 'Not that I know him well but still, he seems quite forceful.'

'Perhaps he really loves her?' Isobel suggested hopefully. 'Opposites are supposed to attract. I see it all the time in my line of work.'

'Someone has to love her,' Alexi muttered.

'I suppose he enjoys being a TV star as well, otherwise...' Cheryl jiggled the baby in arms as her words trailed off.

'I'll go and talk to Marcel about these last-minute changes,' Drew said, grimacing. 'Wish me luck.'

2

'They're well oiled already,' Jack remarked to Alexi when the stags arrived at the hotel from their race meeting, loud and out for a good time. Giles's father's horse had won, so the guys were quids in and high spirited.

'This isn't going to end well,' Alexi replied, aware that the ladies were already ensconced in the upstairs lounge. 'I think Crystabel has an agenda that doesn't allow for the boys to get legless.'

'Ha!' Jack rolled his eyes. 'Good luck with stopping them. It's a stag and getting wasted is kinda the point.'

'I know that but...'

'Cosmo's out of harm's way in here with us.' In

the private kitchen, Jack nodded towards cat and dog to emphasise his point. 'He can't bite any ankles or cause any of his usual mayhem.'

Cosmo looked up from Toby's basket and gave an indignant meow.

Alexi laughed. 'That cat is a prima donna.'

'No question, but he has character.'

'I can't put my finger on the bad feeling I have about this.' She paused, watching the guys through the window as they spilled out onto the terrace, now minus jackets and ties but with drinks in hand. There was a great deal of laughter and raucous comments. Someone emerged from the bar with a tray of shots which were downed with aplomb. Giles and Simon drained their glasses and slammed them down along with everyone else, then withdrew to the side lines, looking intense. The rest of the party didn't seem to notice. Someone shouted, 'Dead ants' and the entire group fell to the floor, wiggling their arms and legs.

'What on earth are they doing?' Alexi asked, looking perplexed.

Jack shrugged. 'Being dead ants, obviously.'

'Why?'

'Because it's a stag. No one said stags were rational. If they were, no one would enjoy themselves.'

'Dead ants don't move.'

Jack laughed. 'Stop it!'

'I thought this was supposed to be Giles's last hurrah,' Alexi said, pointing to a cameraman unobtrusively recording the events for posterity.

Jack frowned. 'Another example of Crystabel's controlling character, I have no doubt.'

'I wonder what they're in such intense conversation about,' Alexi remarked, her journalist curiosity piqued as she pointed towards the groom and his best man. They had moved round a corner that concealed them from the rest of the stags but gave Alexi and Jack a clear view of them from the kitchen window.

'Perhaps Simon is launching a final attempt to get Giles to reassess his options now that his time is almost here.'

'Aren't you supposed to be out there? You were invited.'

'I was hoping no one would remember.'

'Even so, I would love to know why there's so much tension.' Alexi wound her arms around Jack's neck and kissed him. 'I'm sure it's not a product of my imagination.'

'That's blackmail, woman!'

She batted her lashes at him, making him laugh. 'Whatever it takes.'

Jack rolled his eyes. 'The things I do for this place.'

'Have fun.' Alexi frowned, wishing she could shake her feeling of foreboding. 'And don't get so plastered that you forget what you're out there for.'

'Stop worrying.' Jack gave her a reassuring kiss. 'I know you're concerned for the hotel's reputation but lightning doesn't strike in the same place twice. Besides, Crystabel might be a pain in the posterior but at least her main objective is to look good and gain publicity, which can only reflect well upon Hopgood Hall.'

Alexi nodded, failing to look convinced. 'I hear you.'

'I gather she's both liked and hated by the viewing public but impossible to ignore. Ergo, people will talk about the wedding, either in glowing terms or highly critical ones. Either way, it's publicity.'

Alexi smiled. 'That about sums her up. Now go.' She gave him a little shove.

'Yes, ma'am.'

* * *

Jack gave the love of his life a smart salute and sauntered outside. He was greeted with back-slapping and a ragged cheer as a beer was forced into his hand. He'd only met the groom a few times but they'd hit it off and Jack had been invited to attend the stag weeks ago. It wasn't his kind of thing but there was no way he could have politely refused. He'd slip away before it got out of hand, as these things always tended to. To a degree, he shared Alexi's misgivings about the whole situation. The groom looked like a man condemned and the bride definitely had her own agenda. Would someone as ambitious as she was to build her public profile as an influencer use her wedding as a publicity stunt? It seemed like a surreal thought but marriages were no longer made in heaven, Jack reminded himself. No one seemed to imagine that forever actually meant forever any more. It was more a case of 'until death or irrevocable differences do us part'.

Jack rolled his eyes at the cynical turn his thoughts had taken. Even so, the whole shebang did feel more like a business arrangement rather than a love match. Crystabel demonstrated public affection for her handsome groom but that could all be part of the act, for the benefit of the TV cameras.

He would be interested to see what the women

did to crash the party. He didn't have the slightest doubt that was Crystabel's intention; the stag had to be orchestrated, just as every other aspect of the nuptials had been micro-managed by the bride.

'Two hundred quid,' one of the guys told Jack, pulling a pile of notes from his pocket, presumably to emphasise his point. 'Not a bad return for the day.'

'Not bad at all,' Jack replied, feigning interest as he recalled they'd been at the races.

The others crowded round, boasting about their winnings, joshing those who hadn't had the foresight to back any winners. Jack sauntered away, conscious of the fact that Giles and Simon were still absent. He left the stags to their boasting and stood behind a large potted plant, close to the edge of the terrace, where the groom and his best man were conducting a heated conversation. Jack was hidden from their view but able to hear every word.

He could see the two men as well if he peered through the foliage that separated them. The morose groom appeared fraught, tightly coiled. Something was definitely off, Jack sensed. It was none of his business. If the man really wanted to tie himself to Crystabel then good luck to him. But Alexi was worried about the hotel's reputation and Jack would do just about anything to assuage her anxiety. Besides, his own curiosity was piqued. Once a detective...

'Tell her!' Simon's voice was low and insistent. 'It's not too late.'

'I can't, mate.' Giles shook his head. 'I have to go ahead with it.'

'Call me old fashioned, but shouldn't you be madly in love in order to even contemplate marriage? And you sure as hell don't look smitten.'

'You know that isn't what this is about.' Giles kicked at a loose stone. 'I can't humiliate her by...'

'Put yourself first, sod humiliation.'

'You don't understand.'

'I understand all too well. I was there before you, remember, and I know that once she gets her hooks into a man, she'll eat him alive if he lets her. Honestly, mate, the only person she loves is herself.'

'You escaped unscathed.'

'Only just and then only because she moved on to you, making it look like it was her decision for us to split up. I didn't care, just so long as I was shot of her.'

'After what happened on that holiday, I don't see how you can...'

'Let's not go there. We agreed never to speak

about it.' Simon let out a long breath. 'Why do you think she moved her hen party here?'

A loud bark of laughter from the other guys momentarily drowned out their conversation.

'I think the place where they intended to stay was overbooked,' Giles said vaguely. 'Crystabel sent a message. I didn't take much notice.'

'Rubbish! No establishment would turn down the publicity. She's well known *and* she had TV cameras trailing in her wake. If they were overbooked then it isn't her party that would have been turned away.'

Giles shrugged. 'It's no big deal.'

'It's another example of the way she intends to control you, Giles. Wake up, mate!'

'We both know why I have to do this,' he said so quietly that Jack barely caught the words. 'There's no alternative, so stop banging on about it. It's not helpful.'

'There are always alternatives,' Simon replied with conviction. 'Call her bluff.'

'Come on, you guys!'

Giles and Simon responded to the summons and wandered onto the terrace. Jack waited for a moment, pondering upon what he'd just heard, and then followed them. It shouldn't matter to him –

Giles was a grown man and could do as he pleased – but the fact that he was marrying the awful Crystabel under duress bothered him more than it should.

It bothered him a lot.

For the next hour, Jack joined in the drinking games but the others were already too wasted to notice that he actually drank very little himself.

Several waiters appeared with laden trays and set up the buffet table supervised by Anton Heston, resplendent in chef's whites, his dreadlocks neatly tied back. Anton had been one of the contestants in the cooking contest held at the hotel and had also briefly been suspected of killing one of his fellow competitors.

The Trinidadian had come second in the overall contest, thereby earning himself a year's contract in Marcel's kitchen here at the hotel. Anton idolized Marcel and absorbed everything he taught him like osmosis. But unlike the volatile Marcel, Anton's character was terminally laid back and Jack had never seen him looking stressed. Alexi reckoned their temperaments were perfect foils for one another. Now that the hotel's restaurant was operating at full capacity, she hoped that Anton would accept a permanent position working with Marcel rather than setting up shop alone.

The guys descended upon the food, giving the impression that they hadn't eaten for a week. Jack hung back, wondering if he could reasonably escape and re-join Alexi and Cosmo in the kitchen. Before he could beat a retreat though, a loud bark of feminine laughter preceded the arrival of the hen party with Crystabel in the lead. Her mother, Gloria, who was even more ambitiously domineering was at her side, and the inevitable cameraman was tracking their every move.

Jack stood back and watched the horrified expression on Giles's face. Why he was so horrified, Jack couldn't have said. Even the densest person must have anticipated the inevitable.

'What the heck...' Giles looked like a rabbit caught in headlights.

'Hi, darling.' Crystabel pecked his cheek but Jack noticed her watching Simon rather than Giles with a hungry gaze. Unless Jack was losing his edge, the bride still carried a torch for her future husband's best man: a man who very clearly did not return her interest. 'You don't mind if we join you, do you?'

'Actually, we do.' Simon spoke loudly, his words

slightly slurred, and the camera focused on him. 'Men only in this area.'

'I wasn't talking to you,' Crystabel snapped.

'Please leave. You'll cramp our style.'

Giles spoke with quiet authority, very possibly challenging his fiancée for the first time ever, as evidenced by the astonished glance that Crystabel shared with her mother. Her mouth fell open and she was clearly lost for words.

But not for long.

'Darling, don't be silly.' She laughed, taking Giles's comment as the joke it hadn't been intended as. 'This is the twenty-first century. We're equals. Segregation of the sexes is draconian. Do your worst. Play whatever games you boys get up to on your own. We'll just sit on the terrace and enjoy the last of this lovely day. You won't even know we're here.'

The camera was rolling in the background, but Jack knew the altercation would never be seen by the viewing public.

Giles looked at Crystabel impassively. 'Either you ladies leave or we do,' he said softly.

'Go! Go! Go!' The inebriated stags took up the chant.

The camera continued to whirl. A couple of the slightly more sober stags were recording the episode on their mobiles as they put their support loudly behind Giles. Crystabel noticed, which is perhaps why she didn't continue to confront her future husband. Footage that she couldn't control would be an anathema to her.

'Come along, ladies,' she said with a high-pitched little laugh. 'We know where we're not wanted.'

'Sure about that?' Jack heard Simon mutter *sotto voce*.

A huge cheer erupted as the ladies tottered from the terrace on towering heels with as much dignity as they could muster. Crystabel paused to look over her shoulder as she reached the terrace doors, her eyes shooting daggers.

At Simon.

* * *

Alexi watched the proceedings with Cheryl from the kitchen window. She felt like cheering herself when Crystabel lost that particular skirmish. It was the first time that Alexi had observed her failing to get her way.

'Well, well,' she muttered. 'It seems as though Giles has grown a pair.'

'Too little, too late,' Cheryl replied. 'He will be made to pay for defying her so publicly. Did you see her expression? Thunderous doesn't come close. And her mother looked equally furious. She stepped forward to try and exert herself but Crystabel waved her back.'

'She knew she'd overstepped the mark.'

'There has to be a first time for everything.'

'Remind me never to get married,' Alexi said, walking away from the window and shuddering.

'Come and sit down. We'll eat in here and keep well away from the marauding stags.'

Drew appeared on cue, toting a loaded tray. 'It's bedlam out there,' he said, shuddering. 'How can six men—'

'Seven,' Alexi told him. 'Jack's joined the party.'

'All right, seven. How can they have taken over the entire hotel?'

'The bar and the terrace,' Cheryl corrected. 'But we still have punters in the restaurant and Giles is paying over the odds for the privilege. Never lose sight of that.'

'Trust me, I haven't.'

He decanted the contents of his tray onto the table and invited the ladies to help themselves. Cosmo stirred himself and stalked across to Alexi, wrapping himself round her legs and taking an avid interest in proceedings.

Once they'd eaten, Cheryl and Drew both considered it necessary to attend to Verity, leaving Alexi alone and at a loose end. She thought about returning to her cottage but as quickly dismissed the idea. Jack would want to come back with her and he would be in no condition to drive so she needed to wait for him.

On a whim, she wandered upstairs, curious to see how Crystabel had chosen to gloss over her unexpected dismissal from the terrace. Even in front of her closest female friends, Alexi sensed that she wouldn't want to lose face. Not that she had any actual friends, Alexi thought. Her bridesmaids all appeared to have been recruited on the basis of their relationship to her but Alexi hadn't noticed any particularly intimate or typically girly exchanges between them.

The sound of muted voices floated from the upstairs lounge. Alexi put her head round the door but Crystabel was not amongst the ladies and there was no sign of the cameraman either.

Before her presence could be remarked upon, she withdrew and wandered further down the corridor. Crystabel had been allocated the best room in the hotel. Of course she had, Alexi thought, rolling her eyes. It was the same room that Drew had insisted Alexi inhabited when she first came down to Lambourn after her dismissal from the *Sentinel*, in search of the support of friends she had neglected for too long. Their generous embrace, especially in the light of that neglect, had been humbling. Lambourn had seemed like home almost at once and, two murders notwithstanding, it was the place where she had decided to settle.

It was proving to be a wise decision, despite the murders in question.

The door to Crystabel's room was ajar and she could hear the bride's shrill voice raised in anger. What she hadn't expected was to hear the deep timbre of Simon's voice calmly responding.

'You don't need to put on an act,' he said. 'There are no cameras in here.'

'You forfeited the right to tell me how to behave when you dumped me,' Crystabel replied with venom.

Alexi blinked as she flattened herself against the wall, shocked by the depth of Crystabel's animosity. She hoped no one would emerge from adjoining rooms and catch her eavesdropping. She'd take the chance, she decided. If they didn't want to be overheard then they should at least have closed the door and lowered their voices. The journalist in Alexi screamed that she could be on the trail of a story. Not that she would ever publish. Besides, this was gossip column stuff and she was better than that.

So, Crystabel was still smarting from being rejected by the man she obviously preferred and was marrying his best mate as an act of spite. No wonder this society wedding had seem contrived to Alexi. But why Giles was going through with it was less obvious. He didn't seem smitten so perhaps he had reasons that weren't as apparent as Crystabel's.

'Get over yourself,' Simon replied, his voice calm, taunting. 'I suppose I shouldn't be surprised that you took up with Giles. What does surprise me is that my friend can't see through the ruse.'

'A ruse? I love him!' she shrieked. 'And you're insanely jealous. You can't bear to think of me being happy.'

'Darling, I don't think of you at all. But I do care about my mate's welfare and you will emasculate him. He doesn't want to be a celebrity and have cameras trailing behind him the entire time. He isn't that self-obsessed.'

'And I am?'

Simon chuckled but Alexi couldn't detect any trace of humour behind the sound. 'If the cap fits...'

'I have a successful career. Giles is in line to take over his father's training yard. We have different lives, which will make for a successful marriage.'

'With you in London and him down here?' Simon snorted. 'Well, I guess if he doesn't see much of you, that'll give the marriage a vague chance of success.'

'We will be together for a lot of the time. Besides, we have plans. He's going to help me take my career to the next level.'

'You? Down here in your designer wellies where horses outnumber people? You'll die of boredom.' There was a heavy silence before Simon spoke again. 'Have you actually discussed your living arrangements with Giles or have you simply assumed he'll do as you ask? If so, you're in for a disappointment. Racehorse training is a full-time job. He won't have time to trail after you on the red carpet. Besides, he hates city life as much as you dislike the quiet of the country. Surely you know that much about the man you intend to spend the next few months with?'

'Few months?' she screeched. 'This is a lifetime's commitment.'

Simon snorted. 'I'll give it a year max.'

'You say you don't regret our breakup but I know differently.' Alexi wasn't surprised when Crystabel changed the subject, putting herself firmly back centre stage. 'If you have no feelings from me then you wouldn't be making so much fuss about me marrying someone else.'

'I'd already decided that our marriage would be a disaster before we went away. I planned to tell you during that trip to Greece but then...'

Damn, they'd both fallen silent. Whatever had happened in Greece had obviously been defining but neither of them elaborated.

'You're just saying that to save face.' Crystabel's sullen voice broke the ensuing silence: a silence laden with accusation.

'Believe whatever you want, but know this. I'm standing as Giles's best man because he asked me to, not because I want to be anywhere near you. And if you go through with this parody then don't expect me to be part of your circle.' He paused. 'We both know Giles has only agreed to marry you out of a sense of guilt.'

'Nonsense!'

'Proposed to you, did he?' Simon's voice had taken on a taunting edge.

'It was... a joint decision.'

'You propositioned him.' Alexi peeped through a gap in the door and saw the back of Simon's head as he shook it. 'Caught him at a low moment, flattered him, played on his insecurities, and then this ridiculous marriage train got under way without him realising what he'd let himself in for. Now he feels trapped, which he should.'

'Look, Giles is his own man. If he doesn't want to marry me then he should be here telling me so himself. He shouldn't have sent his lackey to do his dirty work for him.'

Simon chuckled. 'Well, well. At least you're willing to entertain the possibility that you're resistible. Never thought I'd see the day.'

'Just go away.' She flapped a hand. 'I thought you and I... but obviously I got it wrong.'

Alexi slipped into an adjoining room seconds before Simon strode from Crystabel's bedroom, his expression thunderous.

Before she could return to the kitchen, Crystabel's mother emerged from the lounge and tapped at Crystabel's door.

'Ah, there you are,' she heard her say. 'Was that Simon I just saw stomping off? What did he say to you, darling? You look upset. Don't let him get to you. He's not important. Don't have anything to do with him.'

Alexi, curious to hear what the other women had to say without the bride and her mother around, joined the bridal party in the lounge.

'Ladies,' she said, 'do you need anything?'

The four bridesmaids – two cousins of Crystabel's and two work colleagues, all significantly less glamorous than the bride – looked up and smiled.

'We're enjoying a respite,' Jenny, one of the cousins, said with a mischievous smile.

'I don't blame you,' Alexi replied, plonking herself down on a vacant chair. 'Crystabel and her mother can be pretty full-on.'

The ladies nodded in unison and the tension left the atmosphere.

'In fairness,' Abby, one of Crystabel's colleagues said, 'in our line of work, women have to be forceful, otherwise they get trampled on.'

'Surely things have moved on since then,' Alexi remarked. 'Although I have to say, when I started on the *Sentinel*, it was very much a male-dominated field. It's changed now, of course, but I always felt I had to work harder than my male counterparts in order to get myself noticed.'

'There's forceful,' Claire, the other cousin, said,

'and then there's Crystabel. I haven't seen her for five years. You could have knocked me down with a feather when she contacted me out of the blue and asked... no, *told* me that I would be her bridesmaid.'

'You could have said no.'

Claire laughed. 'Hardly. Crystabel always gets what she wants. She was the same when we were kids. Everything had to be on her terms. Still, she's getting married, so maybe she'll mature, change and stop putting herself first.'

Everyone in the room gaped at Claire.

'Well, it could happen,' she protested.

'And I could win the lottery,' Jenny replied.

'You know Giles better than any of us, Nicola,' Abby said. 'What's he really like?'

'How do you know him, as a matter of interest?' Alexi asked at the same time, surprised that the ladies were being so candid in front of her.

'My dad has a racehorse in his father's yard. I've been going there for years.'

'And you went on that infamous holiday to Greece, Jenny.' Jenny turned towards Alexi, her face an unreadable mask. 'Crystabel went on it engaged to Simon, the hunky best man. When they came back, they were no longer engaged and Crystabel has never said why.'

'She was cut up about it, though,' Claire said. 'If you ask me, she still carries a torch for him but Simon doesn't want to know.'

'That's probably why she's stuck on him,' Jenny said scathingly. 'No one dumps Crystabel.'

Alexi wanted to ask Jenny what had happened in Greece but suspected that she wouldn't tell her, and certainly not in front of others. Although her friends expressed no curiosity, it seemed unlikely that they knew anything about a mysterious event shrouded in secrecy. An event that had had a lasting effect upon those who were there.

She heard Crystabel and her mother talking to one another as they made their way back to the lounge.

'More champagne, ladies,' Claire said, sighing and simultaneously plastering on a smile as she reached for the bottle in the cooler. 'Respite's over. It's game time.'

Alexi slipped down the stairs and returned to the kitchen.

'Lightweight,' she said, when she found Jack there, looking commendably sober.

'You can have too much of a good thing,' he replied, winking at her.

3

'Find out anything interesting?' Alexi asked as she sat down at the table. 'I saw you listening to the groom and best man's conversation. It looked pretty intense. My snooping instincts must be rubbing off on you.'

'Nothing gets past you.' Jack smiled at her. 'But don't forget that I'm a professional snoop too. Goes with the territory.'

'There's more fighting than partying going on out there.' Alexi nodded towards the terrace, flooded with an array of pretty lights that had come on once the sun went down. The noise level had gone up several decibels. 'Giles's father and a couple of his inner circle just arrived.'

Jack joined Alexi, who had stood to look out the window. 'Father and son are having a right old barny, by the looks of things,' Jack concluded. The two men were standing in the exact same place as Giles and Simon had done earlier, both throwing their arms somewhat dramatically in the air as they argued.

'There's a lot of tension,' Alexi agreed, sighing. She told Jack what she had learned from the other ladies upstairs and the essence of the conversation she had overheard between Crystabel and Simon. 'I wonder what happened in Greece?'

'Let's hope we don't get to find out,' Jack replied. 'It was obviously something significant, if Crystabel and Simon went there engaged and came back single.'

Alexi nodded. 'A lot of unresolved issues is the impression that I get. I know it's none of our business but it obviously has a lot of relevance to some of the people here.'

'Precisely.' Jack moved away from the window. 'Weddings are supposed to be one of the most stressful experiences of a person's life, right up there with Christmas, moving house and family holidays. Did you know that?'

'I did actually.'

Jack smiled. 'Don't tell me; you did a feature on it once.'

Alexi returned his smile. 'No, but I know someone who did.'

A loud burst of laughter from the terrace caused them both to glance in that direction. Another drinking game was being organised by one of Giles's stags.

'It's getting lively out there,' Jack said. 'Do you want to hang around or head back to the cottage?'

'I said I'd stay for a while and hold the fort. Verity has a bit of a temperature apparently and naturally Drew and Cheryl both think she's at death's door.'

'I hope she'll be okay.'

'I'm sure she will be. I think a doctor has given them an online consultation. Anyway, neither of them will leave Verity so I said I'd hang on here in case someone in authority is required to play referee between that lot out there and the ladies upstairs.'

'Blimey, you're brave.'

'Crystabel doesn't frighten me.' Alexi grinned. 'Well, not much!'

'It's interesting that you imagine Crystabel will be the troublemaker, despite that lot,' Jack said, indicating the stags stumbling around on the terrace.

She shrugged. 'Boys will be boys, as Drew reminded us earlier, but they're basically harmless.'

'Hello.' Jack's head jerked up. 'Simon's joined the argument.'

Alexi followed the direction of his gaze. 'I'd love to be a fly on the wall,' she said, frustrated. 'It's the journalist in me. I can't seem to help myself. There's a story there, I just know it. Why else would they be disagreeing so vehemently? They seem to think no one can see them. They've obviously not taken this window into account.' Alexi tapped her toe as she opened the window in question. 'Damn! There's just too much noise. It's drowning their voices out.'

'I get the impression that Giles's nearest and dearest are averse to him marrying Crystabel.'

'Everyone seems to be but he's stubbornly determined to go through with it.'

Jack shrugged. 'He's a big boy, capable of making his own decisions.'

'I don't know. Crystabel seems to dominate him. Who knows? Perhaps he fancies fame and fortune rather than a life of training temperamental racehorses. Anything's possible. I'll tell you something for nothing though. The ladies are just as adamant as the men appear to be insofar as they don't think it's a marriage made in heaven. In fact, they don't think there should be a marriage at all.'

'No one expect the bride and groom seem to think it should go ahead, but it's their lives so who are we to criticise?'

'True enough. Anyway, have you eaten?' Alexi asked.

'No. You?'

'No. Haven't had a chance, not for hours, and I'm famished. I'll see if I can sweet talk Anton into knocking something up for us.'

'He'll do anything for you, that boy. I'm starting to feel like I have competition. Should I be worried?'

Alexi grinned over her shoulder as she left the kitchen. 'Count on it.' She winked as she crossed the entrance hall.

The stags were in occupation of the bar and the terrace beyond. Their numbers had swelled to include what appeared to be the majority of the guys working for Guy's father and a few locals whom Alexi recognised as regular bar-users. The noise level was ear-splitting, as was the music pumping from the speakers behind the bar.

She glanced at the stairs. Some of the ladies were spilling down them, Crystabel in their midst, looking lethal and far from happy, probably because she wasn't the centre of attention. Significantly, there was no sign of the ordinarily ever-present camera-man. Inevitably, some of the stags had met the ladies half way. They were dancing somewhat precariously on the stairs and a private party appeared to be developing. Crystabel looked on with arms folded and toe tapping, clearly resentful. No one had asked her to dance and there was no sign of her intended.

Alexi took the private corridor behind the bar that led to the kitchens, where service was wrapping up. As Jack had predicted, Anton was happy to provide food for them both and promised to deliver it to the private kitchen very shortly.

Alexi retraced her steps but paused when she heard muted voices coming from an alcove below the stairs. A man and a woman. It didn't take the brain of a rocket scientist to figure out what they were doing there. A part of Alexi wanted to tell them that this was a restricted area; the journalist in her was curious to know which members of the wedding party were misbehaving.

She glanced round the edge of the alcove, feeling like a voyeur, somehow managing to withhold a gasp when she recognised the couple in a tight cinch, oblivious to her presence.

It was Giles and Crystabel's cousin, Jenny.

* * *

Jack smiled at Alexi when she returned to the kitchen. 'Mission accomplished, I have no doubt.'

'Never mind that,' Alexi replied breathlessly, her expression fraught with worry. 'Guess what I've just seen.'

'No idea,' he replied warily. 'Give me a clue.'

Jack, who had seen and heard everything during his years as a detective, was himself shocked when she told him. 'What the hell...'

'Precisely.' Alexi plonked herself down at the kitchen table, for once ignoring Cosmo when he stalked up to her and wound himself round her legs. The cat seemed to instinctively know when there was food in the offing. 'There's going to be trouble, I can sense it. I just hope that nothing happens to reflect poorly upon the hotel. We will never survive another scandal.'

'Oh, I don't know.' Jack bent to pick Cosmo up and held the purring cat against his shoulder. 'Without being morbid, the murder during the cooking contest was excellent for business.'

'Jack!' Alexi's head shot up.

He chuckled. 'Sorry, darling, but you know it's true.'

Alexi flashed a rueful smile and gave a half-hearted nod. 'Well, I suppose fighting relations are par for the course at any wedding. But the groom and chief bridesmaid getting it on... Not so sure about that one.'

'A drunken clinch?'

Alexi shook her head. 'I didn't linger but no, I got the impression there was more to it than that.'

Anton pushed the kitchen door open with his backside and strolled into the room bearing a laden tray. The aromas caused Jack to salivate and his stomach to give an embarrassing rumble.

'You're a lifesaver, mate,' he said, helping Anton to decant the contents of his tray onto the kitchen table.

'Glad to be of service,' he replied. 'Enjoy.'

'It's mayhem out there,' Alexi said, nodding in the direction of the bar. 'Did you happen to encounter a mingling of the stags and the hens in the back corridor?'

Anton shook his head. 'Didn't see anyone.'

'Giles is out there.' Jack nodded towards the window, where Giles stood in the middle of a group of his mates, knocking back shots with them. There were no women in sight. The shots despatched, everyone drifted back inside.

'I'll leave you to it,' Anton said, withdrawing quietly.

'Oh God, this is gorgeous!' Alexi cried, closing her eyes in appreciation as she savoured Anton's coronation chicken.

'It is,' Jack agreed, smiling at her enthusiasm.

'I make a point of not eating here too often. Between this kitchen and Fay's efforts to feed me up,' she said,, 'I'm in danger of becoming as large as a house.' Fay was the adoptive mother of Natalie Parker who had been murdered in Lambourn. Alexi and Jack were instrumental in seeing a local trainer jailed for his crime. Fay now lived in Natalie's cottage in the village.

Jack chuckled. 'The view isn't too bad from where I'm sitting.'

'Only not too bad?' she asked indignantly.

Jack laughed at her as he responded to Cosmo's indignant miaow and placed a dish of chicken on the floor for him, along with a smaller portion for Toby. Cat and dog got stuck in with gusto.

They ate mostly in silence, the sound of loud voices and louder music drifting in from the terrace negating the need for words. Alexi was on edge, Jack sensed, watching the pulse beating at the base of her throat as her glance continually strayed towards the terrace. She was worried that some catastrophe would occur between the very antagonistic members of this wedding party, creating problems for the hotel that it would be difficult to recover from.

Jack felt the same way. There was an atmosphere that he hoped was the product of their joint concern. Concern that had been created by the thinly veiled hostility displayed by some of those present. Alexi having seen the groom romantically entangled with another woman was a more serious cause for concern and gave Alexi a legitimate reason to worry, which worried Jack even more.

Alexi seemed to have settled into life in Lambourn. She had forged friendships and appeared to have made the adjustment to country living surprisingly well. Be that as it may, she was still a city girl at heart. Still an investigative journalist to the core. If disaster struck again in this quiet village, she might decide that she was a jinx and that she'd be better off back in London. Her damned ex, the editor of the *Sentinel*, hadn't given up on trying to lure her back and if he offered to reinstate her previous position as a senior journalist, Jack worried that the temptation would be too great for Alexi to resist.

What he would do if that situation arose, he was at a loss to say. He was totally hooked on Alexi, ready to make a life-long commitment. With his che-quered history and an acrimonious divorce behind him, he had never expected that situation to arise. Once bitten and all that. But he now knew with ab-solute certainty that when it was right it was right. He had no doubts whatsoever about Alexi being the one for him. Whether she returned his feelings re-garding their long-term future was not a subject he had raised. He was a coward; scared of... well, scaring her off.

Drew entered the kitchen as they were finishing their meal. Cosmo had licked his own plate clean and had taken over Toby's.

'How's the patient?' Alexi asked.

'Better, I think. We gave her some Calpol and her temperature's down. She's sleeping now. Cheryl's staying with her. I came to make sure everything was in order here.' He winced as raucous laughter infil-trated the kitchen. 'Well, as in order as these things ever can be.'

Alexi smiled and it was clear to Jack that she had no intention of repeating their concerns to Drew. A wise decision, Jack thought. Despite his bravado, it was obvious that Drew was worried about his daughter. As far as Jack was aware, their little trea-sure had been a picture of health since the day she was born and so it stood to reason that the doting couple would be floored by this first bump in the parental road.

'That's good,' Alexi said, yawning.

'You two get off,' Drew said. 'You've done more than enough. Besides, it looks as though the activities are finally winding down.'

Jack nodded. The music had gone down several notches in volume and the majority of the stags had long since abandoned the terrace in favour of the bar. He smiled across at Alexi, telling her without the need for words that her concerns had been groundless.

'The two parties will be merging now, I dare say,' Alexi remarked. 'The ladies were creeping down the stairs when I last crossed the hall. Then Simon appeared and they scarpered.'

'Are you closing the bar?' Jack asked.

Drew nodded. 'I told them midnight and it's almost the witching hour. I know from experience that damage gets done if the bar stays open too late.'

'Very sensible,' Jack replied.

'And whatever happens upstairs stays upstairs,' Alexi added, grinning.

'Yeah, there is that.' Drew grunted. 'The chief bridesmaid and the best man are favourites. It's kind of a tradition. What?' he added when Alexi and Jack exchanged a glance.

'It's nothing. Don't...' Jack abruptly stopped talking when an ear-piercing, feminine scream emerged from the terrace. 'What the...'

All three occupants of the kitchen ran for the outer door that led to the terrace. They found Crystabel there, hysterical, standing over the bloody body of her future husband with a knife in her hand. Blood dripped from its blade onto the gaping wound in Giles's chest.

Jenny led the charge of women who emerged from the bar. She took the scene in, screamed and fainted.

4

Alexi's heart quailed. *Not again! This can't be happening. Why me?* Her feet remained glued to the spot. She watched Jack's training come to the fore as he took control of the situation. He pushed the stunned cluster of people back with a commanding tone that cut through their inertia. Jack, at least, had kept his wits about him, for which Alexi was grateful. He gently extracted the knife from Crystabel's hand, wrapped a discarded napkin around its handle and placed it carefully aside.

A whole raft of conflicting fears spiralling through Alexi's bloodstream as Jack bent to check Giles's neck for a pulse. It was obvious to Alexi from his blank, staring eyes and the amount of blood that had pulsed from the gaping wound in his chest that he was dead. Jack shot her a look and gently shook his head. The onlookers noticed and an audible gasp erupted.

Jack exchanged a dour look with Drew, both of them aware of the damage this latest disaster would do to the hotel, as he withdrew his phone from his pocket. He would be calling the emergency services, Alexi accepted with a sinking heart. She hadn't been able to shake the fear that something catastrophic would happen tonight, something that would have devastating consequences for herself and her friends. Then she felt bad because she was worried about the hotel's reputation when a young man had lost his life in the most brutal manner.

Facts had to be faced though, she knew, squaring her sagging shoulders. A third murder in sleepy Lambourn was now connected to Hopgood Hall. More significantly, all three of those tragedies had occurred since Alexi had arrived in the village. There hadn't been a suspicious death in the district for decades before that. The locals would put two and two together, decide she was a Jonah, and she would find herself ostracised.

Perhaps she should be, Alexi reasoned, random thoughts tumbling through her head like a washing machine stuck on the spin cycle. This was all her fault. She was an outsider who knew nothing about horses and had no place here. She should not have persuaded her friends to extend the hotel, pushing them out of their comfort zone. She was a city girl; what did she know about running a country hotel? But that trifling fact hadn't prevented her from being determined to show her buddies how to conduct their business efficiently. She remembered how hyped up she had been when she insisted upon investing in the hotel and having a major say in its future. It had felt good to put their interests first.

But bankruptcy was not what she'd had in mind, which was now the most likely outcome.

Some entrepreneur she was turning out to be. Ha! She hadn't even been able to hang onto her position at the *Sentinel*, despite being the editor's significant other. She obviously had an inflated opinion of her own abilities.

'What the hell?' she muttered aloud. How could she be feeling so sorry for herself at such a time?

Jack pocketed his phone, then glanced her way and indicated that she should come and help Jenny. He wouldn't let anyone else get near her.

'It's my son, damn it!' Giles's father shouted,

struggling when two of the stags held him back by his arms.

'I'm sorry, he's dead,' Jack replied. 'Best stand clear and wait for the police. There's nothing you can do for him now and the detectives won't thank you if you contaminate their crime scene.'

'What's to contaminate? It's obvious what happened.' He pointed a shaking finger at Crystabel, his voice breaking on a sob. 'She had the damned weapon in her hand; what more do you need? I warned him not to marry the bitch; I told him she'd mess up his life but he was so damned stubborn. Well, he's paid the ultimate price now. I hope you're happy,' he yelled at Crystabel, who seemed oblivious to his harangue. She stood in the exact same spot, pale, shaking and quietly sobbing. It was obvious that the verbal abuse being hurled her way hadn't broken through.

'There's a procedure.' Jack's soft tone appeared to bring Anthony Preston-Smythe back to reality. He swallowed and fell back on the proverbial stiff upper lip common still amongst the English upper classes.

Alexi helped Jenny to sit up. She had a nasty bump forming on the side of her head and appeared dizzy, disorientated. 'Don't try to stand just yet,' Alexi said gently.

'Is he... I want to...'

'Shush!' Alexi put a lot of emphasis on the one word, which appeared to make Jenny focus. 'There's nothing you can do for him now.'

'But I want—'

'I know.' Alexi took her arm and helped her to her feet. 'Come over here and sit down.' She led the girl, now as compliant as a lamb, towards a chair situated in the opposite direction to the body. 'Put your head between your legs until the dizziness passes.'

Gloria Hennessy slipped an arm around her daughter's waist and led her away from the body of her fiancé. The older woman showed no emotion whatsoever. Her expression was carved in stone but Alexi sensed a sharp, manipulative mind at work. Of the two, she was the more forceful, although she was astute enough to remain in the background and allow her daughter to absorb the limelight. Alexi suspected that she'd wanted to achieve notoriety on the back of Crystabel's success but would not have anticipated becoming a household name because her daughter had been arrested for murder.

A murder that Alexi didn't think she'd committed. Why she should think that when all the obvious evidence implied otherwise, she was at a loss to know. But sometimes, often during the course of her career, she had fallen back on her instincts and they had seldom let her down.

'I didn't...' Crystabel blinked as she emerged from her catatonic state. 'I found him. I didn't hurt him.'

'It's all right,' Gloria said, her voice low, soothing.

Alexi barely caught the words and watched as Gloria led her daughter to a stone bench on the opposite side of the ornamental fountain. She sat beside her, took Crystabel's hand in her own and whispered to her in an urgent manner. Alexi would have given a great deal to be able to hear what was being said but had no excuse to get close enough. Everyone else was giving the bride and her mother a lot of space, contenting themselves with shaking their heads and throwing accusatory glances their way.

The stags, drunk and disorderly a few minutes previously, now seemed like the models of sobriety. Significantly, the TV camera was still absent. Alexi wondered about that. Numb and full of self-pity a few minutes previously, her journalistic brain had clicked into gear. Horrified at the vicious nature of the murder, she was now in damage limitation mode. She glanced at Jack, whose jaw was set in a rigid line. He knew as well as she did that this would be the end of Hopgood Hall's booming business.

No one would want to stay here now.

Drew arranged for the kitchen to supply hot drinks laced with brandy where required to counter the shock. The rumblings of discontent had been reduced to a deafening silence as everyone absorbed the enormity of events. Jenny recovered and accepted a cup of tea. Alexi left her in the company of her friends and returned to Jack and Drew.

'Back into the bar please everyone,' Jack said with authority. 'The police are on their way. I must ask you all to wait here. They will want to talk to everyone.'

A slow exodus took place, everyone muttering. No one seemed to want to walk anywhere near Crystabel and Gloria. Trial by public opinion, Alexi thought, although in some respects, Crystabel had brought at least that much on herself by having the TV cameras following her every move. Well, almost every move. By sacrificing her privacy through choice, she'd set herself up for a fall.

'You okay?' Jack asked, slinging an arm around Alexi's shoulders.

'Better than him,' she replied, turning her back on Giles's body with a shudder.

'It's hard to fathom.' Drew ran a hand through his hair. 'Again. It's like we're cursed. Poor bloke,' he added.

'Do you think Crystabel did it?' Alexi asked.

Jack shrugged. 'If she did, then why scream and keep hold of the knife?'

'If she had a knife with her then it implies intent.'

'Is the knife from the dining room?' Jack asked, turning to Drew, who dutifully glanced at the weapon.

'Never seen it before.' Drew shook his head decisively. 'Looks a bit like a cheese knife but it's not one of ours.'

'Hmm, interesting,' Jack mused. 'It's small but obviously sharp. More like a dagger. Why the hell would anyone bring one of those to a stag or hen party?'

No one responded.

'If Crystabel had found out about Jenny and Giles...' Alexi mused.

'She'd have been more likely to kill her cousin.' Jack's voice was calm, competent. He was accustomed to dealing with violent death, Alexi was reminded. She, on the other hand, hadn't seen a murder victim all the time she'd lived in London.

'She wanted Giles, was determined to have him, so he's no good to her dead.'

'Carrying a knife to threaten someone and actually using it to kill them must be two very different beasts,' Drew said pensively. 'She confronted him about something but probably didn't mean to kill him, so shrieked when she realised what she'd done.'

'The lack of the ever-present TV camera implies that she was up to something,' Alexi said. 'Oh God, how can this be happening?'

'Stop fretting,' Jack insisted. 'What's done is done. We now need to limit the damage if we can, harsh though that might sound.'

Drew nodded. 'We can't do anything for Giles, the poor sod. He was a decent bloke and his dad was right; he was too good for her. She'd have emasculated him.'

The ten minutes it took to hear sirens approaching seemed to Alexi to be more like ten tense hours. Two uniformed coppers came onto the terrace, glanced at Giles and looked completely out of their depth. The elder eventually got on his radio and called in reinforcements, which is what Jack had asked for in the first place. His request had obviously held some sway because not five minutes later, a familiar figure strode onto the terrace.

'We can't keep meeting like this,' said Detective Inspector Mark Vickery, a droll edge to his voice. He accepted Jack's proffered hand, gave it a firm shake, and then repeated the process with Alexi and Drew. Vickery had investigated the murder that occurred during the cookery contest and had with him, once again, Constable Hogan, an attractive female detective. 'What do we have here?'

Jack succinctly outlined the circumstances.

'You don't have much luck at this hotel, do you?' Hogan remarked.

Vickery crouched down to examine the body without touching anything. Jack pointed to the knife, which now sat on a table behind him. Hogan gave it a cursory glance and slipped it into an evidence bag.

'Any ideas?' Vickery asked, straightening up again and addressing the question to Jack. 'Whilst we wait for the troops to arrive. Can't do anything until a doctor gets here and pronounces life extinct, as well you know. Not that we can't tell that for ourselves but we have to follow procedure.'

Jack succinctly outlined the events leading up to Giles's death, including the vital fact that his fiancée had raised the alert with her scream and that she'd been standing over him with the murder weapon in her hand.

'Open and shut,' Hogan muttered.

'Hardly,' Vickery responded. 'Can't see the woman killing her intended, then allowing herself to be found with the weapon in her hand.'

'Shock?' Hogan suggested.

'Drew doesn't think the knife is the property of the hotel,' Jack said.

'Someone brought a dagger with them?' Hogan shook her head. 'Seems extreme.'

'And suggests intent,' Vickery added. 'It's an unusual looking knife. I'll make enquiries. See if I can find out where it came from.'

'We've kept everyone here,' Jack said. 'They're in the bar and I believe your uniforms are actively discouraging anyone from trying to leave. Not that you'll get much sense out of any of them. They're all three sheets to the wind.'

Alexi shivered. 'You're cold,' Jack said, turning to her. 'It's the shock. Go into the bar with the others,' he added with a meaningful nod.

Alexi caught on immediately. Jack had only told Vickery the bare bones. He hadn't mentioned Giles's disagreements with his best man and father, or anything about his liaison with Jenny. He would, of course, elaborate but Alexi knew why he'd prevaricated. She would have a few minutes to chat to people before the police got around to them. They were still in shock and hadn't had time to come up with cover stories. It would be interesting to see if any of them confessed to the arguments and, more significantly, if Jenny confessed to whatever she'd had going with the victim.

If there was any way to minimise damage to the hotel's reputation by pinning the murder on an old dispute or grudge then Alexi wanted to get a jump start on that particular line of enquiry.

As she made her way inside, she tried to convince herself that the similarities between this tragedy and the previous murder were circumstantial. They *were* circumstantial, leaving aside the fact that two young individuals had needlessly lost their lives. The previous victim had been stabbed, but only after death. Giles had clearly died from a single stab wound to his chest. But there was no escaping the fact that they had both died in the grounds of Hopgood Hall. People would think that the place was cursed and once the droves of ghouls had satisfied their... well, ghoulish curiosity by visiting the scene then the hotel would likely resemble the *Mary Celeste.*

'Not if I have any say in the matter,' Alexi muttered through clenched teeth.

She was a journalist, a good journalist with a solid reputation, and she was here on the spot. She would do what she'd done after the previous two tragedies in Lambourn and write an informed article stating the facts and showing the hotel in the best possible light. *Damage limitation*, as Jack would say. She squared her shoulders, took a deep breath and entered the bar.

Jenny was the person she most wanted to speak with but she was surrounded by the other three bridesmaids and there was no possibility of getting her alone. Besides, it was obvious that she was still in extreme shock and there would be little possibility of getting any sense out of her.

Crystabel and Gloria sat apart from everyone else. Or more likely, the rest of the group had distanced themselves from the bride, looking upon her as the guilty party. Crystabel was now dry-eyed, her body rigid with tension and Alexi could imagine her mind whirling as she attempted to justify her behaviour. She craved the spotlight and it was now focused firmly upon her, but not for any reason that would increase her popularity. Alexi had taken a dislike to the ambitious woman who rode roughshod over the feelings and opinions of others but wasn't convinced that she was the guilty party. The cynical part of her brain wondered how Crystabel would spin this tragic event to enhance her public image, always supposing that Vickery didn't lock her up. Case closed.

The stags were on the other side of the room. They spoke to one another in muted tones, a million miles apart from the raucous bunch that not so long ago had been writhing around on the terrace, imitating dead ants. Murder was clearly an excellent antidote to drunkenness.

Alexi felt exhausted and defeated before she'd even begun. Much as it would be impossible to get Jenny alone, it was obvious that the same criteria applied to Simon. With no other choice left to her, she approached Giles's father, Anthony Preston-Smythe, and his companions, who sat slightly apart from the rest of the occupants of the bar.

She had met Anthony a couple of times and he had praised her journalistic efforts. She wondered if he would remember their previous conversations given the crippling loss that he now had to come to terms with. She knew she would be intruding upon his grief and that her probing questions would likely seem insensitive. Even so, she had to try. If Vickery took the easy route and charged Crystabel, and assuming Crystabel was innocent, then the real murderer would walk free. That would play on Alexi's conscience even more than the demise of Hopgood Hall's reputation. She was inadvertently responsible for this tragedy, she reminded herself, if any reminder was necessary. If she hadn't pushed Drew into extending both his property and his aspirations then the wedding would not have been booked at his hotel. Therefore, it was up to her to do all she could to find justice for Giles.

'Anthony,' she said softly. 'I am so very sorry. There are no words to express my regret for your loss.'

Anthony looked up at her through grief-stricken eyes but showed no signs of recognition. He clutched a brandy glass between both hands and had drained most of its contents already.

'Alexi Ellis,' she reminded him, sharing a glance with the two men beside him. One was his assistant trainer, a man not much older than Giles had been. He was a regular here in the bar and restaurant and his name was Martin Hall. The other man was, Alexi thought, Anthony's racing manager. Although he'd been pointed out to her a couple of times in the leadup to the wedding, she couldn't recall his name.

Good manners appeared to overcome Anthony's grief. He stood up and shook Alexi's hand. 'Thank you,' he said, sounding dazed, clearly attempting to hold himself together. 'You are acquainted with Martin,' he added, indicating his assistant. 'And this is Paul Croft, my racing manager.'

Alexi shook their hands and then sat down, un-invited. All three men had stood but they too now resumed their seats.

'Why did she do it?' Anthony asked into the en-suing silence, shaking his head.

'That is what the police will ascertain,' Alexi replied soothingly.

'Why is she still here, amongst us?' Anthony glared at Crystabel, seated a good distance away from him, his eyes shooting daggers. 'She needs to be locked up before she kills someone else.'

'The police have their procedures,' Paul said.

'Excuse me.' Anthony stood abruptly, his face sheet white beneath the designer stubble decorating his jaw. 'I need the bathroom.'

'Me too.' Martin got up as well and guided his boss towards the men's room.

'That was considerate of Martin,' Paul said into

the ensuing silence. 'Giles was everything to Anthony. His only child destined to take over the training yard in due course.'

'And yet he wasn't Anthony's second in command,' Alexi replied in a speculative tone. 'Martin is.'

'Giles worked everywhere. Mucking out stalls, riding out, the whole nine yards. He was learning the trade from the bottom, up. Anthony insisted upon it.'

'And Giles didn't mind? He grew up in the business. Surely he'd already picked up enough...' Enough what? Alexi had absolutely no idea what was involved. 'Martin can't be much older than Giles but he's already installed in the second-in-command's position.' She wondered how that situation had come about and how Giles had felt about it.

Paul flashed a brief smile. 'Giles had been away at university. He graduated six months before his mother died of cancer. It drove him over the edge. He and his mother were close, very close, and Giles felt adrift without her influence. She left him quite a bit of her own family's money. He used it to travel for a couple of years, trying to decide what he wanted to do with his life. He wasn't sure that horses were for him.'

'But he saw reason eventually?'

'Yeah, he came back about a year ago, chastened about something that had happened. I never found out what and I don't think Anthony knows what made him decide to toe the family line either. He was simply glad that he'd come to his senses. Anthony wasn't sure if Giles really understood how much is involved in running a business like a top training yard so I guess he was testing his determination. Do all the donkey work, learn the ropes properly and take it from there.'

'And Giles didn't mind?'

'Nope. He knuckled down and got along with everyone. I certainly never heard of any tension amongst the troops. He would do anything that was asked of him, I know that much, and you won't hear anyone at the yard with a bad word to say about him.'

'Would Martin have been pushed out if Giles stuck the course and became his dad's second-in-command?'

'Not sure.' Paul looked away from her and she got the impression that he was about to be evasive for the first time in their conversation. 'You'll have to ask the governor that. What he says, goes.'

Alexi smiled. Paul had clearly cottoned on to the

fact that Alexi was looking for angles. Other reasons for Giles's death besides a fatal spat with his intended. She wondered how to pursue her point but before she could do so, Anthony and Martin emerged from the gents and were heading back their way.

So too was Vickery and his entourage. Alexi had found out all she was likely to for now and so excused herself and joined Jack, who loitered in the doorway to the bar.

5

Jack smiled at Alexi and grasped her hand. 'You okay?' he asked.

'Not really. I still can't get my mind round what's happened. It's surreal.' She sighed. 'Poor Giles. And poor us. My former colleagues will have a field day.'

'Vickery has a prime suspect. The interest will soon fade.'

'Can we get out of here?' she asked as she watched Vickery's uniformed constables organising the inhabitants of the bar, separating them. He knew they would take individual statements now and follow up on anything important that was said the following day, despite the fact that they probably assumed they had their woman.

'Sure. Let's go back to Drew's kitchen. He went on ahead of us to update Cheryl.'

'Of course. She'll be worried. I should have thought of that.'

'You've had a few other priorities. Put yourself first for once.'

Jack examined her drawn features and cursed whoever had killed Giles and the fact that they had done so in the grounds of Hopgood Hall. He wasn't convinced that Crystabel was the guilty party. But for now his first priority was Alexi. She wasn't as tough as she made herself out to be. He knew this latest murder had knocked her sideways, she was riddled with guilt and was holding it together by a thread. She would be blaming herself and worrying about the hotel's future, Jack knew. It would be a waste of breath to tell her that none of this was her fault. It was simply rotten luck.

All Jack cared about was Alexi's peace of mind and if that required him to delve into the murder and make sure it was resolved as quickly and as quietly as possible then that's what he would do. If he trod on any of his old colleagues' toes in the process then he'd deal with that problem as and when it arose.

They crossed the courtyard, which was now

flooded with artificial light as people in white papers suits swarmed everywhere.

'What are they looking for?' Alexi asked.

'Anything that pertains to the murder. If they simply assume that they have the guilty party in Crystabel, which they almost certainly will, but don't look for alternative evidence, a defence brief will have a field day.'

Alexi nodded. 'You're not convinced that she did it, but does it make me a horrible person if I hope that she did. And that she confesses. Then it will all go away and we won't be held to blame.'

Jack smiled. 'It makes you human, darling.' But life, he knew, was seldom that straightforward.

They reached the kitchen and Cosmo, who clearly understood that some tragedy had occurred, prowled up to them. His rigid tail twitched as he mewled, demanding an explanation in his inimitable feline fashion.

'He wants to know why his services haven't been called upon,' Cheryl said, looking up from her place at the kitchen table, clearly attempting to lighten the sombre mood. But Jack could see that she was fraught with worry and worn down by exhaustion.

Alexi went up to her and gave her a hug. 'I am so sorry,' she said.

Cheryl hugged her right back. 'Why?' She blinked up at her friend. 'None of this is your fault.'

'Of course it's my fault. I encouraged you to offer the hotel for weddings.'

'Alexi!' Cheryl's voice was mildly castigating.

'Bad luck seems to dog my footsteps.'

'Self-pity doesn't suit you, Alexi,' Drew said briskly. He'd already opened a bottle of red. He poured generous measures for them all and handed the glasses round. 'Stop moping, which will achieve nothing, and focus instead on how best to limit the damage to the hotel's reputation.'

'Well said,' Jack agreed, leading Alexi to a chair and forcing her to sit. Cosmo jumped onto her lap. Alexi seemed to find comfort from his presence and smoothed his back with long sweeps of the hand not holding her glass.

'Drew tells me that Crystabel was found standing over the body with the murder weapon in her hand,' Cheryl said. 'That sounds pretty conclusive to me. She will be charged and the press will speculate about a spat between bride and groom that got out of hand. So no blame can be attached to us.'

Alexi shook her head. 'Jack isn't convinced that she did it.'

Everyone turned to look at Jack.

'I didn't say that. I simply know from experience that it's unwise to jump to conclusions. Anyway, speaking of the murder weapon, you sure you don't recognise it, either of you?' Jack took his phone from his pocket and pulled up the shot that he'd taken of the dagger. Drew and Cheryl both looked at it and simultaneously shook their heads.

'It's not ours,' Drew said. 'That handle is quite distinctive. It's bone, I think. Anyway, we don't have any daggers in the hotel. We have steak knives but nothing as vicious as that thing, and nothing with a hook other than cheese knives.' He waved a hand at the phone's screen. 'I've already told Vickery. He asked me just now. I checked with Marcel too and it didn't come from the kitchen.'

'So someone brought a dagger to a stag or hen party,' Alexi mused. 'We need to find out where it came from. I know Vickery will be looking but it won't hurt if we ask questions too.'

'Looks that way,' Jack replied, 'and Vickery's first priority will be to find out who that someone is. Unless he can prove that Crystabel brought it with her with the intention of killing her future husband, it begs the question, who does it belong to, why did they feel the need to bring it with them and did they actually intend to kill Giles with it?'

'Why would Crystabel kill him?' Cheryl asked.

'You said a moment ago that you hoped she'd be charged,' Alexi pointed out gently.

'I hadn't thought it through properly. I simply assumed, I suppose, given what Drew told me, that she had to have done it. Horrible person that I am, I hoped she had, just so that this ungodly mess could be cleared up quickly.' Cheryl paused to absently brush hair away from her eyes. 'But, you know, now I'm not so sure. She was really looking forward to being the star of the show in her televised wedding. I know she was keen to make the front pages as well, but doing so by being dragged out of here in hand-cuffs is probably not what she had in mind.'

'The girl has a temper,' Alexi pointed out. 'And if she thought that Giles was having second thoughts then it might have been enough to push her over the edge. I mean, she's been running a video diary about the build up to the big day and talking about it endlessly on her TV slot. She has big ambitions and this wedding was supposed to be the springboard that launched her national career. She would not thank Giles for humiliating her if he dumped her a week before the big day.'

'Was Giles planning to dump her?' Cheryl asked, sounding surprised. 'Frankly, I don't think he had the backbone to stand up to her. He was a nice boy but weak and malleable.'

Interesting, Jack thought, making a mental note to pursue Cheryl's thoughts on Giles's character weaknesses at a later time.

'I saw Giles and Crystabel's cousin Jenny getting up close and personal not an hour before the murder,' Alexi said.

'Blimey!' Cheryl covered her mouth with one hand. 'Does Vickery know?'

'Not unless Jenny told him,' Alexi replied. 'And I haven't had an opportunity to yet.'

'It's one hell of a motive,' Drew said pensively.

Jack nodded his agreement. It was the missing element that Vickery required in order to charge Crystabel and he would have to be told. It would save the hotel's reputation if a charge was brought within hours of the crime being committed; Cheryl was right about that. No one here could be held responsible for the romantic peccadillos of members of the wedding party.

Even so, a nagging corner of Jack's brain screamed at him that it was all too easy. Crystabel was ambitious and unlikeable but she was nobody's fool. Even if she had murdered her fiancé in a jealous rage, she was too cunning to be caught red-handed with the weapon in her possession. Or to draw attention to herself by screaming the place down for that matter. *And* there was very little blood on her clothing.

'True, but we've no way of knowing if she realised that Giles and Jenny were... well, whatever they were,' Jack reasoned. 'It could just have been a spur of the moment thing between two intoxicated people. A groom who was having last minute jitters and a bridesmaid who disliked her cousin.' He shrugged. 'It happens.'

'Not under a staircase in a private corridor,' Alexi replied. 'That smacks of a rendezvous to me.'

Jack conceded the point with a tilt of his head. 'We're agreed then that there are other lines of investigation rather than just the obvious.' Everyone in the kitchen reiterated their agreement, confirming for Jack that they had doubts about Crystabel's guilt as well. 'But if an overworked police force decides that Crystabel did it then the alternatives will be overlooked. We can't know if she knew about Jenny and Giles. She won't say if she did and the only other person who could is Jenny. And we know that she dislikes her cousin, so her word can't be taken at face value.'

Alexi nodded. 'None of the ladies like Crystabel very much. Even without a romantic attachment between Jenny and Giles, I don't have any difficulty believing that they'd think Crystabel capable of committing murder if her fiancé had had a change of heart. Simon ditched her, then Giles. Her ego couldn't withstand the humiliation.'

'But we will never know if Giles did call the wedding off,' Cheryl said glumly.

'There's a history between the cousins, the best man and the groom. Something to do with a holiday in Greece,' Alexi said. 'Crystabel and Simon went there as an engaged couple and came back separated.' She paused, tapping the fingers of the hand not stroking a purring Cosmo pensively against the side of her face. 'I can't shake the feeling that whatever happened on that holiday is pivotal to the atmosphere I've sensed here amongst the main players.'

'Crystabel still carries a torch for Simon,' Cheryl said. 'We've all seen the way she looks at him, but he seems to actively dislike her.'

'Another motive the police will seize on, no doubt,' Jack said.

'Why?' Alexi blinked up at him. 'Simon would never marry her.'

'They will imply that at the last minute, she decided that she couldn't settle for second best, especially if she knew about Giles and Jenny.'

'Hmm.' Drew slid down in his chair. 'What a tangled web...'

'I had a brief word with Anthony's racing manager just now,' Alexi said. 'Did you know that Giles was unsure if he wanted to take over the yard? His mother died, he went travelling for a couple of years then came back and decided he did want to follow in parental footsteps after all. But he's having to learn the trade from the bottom up. And here's the clincher: Anthony has an assistant trainer not much older that Giles himself. How would he have felt if he was pushed out of his top position by the prodigal son? A son who doesn't seem to have applied himself to anything much since leaving uni.'

'It's worth mentioning it to Vickery, I suppose,' Drew said without much conviction. 'I'm half wanting to let him lock Crystabel up without muddying the waters. I mean, she didn't love Giles, not if the way that she ogled Simon at every opportunity is anything to go by, *and* she isn't a nice person.'

'Even so...' Alexi spread her hands. 'Would you

be able to sleep at night if we didn't tell the police everything we know, or suspect?'

'I don't get to sleep at night anyway.' Drew smiled in an obvious effort to lighten the mood. 'I have a baby, remember.'

'Let's wait until morning before we decide on our next move,' Jack suggested. 'We will know by then if Vickery has gone ahead and charged Crystabel. If he does then we can rethink our strategy based on whatever evidence against her he's unearthed.'

'Other than the fact that she was found standing over the body with the murder weapon in her hand,' Cheryl reminded them all.

'Other than that,' Jack agreed, tight lipped.

'Whichever way we look at it, even if she isn't charged, she'll have her work cut out recovering from this situation,' Alexi said. 'My former colleagues will discover that she was the prime suspect and why. Then she'll be tried and found guilty in the court of social media.'

'It's past midnight,' Jack said, glancing out the window at the floodlight bathing a courtyard that had now taken on a sinister edge; the scene of not one but two murders in less than a year. 'They're taking the body away now and the forensic people are packing up. I doubt whether Vickery will want to talk to any of us tonight.'

'But almost everyone in the bar is staying at the hotel tonight,' Cheryl pointed out.

'I'll stay up and make sure they all get to their rooms,' Drew said, touching his wife's shoulder. 'You should be here in case Verity wakes.'

'When she does,' Cheryl replied, rolling her eyes.

'Is she okay?' Alexi asked. 'What with all the excitement, I'd forgotten that my goddaughter is unwell.'

'She's fine,' Drew replied. 'Sleeping like... well, like a baby. At the moment, anyway. We panicked. Anyway, get on off, all of you. If I'm here alone and Vickery happens to corner me then I can't tell him about Jenny and Giles because I didn't see anything.'

'But it would help us if he does know and draws his own conclusions,' Cheryl said, glancing at Alexi. 'A jealous woman scorned and all that. Like I said earlier, Simon dumped her and now her groom's cheating on her a week before they tie the knot.'

'I'm with Jack on this one,' Drew replied. 'I think all aspects of Giles's life need to be explored before we plump for the obvious. Sorry, love,' he added, glancing at Cheryl. 'I don't welcome the bad publicity any more than you do but I care about justice too much to put our own interests first.' He grinned. 'Well, probably!'

'Come on.' Jack held out his hand to Alexi and pulled her to her feet. Cosmo, still on her lap, gave an indignant mewl, stirred himself and landed gracefully on the floor. He trotted towards the door, aware that they were leaving and making it clear that he wasn't staying behind.

'Even Cosmo isn't keen on murder central,' Cheryl muttered.

Jack saw the agonised expression on Alexi's face and wished that her friend hadn't made such a flippant comment. Whilst Alexi and Cheryl hugged, Jack took Drew to one side and had a quiet word. Drew nodded his understanding.

'I'll see what I can do,' he said.

Jack guided Alexi from the kitchen with his hand on the small of her back. Cosmo trotted along beside them like the dog he sometimes pretended to be. Jack unlocked his car and wordlessly, Alexi slid into the passenger seat. Cosmo jumped onto her lap again and curled up in as tight a ball as a large cat could manage. Jack said nothing as he climbed behind the wheel and fired up the engine. She needed time to think matters through now that they were away from the scene. Once she'd done so, he knew she would have a dozen questions.

'Thanks for not asking me if I'm okay,' she said after they'd driven most of the way to her cottage in silence.

'We're none of us okay.'

'But you handled the situation like a professional which, of course, you are.'

'You have to keep your emotions detached. Detective school 101,' he replied, smiling across at her. 'It's not always easy but training helps. It comes to the fore in situations such as that one. You don't allow yourself to think. You just act on instinct. If I'd dwelt upon the fact that I'd been drinking with the victim not an hour before his death then I would have been about as much use as a chocolate teapot.' Jack paused. 'Men have emotional meltdowns as well as women, you know.'

Alexi snorted. 'Somehow I can't ever imagine you losing control.'

Jack pulled the car into Alexi's driveway and cut the engine. The moment Alexi opened her door, Cosmo leapt from her lap and stalked into the garden, patrolling his domain. It was still warm and Jack knew that Alexi wouldn't want to go to bed yet. Those questions would still be whirling around inside her head. She walked into her living room and threw open the doors to the garden. Jack followed her when she stepped outside and they sat on the patio chairs, listening to the sounds of the night.

'Despite all our speculation just now, Vickery will charge Crystabel, won't he?' Alexi eventually said on a sigh.

'Almost certainly but that doesn't mean that a prosecution will follow. It largely depends upon what the forensic investigation throws up.'

'But her fingerprints will be on that dagger's handle.'

'She's claiming that she came across Giles seconds after the attack and pulled the knife from his chest without thinking.'

'It doesn't sound plausible. What are the chances? The timing, I mean.'

'She did bring her hen party to the hotel for reasons she hasn't shared with us. You thought she simply wanted to have everything under her control, the high jinx between the guys recorded to liven up her TV programme, but we know from all the conversations we overheard that there were tensions between the main players. Something was going on that we know nothing about.'

Alexi grunted. 'Something was definitely going on between Giles and Jenny.'

'It could be that Crystabel went to find him because she wanted to iron out the creases, or at the very least apologise to Giles for crashing his party. We know he wasn't pleased about it and actually stood up to her for once. So, it might be possible that she went to look for him when the party was winding down and she hoped to catch him alone.'

The dim light coming from the sitting room threw Alexi's profile into light and shadow, sufficient for Jack to see her troubled expression. He wished he could reassure her but he wasn't in the business of issuing platitudes if he wasn't in a position to deliver on them, nor would she thank him for it.

'I guess we have to wait for the morning and see which way Vickery jumps.'

'We do, darling.'

'We'll tell him everything we saw and heard?'

'Of course. When he asks. But whatever line he takes, we'll conduct our own investigation in the meantime. It's only Friday and the wedding party is booked into the hotel until Monday morning. That will give us some leeway.'

'They might decide to go home.'

'Vickery will discourage a mass exodos. He will

need to get signed statements from everyone. Find out who was where at the time of the murder. That will take time.'

'But if Crystabel is arrested...'

'All the more reason for him to get his ducks in a row.' He stood up and held out a hand. 'Come on, we're talking round in circles. Let's hit the sack and come at this fresh in the morning.'

6

Alexi woke from a fractured sleep feeling headachy and ill-prepared to face the day.

She extricated herself from Jack's arms, almost resenting the fact that he'd clearly had no problem dropping off, whereas her mind had been too full of the horrific murder and its consequences to make that possible.

She hit the shower and heard Jack stirring as she towelled herself off. Not ready to discuss the murder again yet, she offered him an absent good morning, watching him in the periphery of her vision as he sat up, blinked the sleep from his eyes and ran a hand absently through his tangled hair. She pulled on a dressing gown and wandered downstairs, leaving

Jack to use the facilities. By the time he joined her, she had the coffee going and bread in the toaster. Most importantly, she'd fed Cosmo, who was now fastidiously attending to his own ablutions.

'Morning, beautiful.' Jack kissed her brow. 'Get any sleep?'

'Some,' she replied, decanting toast onto his plate and putting another slice in the machine for herself. She had only just eaten it when her phone rang. She glanced at the display and groaned, although why she was surprised to receive an early morning wake-up call from such a quarter, she couldn't have said.

'Patrick?' Jack asked in a resigned tone.

'Yeah. He survives on about four-hours sleep.' She hesitated and then took the call. Her former lover and editor of the *Sentinel* wouldn't stop calling until she answered him. Although he'd stopped trying to contact her so regularly, she knew he hadn't given up on her and this latest murder gave him the perfect excuse to resume communications. Besides, if she declined his calls, he'd only turn up in Lambourn and that she could most definitely do without.

'Patrick,' she said, taking the call. 'What can I do for you?'

'Another murder? Christ, Alexi, are you okay? What do they put in the water down there?'

A good question, she thought, rolling her eyes. 'I can't tell you anything,' she said curtly.

'I haven't asked for inside information. I just wanted to make sure that you hadn't fallen victim to some axe-wielding lunatic.'

'I'm fine, thanks for asking. But you'll have to excuse me, I'm just leaving.'

'I'll be sending a stringer down but of course, I'll buy the story from you,' he said curtly, all business.

'I'll let you know,' she replied, relieved that he finally appeared to be getting the message. Unsure if he actually was. This could simply be another ruse. Back off, give her space and she was probably supposed to realise what she was missing. Yeah, like that was gonna happen, she thought, sighing.

'Crystabel Hennessy is a TV personality. The stations will be all over this.'

'She has a spot on a local station. She's not exactly a household name.'

'She will be once the news breaks.'

Alexi gave a resigned nod, even though Patrick couldn't see the gesture. She knew he was right, heartless though it sounded. Murder was good for the ratings. 'I guess.'

'She was making a name for herself as an influencer, whatever that is...'

'Hmm.' A growing number of wannabes were influencing the behaviour of impressionable people by becoming what would once have been referred to as trendsetters. The modern brand used social media as their platform of choice. 'Well, she's got her wish but for all the wrong reasons. Anyway, I have to go.'

'Keep in touch, Alexi, and stay safe.' Patrick's voice dropped to the seductive level that would once have made her weak at the knees. 'Remember, I'll pay top dollar for the inside scoop.'

So will all the others, she thought. 'I'll bear that in mind.'

Alexi cut the connection, drained her coffee mug and stood up, ignoring Jack's mildly inquisitive glance. He and Patrick detested one another and Jack likely thought this was Patrick's latest attempt to get up close and personal with her again. He was probably right but she had no desire to talk about it. There was nothing left to be said.

'Ready?' she asked Jack. 'My car's still at the hotel so Cosmo and I will have to cadge a ride with you.'

'At your service, madam.' He offered her a sweeping bow that made her smile.

Cosmo led the way to the front door and stood there, impatiently swishing his tail as he waited for Jack to open it.

'Okay, darling,' Jack said, once they were installed in his car and heading for the hotel. 'It will be bedlam there, you realise that. The word's obviously out.'

'Of course it is.' Alexi rolled her eyes.

'The press will be out in force. Vickery will arrive soon so we don't have much time to talk to the wedding guests off the record.'

'What are we trying to establish?'

'There were undercurrents between the members of both parties. We know that from the arguments we saw and what you managed to find out.'

Alexi nodded. 'And whatever people were arguing about might be pertinent to Giles's death?'

'Right.'

The prospect of a juicy murder that would once have had her salivating as she beat the big boys to the scoop now made her feel weary. 'You don't think Vickery will delve if we tell him what we heard and leave it to him?' she asked, more in hope than expectation.

Jack shook his head decisively before she'd even finished asking her question. 'I don't think we can depend on it, especially when we tell him about Jenny and Giles. That will provide him with the missing motive. And that motive is the only reason I can think of for him not to have arrested Crystabel already.'

'Yep.'

'He'll probably arrest her anyway. I most likely would in his position.'

'If he does then it'll take the spotlight away from the hotel. A spat between future husband and wife that got out of hand. We can't be blamed for that.'

'Come on, Alexi. I know you're in self-preservation mode but are you absolutely convinced that Crystabel's the guilty party?'

Alexi thought of the woman's stunned expression when they'd come upon her the night before, knife dripping blood held in her hand, and slowly shook her head. 'I've never murdered anyone.' She paused. 'Yet. But I'd imagine that thinking about it and actually doing it are two entirely different matters. Even someone as determined and hard-hearted as Crystabel would be unable to control her reaction at the sight of all that blood. And the smell of it. Maybe she didn't mean to stab him but a confrontation got out of hand.' She sighed. 'Whatever, I'd prefer to know for sure,' she conceded.

'Well, there you are then. We're not doing Vickery's job for him. I'm not so arrogant as to suppose he needs our help but I do know how the system works, which means I know that he has too few people to investigate too many crimes. And something as apparently open and shut as this murder... well, he'll be under pressure to close the case given the amount of publicity it will garner and so I can understand it if he takes the easy route.'

'No one seems to like Crystabel very much, not even her own bridesmaids, so I don't suppose they'll be an outpouring of support from them. Even so, someone has to fight her corner and I guess that's us. Innocent until proven guilty and all that.'

'Exactly!' Jack slowed to allow a woman with a pram and a small dog on a lead to cross the road in front of him. She waved her thanks. 'I'm guessing that the ladies will be in the upstairs lounge and the guys in the annexe. I suggested to Drew before we left last night that he put them in there. With a murderer lurking and feelings running high, it seemed safer to keep the two parties separated, especially since everyone assumes that Crystabel is the guilty party. Drew was also going to make the annexe lounge available to Vickery for interviews. It will keep him away from any lookie-loos who get past the police and use the hotel's facilities. There are always some.'

Alexi shuddered. 'Surely you don't think this was anything other than a one-off killing?'

'Not seriously no, but it pays to be cautious. I know for a certainty that the stags and hens will be wary of one another. It's the way of the world, darling. Giles has been murdered and Crystabel is the prime suspect. The guys won't want to be anywhere near her, or her entourage. Count on it. And they can't gather in the downstairs lounge. There's no guarantee of privacy there.'

'No, I guess not.' She let out a long breath. 'I assume Vickery will be here early, but hopefully we'll be ahead of him. It's still not seven-thirty. I'm guessing as well that no one will have slept much. So why don't we split up? You take the guys, and I'll see if I can get anything out of the ladies before Vickery has a chance to grill them.' She paused. 'Jenny in particular.'

'Are you going to mention that you saw her with Giles?'

'Only if I can get her alone, which is far from certain, and then only if I think it will achieve anything. I'll have to play it by ear.'

'Be careful.'

'Damn!' They approached the lane that led to the hotel, to find it jammed with vehicles. Alexi had been expecting it but it didn't mean that she had to like it. And yet, not so long ago she would have been one of the reporters eager for a story. 'Whoever said there's no such thing as bad publicity obviously didn't own a hotel,' she muttered.

Jack removed one hand from the steering wheel and tapped her knee. 'It's okay. We'll get through this.'

Alexi nodded, even though she was unsure if she believed it. She recognised a number of people she knew from the world of journalism but there were a lot more that she didn't. Stringers for the nationals, she assumed. There were a couple of TV cameras and an anchor talking into a microphone. Alexi pulled sunglasses over her eyes and looked away, hoping not to be recognised. Cosmo however felt no such compulsion. Not one to miss an opportunity to steal the limelight, he pressed his face against the car's window and hissed at the gathering. He was noticed almost immediately and all the cameras focused upon him. Jack roared with laughter.

'What a poser!' he said.

'Don't encourage him,' Alexi replied, laughing herself. 'I swear he used to be a human in a former life.'

'And has a much better time of it as a feline with attitude.'

Alexi grinned. 'No question.'

Her expression sobered when Jack was stopped by a uniformed constable as they approached the hotel. He gave his name along with Alexi's and they were permitted past the cordon. The car park was half full of vehicles that Alexi didn't recognise.

'Scene of crime techs are back,' he said, nodding towards a large white van.

'Is that good or bad?'

Jack shrugged. 'Probably good from Crystabel's standpoint. They're looking for more evidence so probably think they don't already have enough. Either that or they're being thorough. Vickery knows this will be a trial by television.'

Jack parked up and as soon as Alexi opened her door, Cosmo leapt from the car, stalked over to the cordon and hissed at the gathering. Alexi called him off, shaking her head when grown men jumped out of the way of a domestic feline. It was a light moment that created much-needed spontaneous laughter.

'He could show Crystabel a thing or two about stealing the show,' Jack remarked as, cat safely back under control, they made their way to Cheryl's kitchen.

They were greeted by the aroma of freshly brewed coffee and the sound of a baby crying.

'What's wrong with my precious girl?' Alexi demanded to know, taking Verity from her mother's arms and kissing her forehead.

'Absolutely nothing,' Drew replied with a goofy grin. 'As you can hear, her lungs are in excellent working order and she's exercising her democratic right to... exercise them. Frequently.'

'She's fine,' Cheryl confirmed. 'One less thing to be worried about.'

'Coffee?' Drew asked.

They both accepted and Alexi handed the baby back to her mother so that she could enjoy hers. As they did so, Jack explained their plans for the morning.

'Yeah, the guys are all in the annexe,' Drew confirmed. 'They didn't take much persuading to decant there. I just had their breakfast sent over. I'm told that they're pretty subdued, which is hardly surprising. A combination of hangovers and shock would have that effect.'

Jack drained his coffee mug and stood up. 'No time like the present then. Vickery won't let the grass grow.'

'He hasn't turned up to arrest anyone yet, which is something,' Cheryl told them, her brow creasing with worry.

Alexi gave her friend a brief hug, careful not to squash the baby. 'Jack says it will turn out okay for us, so we can blame him if it all goes pear-shaped.'

Cheryl's smile almost reached her eyes. 'I feel better already.'

Jack and Alexi went their separate ways. Cosmo protested when he was forced to remain in the kitchen. Toby was delighted to have his friend's exclusive company and dropped a ball at his paws, seeming to think that the cat would be willing to play. A smile graced Alexi's features as she watched the cat debating his options and batting the ball experimentally with a paw. She wouldn't put anything past him.

She made her way up the stairs and could hear muted voices coming from the lounge. She put her head round the door and saw all four of Crystabel's bridesmaids there. But there was no sign of Crystabel or her mother.

'Ladies,' she said, walking into the room. Their breakfast was laid out on a side table but no one seemed to have eaten very much. 'How are you all feeling?' She flapped a hand. 'Sorry. Stupid question.'

Alexi sat down on the nearest vacant chair and took a moment to examine the ladies' faces. They still all seemed to be in shock but Jenny looked as if she was held together by the sheer force of her will. Her eyes were swollen from crying, her face was chalk white and her hair hung round her face in unsightly tangles.

'It's like an out of body experience,' Nicola said, speaking for them all. 'I keep thinking that I'll wake up from a bad dream.'

The others nodded their agreement.

'Nothing will bring Giles back though, no matter how often we wake up,' Jenny said, her voice ragged. 'That bitch!'

'You all think Crystabel actually did it?'

Alexi's question was greeted by four nodding heads and no hesitation.

'You discussed it?'

'No, not last night,' Nicola replied. 'We were all

too traumatised. We just came up and went to bed. Not that any of us slept much, I don't think. I certainly didn't.'

'What's to discuss?' Claire demanded to know. 'Crystabel was found standing over him with the dagger in her hand. It doesn't get much clearer cut than that.'

'Why would she kill the man she loved and intended to marry?' Alexi asked.

'Crystabel only loved one person and that was herself,' Abbey said fiercely. 'She was wildly ambitious and supremely confident that this televised wedding would do wonders for her career, so it does make you think, I suppose...'

'She has a right temper,' Claire said. 'Despite her aspirations, if something happened to severely piss her off then there's no telling how she would have reacted in the heat of the moment. Besides, if she can somehow prove that she *didn't* do it then the resulting publicity will definitely work in her favour.'

Alexi knew that if the ladies spoke as candidly to Vickery as they were to her then Crystabel's fate would be sealed because, the way Alexi saw it, if Crystabel *could* prove her innocence, she would already have done so.

'But she was getting what she wanted,' Nicola

pointed out. 'A society wedding that would make the headlines, a handsome husband, the whole nine yards. Even if she was annoyed about something he said or did, she was too conniving to shoot herself in the foot. Or more to the point, kill the golden goose.'

Alexi glanced at Jenny and noticed her shudder. None of the others appeared to, which implied that they were in the dark regarding Jenny's secret affair with the deceased.

'I think they argued last night,' Claire said. 'I heard them. Well, anyone walking past that small room off the bar would have heard them. I didn't see them mind, but Giles was definitely arguing with someone.'

'Argued about what?'

Claire shrugged. 'I have no idea. Didn't take much notice. I just put it down to Crystabel's latest drama.'

'She is a bit of a drama queen,' Abby said, nodding her agreement, as though that much wasn't already common knowledge to everyone in the room.

'How long was this before he was found dead?' Alexi asked, conscious of Jenny's suppressed gasp at this stark reminder of Giles's demise. Perhaps she should have worded her question more diplomatically but as far as she was concerned, dead was dead. Referring to someone who'd passed away or crossed the rainbow bridge or whatever other analogy amounted to the same thing and didn't really soften the blow.

'Not sure.' Claire didn't seem that interested. Could she really be so naïve that she didn't think it was significant? 'Does it matter?'

'It could be vital. Inspector Vickery will want to know. It would be best if you could remember.'

'Well, half an hour. An hour tops. The party was running out of steam early. The guys seemed flat somehow, perhaps because we'd turned up and cramped their style. I told Crystabel that would happen but she never listens to anything she doesn't want to hear. I was wondering if I'd be missed if I slunk off to bed. I'm not big on drinking too much. My hangovers last for days and are just not worth it.'

'Why did Crystabel insist upon crashing the stag party?' Alexi asked, aware that she wouldn't get anything further about the bride's argument with her intended, mainly because no one else had heard it and those who did hadn't bothered to take an interest. Or, if they had, they weren't about to make that admission. Claire wasn't even sure if Crystabel had been the one arguing with Giles, although Alexi found it hard to imagine that it had been anyone else.

It was frustrating but she wouldn't be able to talk privately with Jenny without creating speculation that she would prefer to avoid. If Crystabel was innocent then Alexi would rather that she didn't find out about Giles and Jenny. It would serve no purpose other than to create a rift between the cousins. Not that they seemed particularly close, but still...

'Isn't it obvious?' Nicola asked. 'She had to be the centre of attention,' she continued, not waiting for anyone to answer her question.

'No, there was more to it than that,' Abby said, frowning. 'I think she didn't entirely trust Giles. She never actually said as much because it would imply something lacking on her part if she couldn't hold his interest even before they were married. It's just that I heard her on the phone once in the office, just before we came away. She didn't know I was there but I heard her expressing her doubts about Giles's commitment.'

'Do you have any idea who she was talking to?'

Abby shook her head. 'No, sorry. And I could have got it wrong. It was just the impression I had.'

'She sounds desperate,' Alexi said, half to herself.

'Desperate to save face, no matter what,' Jenny said, a vicious edge to her voice that caused everyone in the room to glance at her this time.

'None of you seem to like her very much.'

'That obvious, is it?' Claire smiled. 'What gave us away?'

'Where is she now?' Alexi asked, feeling a smidgen of sympathy for Crystabel. They didn't have to agree to be her bridesmaids so perhaps they weren't averse to a little publicity either.

'In her room. Her mother slept in there with her. She hasn't spoken a word to any of us since she was found standing over poor Giles,' Nicola said. 'Will she be arrested?'

'She ought to be if there's any justice in this world,' Jenny said. 'She's as guilty as sin. What are the police waiting for?'

The others all nodded and Alexi knew she'd got as much out of them as she was likely to, which wasn't a great deal but more than enough to seal Crystabel's fate. Her arguing with Giles on top of all the other evidence did not look good for the young woman.

'I'm going to hit the shower,' Claire said, standing.

'Me too.' Nicola got up as well.

Alexi wished Abby out of the way so that she could question Jenny. Her instincts told her that she wanted badly to talk and wouldn't take much persuading. Alexi also knew that time was running out. Vickery and his entourage would be here soon and he wouldn't look kindly upon Alexi poking her journalistic nose into his investigation.

As if in answer to her prayers, Abby's phone rang. She glanced at the display and sighed.

'It's work,' she said. 'They must have heard. I need to take this. Excuse me.'

Left alone with Jenny, Alexi allowed the silence to work for her. It wasn't long before Jenny broke it.

'What happens now?' she asked.

'The inspector will want to talk to you all again.'

She spread her hands. 'I don't see why.'

'He will want to know where everyone was at the time of Giles's death. Or just before.'

'None of us had reason to kill him.' She threw up her hands. 'Why would we?'

'Crystabel can argue that she had less reason than anyone,' Alexi replied calmly.

'True, but for the fact that she was found with the weapon in her hands and blood all over them.'

Jenny was getting worked up and Alexi knew that it was important to keep her calm and focused.

'Do you think Abby got it right and Crystabel did suspect Giles of having an affair?'

Jenny's pale cheeks bloomed with colour. 'How would I know?'

'Take some advice from me, Jenny. Don't lie to the police. You'll be found out in the end and it will cast suspicion on you.'

'Me!' She pointed at her own chest for emphasis. 'I'm the last person in the world who would hurt Giles. Why would I?'

'Because you were in love with him and he with you but you couldn't persuade him not to go through with the marriage to Crystabel?'

7

Jack made his way to the annexe, shuddering when he recalled that the victim in the cookery contest had been found in one of its rooms. Even if the stags also knew it, they would have had other priorities, Jack reasoned, like getting their minds round the brutal killing of their mate. They'd come here to get him paralytic before his big day, not to witness his murder. They were guys so they'd tough it out but it would still have been one hell of a shock.

Jack entered the lounge and found all five of them gathered there, draped over chairs and settees, awake after a fashion. Jack reckoned that they hadn't slept much, if at all and had spent the night dozing in the chairs they occupied. He recognised their clothes from the night before. Dishevelled hair, haunted faces and a cacophony of groans confirmed their hangovers, as did the empty bottles and glasses littering every surface. Clearly, they had continued drinking once they got here and had probably done so for the majority of the night. He wondered what they'd said about the murder amongst themselves and what conclusions they'd drawn. Not that anyone had expressed much doubt as to the identity of the culprit the previous evening but slightly clearer heads might now question their initial conclusions.

Crystabel had already been condemned in the court of public opinion and perhaps rightly so. It was always easy to point the finger of suspicion towards a person who was unpopular, Jack knew, but despite all the evidence to the contrary, he remained to be convinced of Crystabel's guilt. Part of him thought he should back off, let Vickery do his job and if Crystabel was charged, it would not only make the matter go away but also limit the damage to Hopgood Hall's reputation. The evidence against Crystabel was compelling but not set in stone. A good brief would create enough doubt to see her acquitted.

Probably.

But the detective in Jack baulked at the idea of

not digging deeper. Something about this entire business wasn't right. It was all too convenient. His mind dwelt upon those heated discussions between the groom and his best man. Between the groom and his father. To Simon's previous engagement to Crystabel. Why had it broken up and why was there so much animosity on Simon's part? It was obvious that Crystabel still carried a torch for Simon and that he didn't return her feelings. Why had Crystabel insisted upon crashing the stag party? What was it that she'd wanted to control?

There were simply too many anomalies for Jack's liking. Damage limitation notwithstanding, he wouldn't be able to sleep at night if he thought an innocent person – even one as hard to like as Crystabel – had been charged with a crime that she hadn't committed.

'Morning.'

Five heads nodded in acknowledgement of Jack's greeting but no one spoke at first, other than to groan. Nodding was clearly a painful enough challenge. Breakfast had been laid out on a table but only the coffee appeared to have been attacked.

'A fry-up's the best thing for hangovers,' Jack said, nodding towards the covered serving dishes.

'Just sayin',' he added when verbal abuse was hurled at him.

'Anything's worth a try,' Simon said, getting up and helping himself.

The others did likewise, showing little enthusiasm. Jack sat by, willing them to eat quickly. He knew he wouldn't get anything out of them until they felt vaguely human.

'What happens now?' Simon asked, pushing his half-finished breakfast aside and standing to refill his coffee cup. He ran a hand through his hair. His eyes were bloodshot but he seemed more alert than the others.

'Vickery will be here soon. He'll want individual statements from you all.'

'Not much we can tell him,' a guy called Will replied. The others nodded their agreement. 'The party had pretty much broken up. The women's arrival had turned it into a damp squib. Even though we'd banned them from the bar, we still knew they were upstairs and speaking personally, that made me uncomfortable.' The others again nodded. There were no dissenting voices. 'Anyway, we were all in the bar, having a final snifter. Giles had been missing for a while and, to be honest, hadn't exactly been the life and soul when he was with us. He had something on his mind, is my guess. Second thoughts perhaps.'

'Did he tell you that?' Jack asked.

'Nah. Guys don't go in for all that soul-searching; you know that. Anyway, most grooms get the jitters when the big day draws near, don't they?' Will shrugged. 'Wouldn't know myself. I've never taken the plunge.'

Terry, a bespectacled guy who Jack had heard referred to as a boffin, nodded cautiously. 'Giles seemed more like a condemned man at times, rather than one who was about to marry the woman of his dreams; that much is undeniable. The party wasn't spontaneous. It was forced gaiety, if you know what I mean.'

Jack nodded. He did know. He'd been there and experienced the tense atmosphere for himself.

'I'd have been in the front row applauding if he did call it off.' Arthur rolled his eyes. 'The woman's a barracuda and she would have eaten Giles for breakfast. He'd never have found the backbone to stand up to her. And, just so you know, I'm not speaking ill of the dead and not saying anything to you that I didn't say to Giles's face but he didn't want to hear it. He just shrugged and walked away from me.'

'When did you have this conversation?' Jack asked.

'Last night, early on.' Arthur blinked his bleary eyes. 'Why? Is it important?'

Jack shrugged. 'No idea. Best tell Vickery.'

'And hammer another nail into Crystabel's coffin,' Will said quietly.

Jack shook his head. 'It was Arthur giving advice. No one will ever know if Giles took it. Even so, it's best to be open and honest about what was said. Who knows what could be important?'

'We all thought he was being led to the altar by the balls,' Simon remarked, 'but I can tell you now that he was dead set on going ahead with the wedding, and not because he was head over heels in love.' Simon frowned. 'There was something else making him determined to go through with it and don't bother asking me what it was because I have absolutely no idea. All I can tell you is that neither I nor Giles's dad, who had considerably more bargaining power, could talk sense into him.'

'His father threatened to disinherit him, I gather.'

Simon looked surprised. 'Where did you hear that?'

'Is it true?'

'Yeah, but he wouldn't have done it. He could see through Crystabel and knew she'd make a terrible trainer's wife but he also told me that he'd give the marriage two years tops. Personally, I thought that was optimistic.'

'You and Crystabel were engaged once, I hear.'

'Until I realised the error of my ways.' Simon shuddered. 'I was briefly swayed by a pretty face and a glamorous lifestyle but I soon realised that Crystabel only has the capacity to love one person, and that's herself. She's also strong-willed, high-maintenance and don't get me started on that mother of hers. Anyway, I came to my senses and had a lucky escape.'

There was a great deal more to his relationship with Crystabel and the subsequent breakup that he wasn't telling. If Jack was a betting man, he'd put a hefty wedge on it being pivotal to this investigation. But Jack knew that Simon wouldn't open up in front of his mates. He wasn't convinced that he didn't have his own views on why Giles was determined to marry Crystabel but even if Jack could get him alone, he had no authority to grill him and Simon would be well within his rights to tell him to take a hike.

Jack put that mysterious Greek holiday that kept

intruding into his thoughts on the back burner, out of sight but not forgotten.

'Crystabel controls everything and everyone who comes within her sphere,' Simon said, filling the silence that Jack had permitted to stretch between them, broken until then only by the yawning and groaning of the other men. 'She would have emasculated Giles, no question.'

'It was almost like she had some sort of hold over him,' Pete said, speaking for the first time and simultaneously munching on a sausage. 'Simon's got that part right. And, for the record, she was an outrageous flirt. She came on to me last night. I couldn't believe it.'

'I can,' Simon said. 'Giles stood up to her, probably for the first time, in front of us all and her pride took a bashing. She needed to feel in control again.'

'Yeah well, she was out of luck,' Pete said with a careless wave. 'I don't do other men's women. And especially not those who are engaged to mates of mine.'

The others all grumbled their agreement.

'Tell me more about Giles's father's opposition to the marriage,' Jack said, himself yawning behind his hand. He knew Alexi had barely slept the previous night. He knew because he hadn't either. Not for a moment did he think that Anthony had killed his own son, but his opposition to the marriage and the financial hold he had over Giles had placed stress on the engagement.

'Simon's already said it all. Anthony disliked Crystabel on sight and saw her for the conniving bitch that she is,' Will said with venom in his tone. 'Shame Giles didn't take any notice of his father's warnings. Although, to be fair, even I didn't think she'd attack him with a dagger simply because he'd embarrassed her.'

'Is that what you think happened?' Jack asked.

'Well, what other explanation can there be?' Will glanced at the others for support and they all nodded but Jack knew they hadn't thought it through with the brain of a detective and had allowed their own prejudices to cloud their judgement. They knew what they'd seen, feelings were running high, and it was enough to condemn her. They hadn't stopped to wonder why she'd gone armed with a dagger in order to confront her intended about their earlier spat, or where the dagger had come from in the first place for that matter. They also didn't seem to realise that if she had armed herself then it implied premeditation. Ergo, if charges were brought, they would be for murder not manslaughter.

'Perhaps he did take his father's warnings on board at the eleventh hour,' Terry suggested. 'I saw him and his father having a heated discussion. You were there, Simon. What was that all about?'

'Oh, it was Anthony reinforcing his opposition to the marriage but Giles was still determined to go through with it.'

You're holding something back.

'Giles is... was malleable. He never stuck to things for long,' Will said. 'All that drifting around the world for two years, doing bar work, picking fruit, living off the money his mother left him. It was a good sum but he ran through it all. I think that's probably why he came back in the end.'

Simon and Terry exchanged a look and nodded.

'I don't think he was that interested in training racehorses, which is why he took himself off in the first place,' Simon said. 'Too much like hard work and too much responsibility, he once told me. Giles wasn't big on taking responsibility, which is probably how Crystabel got her hooks into him so easily.'

'Heir to a thriving training yard.' Will nodded. 'Makes sense. She probably pictured herself at the races, tarted up to the eyeballs, leading in winners.' He rolled his eyes. 'The silly bitch!'

'Do you really think his father would have made good on his threats to disinherit his only son?' Jack asked.

Simon shrugged. 'Probably, at the time. But if the marriage went ahead, tempers had a time to cool... who knows? He didn't approve of Giles wafting round the world, trying to find what it was that he actually did want to do with his life, and didn't hesitate to say so. Anthony is nothing if not forthright in the expression of his views.' Simon bit into a slice of toast and wiped the crumbs from his chin with a napkin. 'As to Giles, he obviously didn't find that elusive something because he finished up back where he started, none the wiser.'

'Perhaps he did decide to take his father's advice and broke it off with Crystabel that evening,' Pete said speculatively. 'That would be more than motive enough for Crystabel to take her revenge. The humiliation, when she'd made such a big deal of her nuptials both online and on her TV show, would have been unthinkable and in the heat of the moment...'

Given what Jack knew about his association with Jenny, that seemed plausible. Giles was coming across as a weak individual but if he really did have feelings for Jenny then coupled with his father's threat to cut him loose, perhaps he'd developed a backbone, confronted Crystabel and called off the wedding.

Even so, Jack sensed there was more to it than that. Giles might have been weak but he also had a hidden agenda. Something in his and Crystabel's shared past that had made him feel obliged to marry her.

'Bloody hell!' All heads turned in Terry's direction. He was gawping at something on his phone. 'Look at this, guys.'

Jack's chin almost hit the floor when confronted with a tearful image of Crystabel, without makeup in public for probably the first time in her entire adult life, telling her adoring public on her YouTube channel about the brutal murder of her fiancé.

'And I found him,' she sobbed, biting her lower lip. 'He was the love of my life but the police think that I killed him.'

'Any lingering doubts I might have had about her guilt have been eradicated by that self-serving bullshit,' Simon said bitterly, shaking his head, sounding and looking disgusted. 'How could she? Does she really think people will buy it?'

'I sense her mother's hand behind this publicity stunt,' Will replied. 'She's the driving force behind her daughter's ambitions and as hard and conniving as they come.'

'Look at all the comments,' Terry said, scrolling through his phone. 'There are hundreds and this only went up a few minutes ago. The majority are sympathetic.'

Which, Jack knew, would have been the idea. Crystabel's video had been short on fact and heavy on emotion. She knew she was the prime suspect and wanted public opinion on her side, making it that much harder for the police to arrest her.

'A hell of a way to go about proving her innocence,' Pete muttered.

'What happens now?' Terry asked, stretching his arms above his head and wincing. 'Christ, I need a shower.'

'Goes for us all,' Will added, sniffing his own armpit.

'I'd suggest you hang out here,' Jack said. 'The police will be here shortly to take statements from you all.'

The guys nodded and drifted towards the bathrooms. Simon was the last to leave but Jack didn't attempt to detain him. He knew he'd gotten everything he was likely to from the best man, at least for now.

Sighing, he left the annexe and returned to Cheryl's kitchen, wondering what success Alexi had managed.

8

Alexi watched Jenny closely, waiting for a denial. An outraged reaction. Something to convince Alexi that this likeable young woman hadn't been the cause or the instigator of Giles's untimely demise. But instead of fighting her corner, she settled for a doe-eyed look that put Alexi in mind of a rabbit caught in a car's headlights and sighed, tears pouring down her cheeks.

'Yes,' she said simply, lifting her head defiantly. 'I was in love with Giles.'

'Presumably your feelings weren't reciprocated, otherwise he wouldn't have been so determined to go ahead with the wedding? And yet, the two of you...' Alexi shook her head in confusion. There was no denying the total investment behind the clinch that Alexi had seen them in. They had been completely oblivious to her presence. A bomb could have exploded and they probably wouldn't have noticed. It was more than a drunken fumble, a spontaneous fling that could be blamed on copious amounts of booze. But Giles was engaged to another woman so why would Jenny agree to an affair?

'He wasn't going to marry Crystabel. He'd finally come to his senses. He told me last night that he'd made a mistake and was going to break it off with her. Then we'd be together.' Jenny folded her hands neatly in her lap and a quiet dignity briefly overcame her crippling grief. Alexi didn't doubt for a moment that the embrace she'd witnessed had been celebratory but there was no way to prove it. Only two people knew the truth and one of them was dead.

'And that's why you were in the kitchen corridor.'

Jenny blinked in evident surprise.

'I saw you,' Alexi explained. 'But you were too preoccupied to notice me.' Or anyone else, she thought. It would take more than a door with a sign saying 'Staff Only' to keep Crystabel out if she'd seen Giles and Jenny disappearing in that direction, so who was to say who else had seem them?

'Yes,' she replied simply.

Alexi had a dozen questions crowding her mind but asked the most obvious one first. 'Do you know if he actually did confront Crystabel?'

Jenny shook her head. 'No. That was the last time I saw or heard from him. He promised he'd message me when the deed was done. He intended to tell her last night and so I waited, hoping, but I never heard from him again.'

She shook her head as fresh tears slid down her cheeks. Her grief, Alexi knew, was genuine but she would have to keep it under wraps in front of the others. For that reason, she probably welcomed this opportunity to pour her heart out to Alexi, who was a sympathetic listener. She had learned during the course of her career to conceal her personal feelings and appear supportive to the views of others. She was experienced enough to accept that Jenny's grief was heartfelt, but whether her account of Giles's intentions was accurate rather than an extension of her own desires, a way to make her feel better about herself, Alexi had yet to decide.

'Tell me how it started, you and Giles,' she invited, squeezing Jenny's hand.

'Horses,' she said succinctly. 'Crystabel regularly drags me and my mum out of the woodwork when she wants to show off and, fools that we are, we obediently trot along. She likes to pretend that we're one big, happy family, whereas in fact, my mother and hers are barely on speaking terms.'

'They're sisters?'

'Yes, but as different as chalk and cheese. My mum is down to earth and doesn't have an ambitious or pretentious bone in her body. Gloria, as you've probably seen for yourself, makes up for her own disappointments by living vicariously through Crystabel.'

'What do you mean by that?' Alexi asked, thinking she knew very well.

'Gloria is all about the way she looks. She tried and failed to get her modelling career off the ground when she was a teenager. The only alternative was paid employment and she didn't fancy that, so she used her looks and figure to snare two wealthy husbands. Neither marriage lasted for long and she didn't do especially well financially out of either relationship which, I think, is one of the reasons why she pushes Crystabel to make the most of her opportunities.'

Jenny paused to draw breath. Reluctant at first to speak, she now seemed anxious to vent. 'Of course, it's a lot easier but also harder to get noticed now that social media rules. Anyone can set up a You-Tube channel but getting people to watch it is another matter entirely. And controlling the nasty comments and the inevitable trolls is impossible. You have to take the rough with the smooth.'

'But Crystabel has a regular spot on local TV.'

'A relatively small weekly appearance on a chat show that she's used to build her online presence. She sold the network on featuring her wedding, the build-up, the dress fittings, the whole nine yards, and she's gotten quite a lot of favourable feedback as a consequence, as she never loses an opportunity to remind us. People love a wedding.' Jenny fished a tissue out of her bag and dabbed at her eyes. 'Now, she'll use Giles's death to make herself look like a tragic victim herself.' Disgust radiated from the girl's eyes and her slim figure vibrated with emotion. 'You just see if I'm not right. Whereas I can't even publicly grieve for the man I adored and intended to spend the rest of my life with.'

'How are you and Claire related?' Alexi asked, having allowed a moment for Jenny to compose herself.

'We're not but we are both Crystabel's first cousins. Claire's mum and Crystabel's dad are brother and sister.'

'Ah, one of the rich husbands who didn't hang about for long. Does Crystabel's father ever see her? I haven't seen his name on any of the guest lists for the wedding.'

Jenny shook her head. 'Gloria refused to give him access to Crystabel as a child. She was very bitter about the separation, as you can imagine.'

Alexi nodded. She could imagine very well indeed. 'I assume he supported his daughter financially.'

'He did, and he set up a trust fund for her.'

'Ah, I didn't know that. Not that there's any reason why I should. Does she have access to it?'

'Not until she's twenty-five, in a year's time.' Jenny adjusted her position in her chair and crossed her feet at the ankles. 'He tried to make contact with her when she turned sixteen but her mother had poisoned her mind against him by then and she didn't want to know. Crystabel doesn't take rejection well, which I know worried Giles. He couldn't antici-pate how she'd react when he broke things off, or how she'd get her revenge.' Jenny sniffed. 'Well, we know the answer to that one now, don't we. Even he didn't think she'd resort to murder.'

'Tell me more about her father,' Alexi said in an effort to distract Jenny.

'Not much more to tell. She accepts his money but that's about it, as far as I'm aware.' Jenny twitched her nose. 'Even if she wanted to see him, she would almost certainly be put off by the fact that he's married now to a girl not much older than Crystabel herself. A stunner by all accounts. Claire knows and likes her so she can tell you more about that than I can. But Crystabel refused to meet her, claiming that her dad treated her mum abominably and that she wants nothing to do with him. Other than his financial support, obviously.' Jenny rolled her eyes. 'Crystabel has a vlog and talks about her father's new wife on there if you're interested. Forget the righteous indignation though. It boils down to the fact that neither Crystabel nor Gloria would appreciate the competition from a better-looking woman.'

'I see.' At least, Alexi thought, there didn't appear to be any reason why the absent father would do away with Giles. Besides, to the best of Alexi's knowledge, he'd never set foot in Hopgood Hall. 'Did you go on the holiday to Greece?' she asked in an abrupt change of subject. She had no idea how long they would be left alone and whether she'd get another opportunity to speak with Jenny alone.

Jenny shook her head. 'No. I was invited but I had a competition.'

'Competition?'

'Amateur three-day eventing.'

'Ah, horses. I see.' Alexi would come back to that. 'Claire went to Greece, I gather, and Crystabel and Simon went as an engaged couple but came back separated. Do you know what happened?'

Jenny shook her head. 'Crystabel said she broke it off because she'd decided it wouldn't work but none of us have ever believed that. We all agree that Simon dumped her but, of course, she'd never make that admission.'

'Did Gloria go?'

'No.' Jenny turned to give Alexi her full attention, squinting with suspicion, as though she'd suddenly realised that she was being interrogated. 'I know who you are and I know you're trying to find out what happened to my Giles although, if you ask me, it's obvious. Giles must have broken off the engagement like we agreed and she couldn't handle the humiliation; not for a second time and certainly not when she'd gone so public with the preparations.' Jenny sniffed. 'If he told her about me then that would have been enough to tip her over the edge. She couldn't stand competition of any sort, like I just explained, especially from other women. She felt safe with Claire and me because she knows she is much better looking than either of us and that we both dislike being the centre of attention. That left the stage clear for her, with us in supporting roles.'

'Giles clearly preferred you and I can see why.'

'Thanks, but I'm not the glamorous type. I'm more comfortable in wellies, mucking out stables and going to the local for a pie and a glass of wine.'

'You and Giles clearly had horses in common but I can't see that he and Crystabel would have had anything much to talk about, which makes me wonder why he stuck with her for so long, especially if he was in love with you.'

'That's what Giles said. He'd been running away from horses for some years. He held them responsible for his mother's death, you see, and had no one to help him make sense of a senseless situation. So, he took himself off to try and work things out on his own. Silly, I know, but grief can play tricks on the mind. Anyway, when we met and got chatting and my enthusiasm for equestrian sport became obvious, we were speaking the same language and he realised how much he'd actually missed it. And, well... things went on from there.'

Alexi blinked. 'I heard his mother died of cancer.'

'She did but she ignored the signs until it was too late for any treatment to save her. Giles was convinced that she neglected her health because his father depended upon her input in the training yard. She held the place together, taking responsibility for all the admin, and there's a huge amount of it.'

'I'm sure, but although I haven't been in Lambourn for long and know next to nothing about horses, I have learned that trainers charge a fortune for their services. Presumably Anthony employed good people to fill the major roles.'

'Of course, but they have to be supervised, to say nothing of the social obligations that have to be fulfilled. Entertaining owners at the yard and at the big race meetings amongst other things. That takes a lot of time. She did all of that and excelled at it. Anthony took her contribution for granted and didn't even notice that she was unwell.'

'She could have said something,' Alexi pointed out gently.

'Yes, she could have and perhaps she did. I have no way of knowing and frankly, neither did Giles. He felt guilty because he himself hadn't noticed the deterioration in his mother's health but he was at university at the time, so how could he have?'

'He transferred his own guilt onto his father's shoulders, presumably.' Alexi sighed. 'We always regret the things we didn't do when it's too late to change things. I found that out early on my career as a journalist. Anyway, what you just told me explains why he baulked against toeing the family line for a while. He was working through his grief and resentment.'

'Yes, he was. Anthony has a partner now: a woman twenty years younger than him who's moved in and taken over his mother's role. Giles hated her.'

'Crystabel introduced you to her intended and if you're right then she didn't fear the competition,' Alexi said, half to herself. 'But she neglected to take into account your passion for horses.'

'Exactly. Giles said he tried to run away from horses but that they're in his blood. I understand that. I could ride almost as soon as I could walk and can't imagine a life without horses in it.'

'Which makes Giles's determination to marry Crystabel all that much harder to fathom.' Alexi paused. 'Although in some respects, perhaps it doesn't. He didn't think he wanted a wife who would be forced into the same role as his late mother. Then he met you and realised that if a man and wife share the same passion, it becomes a joint enterprise. A labour of love. A common goal.' Rather like her and Jack, she thought but did not add. She was an investigative journalist; he was an investigator. They complimented one another.

'Yes.' She gave a tremulous smile. It lit up her features and Alexi could see what it was about her that had attracted Giles. She was pretty rather than head-turning gorgeous but there was a wholesomeness about her, a vulnerability that was at complete variance to Crystabel's brash self-confidence, which would appeal to most men's protective instincts. 'It's funny but those were almost precisely Giles's words. We had plans and were excited about the future.'

'Had he told his father about you?' Alexi rather doubted it but had to ask.

'No.' Jenny shook her head, sending dark curls dancing over her shoulders. 'He said he wanted to square things with Crystabel first. She deserved at least that much.'

'Why do you suppose he changed his mind so abruptly? You had clearly discussed a future together but as recently as yesterday evening, he was ignoring heartfelt entreaties to call the wedding off.'

'We had talked about a future in abstract terms:

that he wanted to be with me but that it simply wasn't possible.'

'But you just said you had plans.'

Jenny sighed. 'They were a pipedream, or so I thought. He said it was what he wanted but that he had to go through with the marriage. I couldn't get him to tell me why. I know he was very conflicted.' She frowned. 'Conducting an inner battle with his conscience, I guess you could say. Anyway, all I know is that something was preventing him from calling off the wedding; something stronger than his own will.'

Alexi frowned. 'But if he didn't love her but instead loved you...'

'I know.' Jenny threw up her hands. 'There was something, some hold Crystabel had over him. Like I say, he never told me what it was.' She gave a little laugh that sounded contrived. 'And then, last night, he told me that he'd been an idiot, seen the light and that he would put his own interests first.'

'What did he mean by that?'

Jenny shook her head. 'I have no idea. I did wonder if Crystabel was blackmailing him but I can't begin to imagine why she would do so, even if she had the means. Someone who looks like Crystabel could have just about any man she wanted.

She would be mortified if she had to turn the thumbscrews, I should have thought.'

'Not all men prefer women who'd likely emasculate them.'

'True, but Crystabel comes over all sweetness and light on TV, and in person when it suits her purpose. She knows how to keep her aggressive side under wraps.'

'I suppose...'

'I'm telling you the truth, Alexi. That's the way it was between Giles and me and I was forced not only to accept that the man I loved was marrying my cousin, but I also had to be a part of the wedding party, with a smile plastered on my face. It was eating me up inside. Then Giles messaged me, asking me to meet him in that corridor. I almost didn't go. I knew it would be painful but I never could resist him. Anyway, he said that now it was crunch time he couldn't go through with the wedding. I was the one he wanted. He was going to tell Crystabel that he was calling it off. He wanted to tell her there and then but I suggested waiting for the morning when they'd both be sober so that there could be no misconceptions.'

'So the chances were that he didn't tell her last night?'

Jenny shrugged. 'Unless she confronted him, they argued, he got angry and blurted out the truth. It could have happened that way.'

'Possibly.' Alexi conceded the point with a nod. 'Why did Crystabel move the hen party to this hotel?'

'She said it would be more fun. She was never big on all female company, even when she was star of the show. She said it would liven up the TV aspect if they got coverage of the guys behaving badly at the stag.'

'You don't believe that?'

'Not for a minute.' Jenny shook her head emphatically. 'I think she sensed that Giles wasn't too enthusiastic about the wedding. She knew for definite that his father was firmly opposed to it going ahead.' Jenny tapped a finger pensively against her lips as she articulated her thoughts. 'She probably also realised that the stag would be the last opportunity for his father to change his mind and that Giles would be more malleable when surrounded by men who didn't want to see it go ahead. She dominated him, you see, and he went into his shell when she was around.'

'And yet he stood up to her when she tried to crash their party.'

'I know.' Jenny's smile was full-on this time. 'No one saw but he winked at me when she turned her back on him and I knew then, or hoped, that he'd finally come to his senses.' She sighed. 'I shall treasure that memory. It's all I have left of him.'

'I'm sure you will.'

'Why are you asking me all these questions, Alexi? Are you going to write about the murder once Crystabel has been tried and convicted? Is this for background?'

'I want to be sure that the police get it right, that's all.'

Jenny gasped. 'Surely there can't be any doubt.' She puffed out her chest and looked on the verge of tears again. 'Crystabel was caught red-handed *and* she had motive. Giles was going to dump her, for goodness sake. He must have told her after all and if she was tipsy then she would have likely acted without thinking it through.'

'Calm down, Jenny. I'm simply making sure that there's no margin for error. Crystabel will get an expensive defence lawyer if she's charged—'

'If?'

'An expensive lawyer's job is to cast doubt upon her guilt by finding loopholes. For instance, we don't know that Giles actually broke off the engagement.'

She waved a hand to silence Jenny's protest. 'I know what you just told me but Giles isn't here to back you up and if he did tell Crystabel, you can be sure that she won't admit it.'

Jenny's shoulders slumped. 'I see.'

'And at the moment, the police lack motive. She can argue that she had every reason in the world to want Giles alive and that she really did come upon him just seconds after someone else killed him.'

Jenny blew air through her lips but reluctantly nodded. 'I see what you're getting at.'

'Her mouthpiece might also suggest, when your association with Giles comes to light, that you were obsessed with him and that he didn't return your feelings. You were furious when he refused to break off the engagement and killed him in a fit of jealous rage.'

'But that's ridiculous!'

'I know that,' Alexi said calmly, 'I'm just playing devil's advocate here. I covered enough trials during my time on the *Sentinel* to know how the justice system works. For a jury to acquit someone who looks as guilty as Crystabel, they have to have a viable alternative suspect.'

'Well then, I won't tell the inspector anything about Giles and me.'

'You have to, I'm afraid. You'd be withholding vital evidence if you don't.'

'It will make what Giles and I had seem tawdry.'

'Some might say that it shows he had good judgement.'

Jenny gave a timid smile. 'Thanks.' She sighed. 'But I don't expect the inspector will really believe that Giles preferred me to Crystabel.'

Such little self-confidence, Alexi thought with a sad shake of her head. 'I dare say there are text messages between you.'

Jenny brightened fractionally. It seemed she would prefer to be a potential murder suspect rather than have the world believe that Giles didn't love her. 'Yes. Yes, I do.'

'Including the one asking you to meet him in the corridor leading to the kitchen.'

'I've never deleted any of his messages.'

'Well, there you are then. And I can tell Vickery that I saw you there with Giles. That will leave no further doubt. I mean, if he'd decided not to break up with Crystabel, he'd hardly have been kissing you quite so passionately, would he?'

'No, of course. Thank you, Alexi. I will tell Inspector Vickery everything when he gets round to talking to me.'

'It's for the best. These things have a habit of coming out and it will look suspicious if you don't volunteer the information.'

Before Jenny could respond, her phone pinged an alert. She instinctively glanced at it and gasped. 'I don't believe it. Of all the irresponsible...'

She seemed incapable of articulating her obvious anger and instead covered her mouth with a shaking hand. Alexi glanced over her shoulder and was almost as disbelieving.

'Trial by social media,' Alexi muttered, watching Crystabel's convincing performance on her YouTube channel. 'She's making it harder for Vickery to arrest her, or thinks she is, but she's actually doing herself no favours whatsoever.'

'If I didn't know better, even I would be half convinced of her sincerity,' Jenny said, shuddering. 'It's sickening, especially since her grief isn't even genuine. Crystabel is incapable of loving anyone other than herself.'

'Vickery won't be pleased.' Alexi tapped her fingers, aware that the recording had been made in the room along the hall; Alexi recognised the wallpaper. She ought to make Crystabel take it down but she had no authority. Besides, the damage was done. She did need to let Jack know about this latest development though. He probably hadn't heard but would know how to handle it.

In the end, the opportunity to limit the damage was snatched away from her. She heard heavy footsteps in the corridor that stopped a few doors down. Alexi and Jenny got up and exchanged a wary glance, watching as Vickery knocked at Crystabel's door. It was opened by her mother.

'Yes, Inspector,' they heard her say. 'What can I do for you?'

'Miss Hennessy needs to come with us,' Vickery replied calmly. 'She is under arrest on suspicion of the murder of Giles Preston-Smythe.'

9

Jack and Alexi met in the front hall as they watched a subdued Crystabel being led from the hotel by two of Vickery's uniformed constables. The women were still upstairs, the stags in the annex, oblivious to the drama being played out. No one was loitering to see Crystabel's humiliation, at least not inside the hotel itself. Outside was a different story. The paps were clustered there, bored as they chatted amongst themselves. They sprang into action when Crystabel and her escort emerged through the front door, cameras and microphones to the fore.

Alexi watched the wannabe influencer, interested to see how she would respond to publicity that was for once not courted. She looked suitably desolate and convincingly afraid, probably because she was. Being arrested so publicly would be humiliating, especially if she was innocent. She gave the reporters a brave little wave, head held high, but didn't answer any of the questions that were shouted at her.

'No such thing as bad publicity then,' Alexi muttered.

'She's putting on a show,' Jack replied. 'Can't seem to help herself.'

'The case against her is far from watertight. Fortunately for her, they didn't slap on the handcuffs so she can make it seem as though she's helping voluntarily with enquiries.'

'We didn't use cuffs, nor did we beat a confession out of her,' Vickery said, walking up to Jack's shoulder. 'Unfortunately, those days are behind us.'

'Life was so much easier then,' Jack said, nodding in faux sympathy.

'She really does love herself, doesn't she?' Alexi remarked, watching her through the window as she paused at the rear door of a police car that had been opened for her, wiping a tear, real or imaginary, from her left eye.

'There's tomorrow's front-page picture,' Vickery remarked drolly.

'You think you have your woman?' Jack asked.

'Looks that way. The evidence is stacking up and it's pretty compelling.' But Jack could see that Vickery wasn't absolutely sure. 'Still haven't found a motive, though.'

'Seems to me you need to discover who owns the dagger that was used.' Jack flapped a hand. 'I'm sure you're already all over that. Just sayin', is all.'

Alexi opened her mouth in order to tell Vickery about Jenny and Giles but held back at the last second and closed it again. Jenny had promised to enlighten him and it was her story to tell. She and Jack could use the intervening time to delve a little deeper.

'You'll be taking statements from everyone?' she asked.

'For what it's worth.' Vickery sighed. 'Preliminary statements last night resulted in everyone either being several sheets to the wind or back in their rooms. No one had seen the groom for a while; that much they all agree on. We're trying to establish time of death but, as you know, it's not an exact science, so tracking down who last saw Giles and when is vital.'

'Good luck with that one,' Jack said, slapping Vickery's shoulder. 'Even so, time of death can be calculated pretty accurately. He was still pumping blood when he was found, so death had to have happened minutes, or seconds before that.'

Vickery sent Jack a droll look. 'True, but I'd still like to know when he was last seen and with whom. At present, it seems as though he disappeared off the face of the earth.'

'What do you need from us?' Alexi asked. 'What are you doing here?' she added, bending to scoop Cosmo into her arms when he stalked up to her and rubbed his big head against her shins before hissing at Vickery. He appeared to have gained yet more weight. Alexi made a mental note to feed him less, if he let her get away with reducing the size of his portions. 'You were shut in the kitchen where you can't get into any mischief.'

Vickery chuckled when the cat continued to spit at him. 'I think he likes me.'

'He thinks he's a guard dog,' Jack replied, scratching Cosmo's flat ears.

'If you want to help, you could have a word with the staff who were on duty at the time,' Vickery surprised Alexi by saying. She had anticipated being told that he had the situation under control. 'They at least will have been sober and more likely to recall when they'd last seen Giles, and with whom.'

'Consider it done,' Jack replied.

'Okay, I'd best get back to the station. I will have officers here all day taking statements from both groups.'

'The stags are in the annex and the lounge over there has been set aside for your use,' Alexi told him.

'Appreciate it.' Vickery patted his pockets, appeared satisfied that he had all his possessions about his person, and sighed. 'Christ, it's gonna be another hot one. I should be on a sodding beach somewhere, not trying to coerce confessions out of a killer. Anyway, keep in touch. I'll be back later.'

Alexi and Jack shared a look as they made their way into Cheryl's kitchen. She put Cosmo down and he retreated to Toby's basket, taking up most of the space. The little dog wagged his entire body, more than happy to be squeezed into a corner. The coffee had been brewed but there was no sign of Cheryl and Drew. Alexi hoped that Verity hadn't taken a turn for the worse. Jack poured coffee for them both, almost tripping over when Cosmo decided to join him and wound himself round Jack's legs.

'Steady, big guy.' He placed Alexi's coffee in front of her and took the seat beside her. Cosmo jumped onto Jack's lap. Toby yapped in protest. 'Well, how did you get on with the ladies?' Jack smoothed Cosmo's back and was rewarded with a cacophony of purring. 'Come on, I can see you're bursting to tell me.'

Alexi proceeded to do so and could almost see the cogs in Jack's quick brain churning as he took it all in.

'Well, there's Vickery's motive,' he said when Alexi ran out of words.

'I know. That's why I didn't say anything just now. Should I have?'

'Not if Jenny's going to tell whoever interviews her, but obviously Vickery does need to know, and sooner rather than later.'

'And part of me wonders why I held back.' Alexi frowned. 'It would make life much simpler for us here at the hotel if the case was wrapped up today. I don't know why but...' She paused, unsure how to articulate her nebulous doubts.

'It's annoying, having a conscience, isn't it?' Jack replied, winking at her.

'Yeah. I don't like Crystabel but I remain to be convinced that she killed Giles. I mean, if she was facing him and plunged a dagger into his chest, wouldn't there have been blood splatter all over her clothes? There always is on TV shows. But apart from her hands, which only had a little blood on them, and that could be explained away if she really did pull the dagger out, her clothing was spotless.'

'Possibly.' Jack waggled a hand from side to side. 'Probably but not necessarily. Depends upon a lot of things. The angle that the dagger was thrust at, where she was standing at the time, and so on. Besides, if she's telling the truth and the killer left the knife in Giles's body then the blood would only have spurted when it was pulled out if he was still alive and his heart was pumping. There are a lot of imponderables.'

'That makes sense, I suppose, because I didn't notice anyone wearing blood-stained clothing immediately after the discovery, and there would have been no time to change.'

'Vickery will be waiting to hear from the pathologist, who will be able to tell whether blood fountained by the depth and angle of the wound,' Jack said. 'But bear in mind that there was no obvious splatter on the flagstones where Giles was killed, just the blood that spilled from the wound itself. Also, Vickery still needs to put Giles and Crystabel together at the vital time.'

'Despite the fact that she was standing over the body with the dagger in her hand, screaming blue murder?' Alexi made a dubious face. 'It doesn't seem like the reaction of a conniving female who'd just killed a man in a fit of jealousy.'

'Stabbing a person isn't as easy as you'd imagine. Well, it's easy enough, I guess, but you don't know how you're going to react until you've actually done the deed. Blood splurting, the smell, the shock, all of the above combine to overcome a person's detachment, for want of a better word. So, Crystabel might well have stabbed him in a fit of rage, then realised what she'd done and lost control.'

'You think Crystabel's reaction was instinctive?' Alexi asked.

'I do and that's why I want to do a spot more digging, just for my own satisfaction.' Jack chuckled. 'You can take the detective out of the Met...' Cosmo mewled indignantly when Jack stopped stroking him and picked up his coffee instead. 'Crystabel's reaction could have been that of an innocent person who'd come across her dying fiancé by chance, which is what any half-decent defence brief will suggest, or it could have been the shocked reaction of a woman who'd just murdered her intended, as the prosecution will insist. "Oh my God, what have I done?" Like I say, almost anyone is capable of committing murder, given sufficient provocation. It's how that person deals with the immediate aftermath that gives them away and Crystabel's reaction didn't set alarm bells ringing.'

'If Giles did tell Crystabel about him and Jenny then I'd say that she had more than enough provocation.' Alexi rested her elbow on the table and her chin on her fisted hand. 'It doesn't look good for our princess.'

'Right. My guess is that she will be interviewed and released on police bail. Of course, that could all change when they speak to Jenny and have their missing motive.'

'The more I hear about Giles, the more he comes across as a weak individual who didn't know his own mind,' Alexi said pensively. 'A bit spoiled, if you ask me.'

'I agree. That's more or less what the guys said. But they also think his father was serious when he threatened to disinherit him if he married Crystabel.'

'I think we need to talk to Martin Hall, Anthony's assistant trainer. He had the most to lose if Giles ditched Crystabel and toed the family line.'

'We don't have any reason to speak with him but I'd certainly like a word with Anthony.'

'And his new partner. Jenny didn't say how soon

she moved in after the death of Giles's mother but we do know, if Jenny told the truth, that Giles wasn't at all happy about the relationship.'

'Anthony's woman didn't kill Giles, darling. She wasn't even here.'

'I know, I'm going off on a tangent. My journalistic nose is twitching and I can't help myself.' She grinned at Jack and placed a smacking kiss on his cheek. 'That's my excuse for being nosy. Anyway, it's another tenuous lead to follow. Someone didn't want Giles to get married. If he intended to go ahead with the ceremony then Jenny has to be a suspect, even though I don't actually suspect her, if that makes any sense.'

'None whatsoever,' Jack replied, smiling. 'But I'm sure you won't let that stop you.'

Alexi punched his arm. 'I believed Jenny when she told me that Giles had decided to call the wedding off.' She turned sideways on her chair to face Jack. 'The passion in their embrace would be impossible to fake. Besides, they wouldn't have been kissing like that if Giles had just told her that he'd decided to go through with the marriage.'

'Okay. If Crystabel knew of his change of heart then I won't lose any sleep over her being charged with premeditated murder.'

'Who takes a dagger to a hen party though?' Alexi muttered. 'That's a vital question that needs answering. We need to discover where that knife came from.'

'We do, but Vickery's already on it. We have limited time and other priorities. That aside, we're back to the people who had compelling reasons to stop the marriage. Giles's father, Martin Hall, Jenny and we have to add Simon's name to that list, at least until we find out why he and Crystabel actually split.'

'Simon appeared to actively dislike her.'

'Appeared to,' Jack emphasised.

Alexi nodded. 'We ought to add Gloria's name. Jenny tells me that she pushed Crystabel to make a public name for herself in order to achieve her own ambitions vicariously.'

Jack rolled his eyes. 'I've met pushy parents like her more times than enough during the course of my career.'

'Right, well just suppose that Giles did confront Crystabel. She would have been distraught, to say nothing of furious if he was stupid enough to tell her that he'd transferred his affections to Jenny. Jenny reckons that Crystabel liked to have her cousins around her on public occasions because it made them look like a cosy family unit and because Jenny and Claire were no competition in the looks department.'

Jack tutted and shook his head. 'She really is a piece of work.'

'She really is. Anyway, Crystabel was dumped by Simon and that still smarts; we know that much from her reaction to him here. But at least Simon didn't have another model waiting in the wings. Giles, on the other hand did and to add insult to injury, that model wasn't a stranger but Crystabel's own cousin. How would that feel to someone as self-obsessed as Crystabel?'

'You're doing Vickery's job for him. That's precisely how he'll be thinking when he knows the truth.'

'If Crystabel is the guilty party and acted in the heat of the moment then Jenny's had a lucky escape if you ask me. If she'd had time to calm down a bit then Jenny would more likely have been the victim since Crystabel would look upon her behaviour as the ultimate betrayal.'

'Right, but just supposing that Crystabel only knew that Giles had decided to call off the wedding but not why,' Jack remarked in a speculative tone. 'She couldn't talk him out of it and saw all her carefully orchestrated publicity going up in smoke, making her a laughing stock in the process. She would have gone back to the room she shares with her mother, distraught. Gloria would have found out why and stormed off to talk sense into Giles.'

'A mother hen protecting her chick.' Alexi nodded. 'Yeah, I can buy that.'

'They argued, Gloria had the dagger with her for some reason.'

'That dagger is the stumbling block. We have to find out who brought it to a stag or hen party,' Alexi reiterated.

'Agreed. Anyway, I can see Gloria stabbing a man in a blind rage and walking calmly away. She simply didn't expect her daughter to stumble upon Giles so soon after the event and do what she did.'

'So, what do we...'

Alexi abruptly stopped talking and turned towards the door when it flew open and slammed against the wall. Cosmo arched his back and hissed at a dishevelled Gloria, who stood on the threshold, looking like a wild woman.

'You have to help me!' she cried. 'They've arrested the wrong woman. It wasn't supposed to be this way.'

Alexi glanced at Jack and then held out a hand

to Gloria. 'Come and sit down,' she said. 'Have some coffee.'

'I don't want coffee, I want action, damn it!'

'If you want our help,' Jack said calmly, 'then I suggest you adjust your attitude and explain what you think it is that we can do for you.'

Gloria expelled a long breath. 'Sorry,' she said in what was for her a meek tone. 'It's the stress. The in-justice... It's awful.'

'Not as awful as things are for Giles.'

Jack's expression was set in stone. He was disgusted by the woman's selfish approach and could see that Alexi was too, although why Glo-ria's self-serving behaviour should surprise him, he was at a loss to know. What did surprise him was their being Gloria's first port of call. Pre-sumably she was aware that they'd solved two previous murders in Lambourn. Be that as it may, this was the first occasion upon which Gloria had addressed a single voluntary word to Jack and, as far as he was aware, to Alexi as well. The hired help was ordinarily beneath her notice.

'Of course.' Gloria dipped her head. 'Sorry. It's all such a massive shock and I'm not thinking straight.'

'Have you arranged for someone to represent Crystabel?' Alexi asked.

Gloria's head shot up. 'She doesn't need a lawyer. Why would she? She hasn't done anything wrong.'

'Don't be so naïve. She's been arrested so the police must think they have a strong case against her.' Alexi leaned forward. 'They do have a strong case. Wake up, Gloria, and face facts. This is real life, not manipulative TV.'

Jack extracted his phone from his pocket, scrolled through the contacts and made a call. He conducted a short conversation when it was answered and placed his phone on the table.

'Ben Avery, a local solicitor, will meet Crystabel at the station.'

'Thank you,' Gloria said, but it seemed to Jack that it took a mighty effort of will to get the two words past her artificially plump lips.

He picked up his phone again and got straight through to Vickery's mobile. He told him not to start the interview until Avery arrived. By the time Jack hung up again, Gloria seemed reluctantly impressed by his efficiency and a little less frazzled.

'Right, Gloria,' Jack said, sitting across from her and fixing her with an unsmiling look. 'I'm not sure what you think it is that we can do to help your daughter. The evidence, as things stand, is compelling.'

'But she didn't do it!' Gloria screeched.

'It's natural that you'd think so but how can you be sure? Were you with her at the end of the evening the entire time?' Jack raised a hand to prevent her from answering his question. 'I'm assuming not, otherwise you would have told Vickery so last night and he wouldn't have been so quick to haul your daughter in.'

'We weren't apart for long. I went to bed ahead of her. She said she had something she needed to do.'

'I hope you didn't tell Vickery that, without also telling him what that something was,' Alexi said with feeling.

'No, of course not. I simply said that I went up to bed about ten minutes before Crystabel.'

'And how long was the actual gap?' Jack asked.

Gloria examined her fingernails for a prolonged moment. 'About half an hour,' she mumbled.

'During the crucial time when Giles was being stabbed,' Alexi said, shaking her head.

'But she wasn't with Giles. She didn't see him until she came across him already dead.'

'Then where was she?'

Gloria allowed a long pause. 'Talking to Simon,' she eventually said.

Alexi and Jack shared a glance.

'Why?' they asked together.

'They have a personal history. They were engaged, it ended badly and there's a lot of animosity. With Simon being best man, Crystabel wanted to clear the air between them so there would be no tension on the big day. That's one of the reasons why she moved the hen party to the hotel. She thought it would be a good opportunity to get Simon alone but she had no chance earlier in the evening.'

Jack knew that wasn't true. Alexi had overheard him and Crystabel arguing. Perhaps Crystabel had gone in search of him again in an effort to clear the air. It was possible but if that was the case, why hadn't Simon mentioned getting up close and personal with the woman he appeared to dislike? Why hadn't he told Jack about his argument with her earlier in the evening, come to that? Jack hadn't asked him if he'd seen her but assumed he would have said so if he had. Unless he had a reason to dislike her even more than he appeared to and saw hanging her out to dry as the ultimate form of revenge.

He made a mental note to have another word with Simon as soon as he could. Whether he would open up to Jack, who had no authority to ask questions, was another matter. Jack suspected that he would. Jack's friendship with Vickery must have been obvious the previous evening and Simon would realise that if he didn't offer up an explanation then Jack would simply to go Vickery, who *could* insist upon getting answers. In which case, if he had seen the bride minutes before she stumbled upon Giles's body then it would look suspicious if he didn't say so.

'What caused the break up in their engagement?' Alexi asked.

Gloria looked up and met their gaze directly for the first time. 'I don't know, not for sure.'

'Sorry,' Alexi replied, 'but I thought you and your daughter shared everything. If you aren't honest with us, no matter how bad the truth might look, we can't help you.'

'Truthfully, I really don't know.' Gloria spread her hands and looked almost convincing in her denial. Almost. 'She went to Crete with Simon and a party of friends, including Giles. I was charged with making wedding arrangements for her and Simon, choosing a venue and what have you, but when she got back she said it was all off. She looked terrible and refused to talk about it but I know for a fact that her heart was broken.'

She wasn't so heartbroken, Jack thought, that she didn't latch onto Giles with a speed that defied gravity.

'Why would Crystabel murder the man she planned to marry in a ceremony that was being televised?' Gloria asked. 'It makes no sense.'

'You're aware that Giles's father was opposed to the match?' Alexi asked.

Gloria waved the suggestion aside with an impatient tut. 'She wasn't marrying that pompous prick, Anthony, who thinks he's too good for the likes of us. Do you know, he had the temerity to describe the coverage we've attained, which promotes his training yard I might add, as "tacky". He told Giles to ensure it was toned down, or at least left his business out of things. I mean, who doesn't want free publicity in this day and age? Anthony should have thanked us, not put up objections.'

'You're not aware that Anthony had threatened to disinherit Giles if he went ahead with the wedding?' Jack watched her closely as he spoke and noticed her complexion pale when his words struck home.

'No, I wasn't aware, but he wouldn't have cast his

only child aside. That was all hot air and anyway, Anthony had come to terms with the idea of the wedding weeks ago.'

'He might have given that impression, although I rather doubt it. Anthony isn't the type to mince his words.' Jack shook his head emphatically. 'He reiterated his position last night, in fact. I heard him myself and it didn't sound as though he was making empty threats to me. Perhaps that would have been enough to make Giles reconsider.'

'Never! Giles was a man of his word, more than willing to take his father on. In fact, I think he would have relished the opportunity. I gather that things hadn't been comfortable between them since the death of Giles's mother. Anyway, Giles didn't see a long-term future for himself in his father's training business. He had other plans.'

'What other plans?' Jack and Alexi asked together.

'Giles was a whizz with computers. He wanted to take some of the load off my shoulders and do Crystabel's online promo.'

Jack and Alexi exchanged an astounded look. Jack didn't believe a word of it and he could see that Alexi didn't either. Had Gloria made it up in an effort to point the finger of blame towards Anthony? If so, it wouldn't wash. If Anthony loved his son so much that he wanted to save him from a train-wreck of a marriage, Crystabel would have been his target, not the son in question. Gloria was clearly thinking on the hoof and making a piss poor job of things.

'I'm surprised to hear it,' Alexi said with commendable calm. 'I've seen quite a bit of them both over the past couple of weeks and they didn't strike me as being besotted. I never saw them so much as holding hands in fact, unless Crystabel instigated matters.'

'They weren't into public displays of affection but you can take my word for the fact that they were both committed to the marriage. Anyway, the inspector needs to know about Anthony's thuggish threats.'

'He already does,' Jack replied.

Gloria's gaze dropped to the table top and her shoulders fell right along with it. 'Surely, if Simon says that he and Crystabel talked and confirms what time they parted, then it will put Crystabel in the clear.'

'Did she tell you that she actually ran him to ground and that they did talk?' Jack asked.

'Well, no. Obviously, she was too traumatised last night to say anything, other than that she didn't kill Giles. She was really upset. I've never seen her so devastated. This will destroy her.'

The cynic in Jack wondered if Gloria was referring to her daughter's finer feelings or to the death-knell for the career that the two women had gone to such pains to build up. The wedding would have been her launching pad to greater things, or so she had hoped. Being accused of murdering the groom would definitely not be good for business and was a setback that Crystabel was unlikely to recover from.

'I made her take one of my sleeping pills,' Gloria said. 'And then, this morning, she'd barely woken before she was carted off.'

'I spoke with Simon earlier and he didn't mention having seen her,' Jack said.

'Oh God!'

Gloria buried her face in her hands and her shoulders shook. Jack still couldn't decide if she was upset for her daughter or for her own ambitions which were shattering before her eyes. She would be getting all the publicity she'd ever dreamed of now, but for the wrong reasons.

'In order to cast doubt on Crystabel's guilt,' Jack said, aware that he would do no such thing unless he could convince himself that she hadn't done it, 'I need to know if there was anyone in Giles's life who bore him a grudge. Anyone who was here last night.'

Gloria shook her head. 'Not that I'm aware. If there was such a person then he never shared that information with Crystabel. She would have told me. Mind you, there was a lot of tension on that Greek holiday, I do know that much, but that was a couple of years ago. Water under the bridge.'

'Only Simon and Claire were involved, as far as I've been told,' Alexi said.

'Well yes, but the hotel bar was open last night and a lot of people unconnected to the wedding party were here. Horsy types who'd have access to daggers.' She allowed a sinister seeming pause. 'Jenny's firmly in the equestrian set. She would know who they were.'

Jack and Alexi exchanged a look.

'Not anyone known to Giles presumably,' Alexi said. 'Besides, it would have been apparent if a friend who'd gone to Greece with them was here. Either Claire or Simon would have said something.'

'What will happen now?' Gloria asked in a defeated voice.

'The police have a strong case against Crystabel,' Jack said, softening his tone slightly. 'There's no glossing over that fact. What they don't have is a motive.'

Gloria nodded. 'I know.'

'And the dagger. You were right to mention it. Do you recognise it?' Jack pulled the picture he'd taken of it up on his phone and handed it to Gloria. She took the phone from him, barely looked at the picture and shook her head.

'Doesn't it belong to this hotel?' she asked.

'No,' Alexi said. 'It's a dagger, not a table or chef's knife. If we can find out who brought it with them, it could change the direction of the entire investigation.'

'I see.'

'Can you think of anyone else who might be able to vouch for Crystabel at the vital time, given that we can't be sure she saw Simon?' Alexi asked. 'She found his body at just before midnight and we know he hadn't been dead for more than a few minutes, or if he was actually dead when she found him for that matter, so think hard.'

Gloria plucked at her lower lip. 'Her father, possibly,' she said bitterly.

Jack and Alexi looked at one another but before either of them could speak, Drew burst in through the door that led to his private quarters.

'Have you seen this?' he demanded to know, brandishing his phone.

'Hell, no we haven't!' Jack glanced at the phone and then turned accusatory eyes on Gloria. 'What the hell?'

'Oh, I didn't see you there,' Drew said at the same time.

'I had to do something,' Gloria said defensively. 'I'm Crystabel's agent. I have her best interests at heart. I had to do something to stop trial by public opinion. There are people out there who are jealous of Crystabel's success and will use this situation to destroy her reputation.'

'Live by social media,' Alexi muttered. 'I thought you were her mother,' she added.

'And her agent too. When she was taken this morning, she asked me to fix the publicity.'

'That was her first thought?' Jack wondered why he was so surprised to hear it.

'Another reason to think she must be innocent,' Gloria countered. 'If she'd done it and imagined that the police could prove it then her thoughts would have been very different. But she knows they can't prove it,' Gloria added, lifting her chin defiantly, 'because she didn't kill Giles.'

'Even so, Gloria, this isn't helping,' Jack said,

watching Gloria on her daughter's YouTube channel, telling the world that Crystabel was under suspicion. She stared straight into the camera and said
that she couldn't have done it because she'd been
elsewhere at the time. She'd told the police that but
they were going for the easy option.

'Take it down, Gloria,' Jack said with a weary
sigh, 'and if you want to help Crystabel then don't
put anything else on social media until the situation's been resolved.'

'But her followers. If she goes quiet, it will imply
guilt.'

'Her fiancé has just died under violent circumstances,' Alexi said, her expression showing distaste
as she leaned towards the woman. 'Why would
anyone expect her to say anything publicly when
her grief is so raw?'

Gloria looked set to argue but presumably
clocked the disgust in Alexi's demeanour and acqui-
esced with bad grace. 'Very well,' she said, jutting
her chin pugnaciously. She extracted her phone
from her pocket, hesitated for a telling moment,
then pressed a few buttons and nodded. 'It's gone,'
she said. 'Happy now?'

10

'You mention before Drew joined us that you thought Crystabel had seen her father,' Alexi said, receiving a barely perceptible nod of approval from Jack, who'd clearly intended to ask the same question. 'But it's my understanding that she'd never had anything to do with him. When did that situation change?'

Drew had taken a seat at the table and an active interest in the conversation. Alexi sensed that Gloria would prefer for him to leave. She almost smiled when she imagined the reaction the woman would get if she told Drew to leave his own kitchen. Eventually, common sense prevailed. She probably realised that her performance on YouTube had

adversely affected Alexi's desire to help her, as it un-
doubtedly had Jack's. She needed to regain their cooperation if she thought they could be useful to her
and so addressed her attention to Alexi's question.

'I never tried to poison Crystabel's mind against
her father, if that's what you're thinking,' she said
defensively.

Oh yes you did! 'Even if nothing was said, by
denying him access to his daughter as a young child,
you clearly affected her attitude towards him.'

'Luke Farrington didn't want to be a father—'

'Crystabel took your maiden name, I'm guessing,' Jack said.

'Why would she take his?' Gloria countered, a
hard edge to her voice.

This was not, Alexi realised, a lady whom it
would be wise to cross without good reason. She
clearly knew how to bear a grudge, was fiercely protective of her only child and didn't possess a forgiving nature.

'Farrington. I know that name.' Alexi rubbed her
chin as she searched her memory for clues, snap-
ping her fingers when it came to her. 'He's a property
developer. His name is plastered over billboards on
various building sites around these parts. There was
some sort of scandal a while back, before my time.'

'There was a big hoo-ha when he got planning permission to build on a greenbelt site. The protestors got violent, the popular press took the protestors' side and painted Luke and his partner as money-grabbing destroyers of wildlife.'

Gloria's derisive tone when speaking of a legitimate protest revealed more about her lingering feelings for Crystabel's father that she'd probably be comfortable with them knowing anything about, Alexi thought. She wondered too if Gloria was aware that she still hankered after the father of her child's affections. It would explain the hostility that she displayed at the mere mention of his name.

'These things happen,' Jack said.

'It was after we split so I wasn't involved.' Gloria paused, her eyes sparkling with malice. 'Luke was doing well when Crystabel was conceived but said he didn't have time to be a father. He blamed me for not taking more care.' She sniffed. 'As though it doesn't take two. Anyway, his workload had nothing to do with his disinclination for parenthood. He was too busy chasing anything in a skirt to settle down and be a hands-on family man. So I threw him out.'

'Presumably you'd discussed starting a family before getting pregnant?' Alexi said.

'Well, not exactly.' She waggled a hand from side

to side. 'We wanted one eventually. Crystabel was an accident but I didn't think it would be a problem. I mean, it wasn't as though we couldn't afford an addition to the family. But he wasn't best pleased when I told him, which is why we split.'

'He wanted you to have an abortion.'

'It was implied but not something I considered for a single moment. Anyway, Luke had disappeared from the scene long before Crystabel was born. He worked abroad for the first five years of her life and didn't even attend her christening.' Gloria wrinkled her nose, or attempted to. Her face was so heavily botoxed that almost nothing moved. 'Then he returned to the UK from the Costa del something-or-other and simply assumed that he could become a part of Crystabel's life.' Gloria stiffened her shoulders and sat a little straighter. 'But he assumed wrongly. He hadn't been there when I needed him and it was too late to make amends. Besides, I'd married again by then and my daughter had a father in Philip who actually took a real interest in her.'

'What happened to him?' Jack asked.

'What happens to any man when he hits a midlife crisis?' Gloria dismissed thoughts of her second husband with a negligent swipe of one hand. 'He couldn't keep it in his pants. I learned then that there was only one person I could depend upon to give my daughter a stable upbringing and that was myself. She was heartbroken when Philip upped and left so I wasn't about to risk letting Luke into her life, only for history to repeat itself.'

'But you think they made contact anyway?' Drew asked, speaking for the first time.

'I know they did. Crystabel has never been able to get one over on me. Not only did I see his name on her phone but I also know immediately if she's being economical with the truth, which is how I can be sure that she didn't kill Giles, no matter how damning the so-called evidence against her happens to be.'

A mother who monitors her adult child's phone, Alexi thought, sharing a glance with Jack and raising one brow.

'When did she first make contact with him?' Alexi asked.

'Just after she came back from that Greek holiday, after she'd broken up with Simon. She makes excuses to go places and I know she's actually meeting her father and his latest floozie.'

'I'm sorry,' Alexi said, frowning. 'But Crystabel is a grown woman. Why would she need to make excuses for her activities or explain herself to you?'

'We work together promoting her image online so we have to keep a close watch on one another's diaries. I will admit that I was hurt when I knew she'd gotten in touch with her father and *her*.' She rippled her shoulders indignantly. 'The woman is only a year or two older than Crystabel. It's obscene and Luke is making a right fool of himself. The stereotypical older man with deep pockets and a gold-digger on his arm. It's laughable.' But Gloria wasn't laughing. Instead, jealousy radiated from her in waves.

'Why do you suppose she got in touch with him, given your antagonism?' Jack asked. 'You and she are very close and she must have known how much it would upset you.'

'You'll have to ask Crystabel for her reasons. It's not a subject that I can raise with her.' She sighed. 'I won't deny I'm disappointed that she chose to reach out to him without at least talking to me about it first. But, if I had to guess, then I'd say that she's looking for backing.'

'Financial backing?' Alexi asked.

Gloria nodded. 'Crystabel is making a name for herself as an influencer. She has a substantial number of followers: people who want to hear what she has to say, what recommendations and secrets she has to share. People who want to be like her. The televising of her wedding would have vastly increased her fanbase and she was going to use it as a launchpad to start her own TV production company.'

'Production company?' Alexi and Jack said together. Drew's mouth fell open.

'Sure. Why not? Times have changed and it isn't just the big boys who can decide what the viewing public want served up to them. With the advent of social media, the masses have an opportunity to express their views and be heard. Crystabel wants to be a pathfinder in that regard and make her own programmes for television that she can sell to the networks. She wants to include participants from her fanbase who have problems with their appearance, their size, their eating habits, coping with today's life in the fast lane. Unlike the established companies, she's down to earth and understands what hang-ups ordinary people have.'

'I see,' Jack said, looking as perplexed as Alexi felt.

Gloria leaned towards Alexi, presumably in the hope of garnering feminine support for a scheme that Alexi thought ridiculous. 'We had it all planned out and Giles was going to play an active role on the promotional front. He and Crystabel would have been the golden couple. The modern equivalent of the Beckhams.' Ambition radiated from Gloria's eyes. 'He was excited, could see merit in the plan and encouraged Crystabel to go for it, to reach her full potential. So why would she kill him, and kill off her aspirations in the process?'

Alexi broke the silence that followed Gloria's assertion. 'I still don't understand why her father might have been here last night,' she said.

'I don't know if he was, not for sure, but I do know that he wanted to come to the wedding. I overheard Crystabel on the phone to him. She insisted that he couldn't come out of deference to me but she did say that she wanted him to meet Giles and that he could do so here towards the end of the stag. She'd find a way when the party was winding down and everyone was too pissed to notice.'

'Which could be why she moved her hen party to the hotel,' Jack said quietly.

'Why couldn't she have introduced her father to Giles when she went to meet him for dinner. If she did?' Alexi asked.

'Again, that's a question that you'll have to put to her. Timing is my guess. Luke is in and out of the country all the time. He's got other interests now, as well as the property development, and they regularly take him away to exotic locations.'

For someone who despised her ex-husband and wanted nothing to do with him, Gloria appeared to know a very great deal about his business affairs, Alexi thought, which backed up her earlier suspicions in that regard. She appeared to actively hate him but the dividing line between love and hate, she knew, was thin enough to be diaphanous. *I'd rather hurt than feel nothing at all.*

'Do you have an address for him in the UK?' Jack asked.

'No.' Jack simply looked her in the eye and said nothing. 'I think he has a pile outside of Winchester in a village called Shawford,' she added ungraciously, 'but don't quote me on that.'

Alexi suspected that she knew the precise address, right down to the post code, but also knew that she'd let her daughter be convicted of murder before she made that admission. With such a role model as her only influence, Alexi was beginning to see why Crystabel had turned out the way that she had: self-important, assertive and too ambitious to allow any impediments to slow her progress. Alexi felt almost sorry for Crystabel.

Almost.

'That's interesting. I'll ask around and see if anyone saw Luke here last night,' Jack said, stretching his arms above his head and yawning. Cosmo, still on his lap, gave a mewl of protest because the gesture disturbed him. He leapt agilely to the floor and re-joined a delighted Toby in his basket, where dog and cat settled down together for a doze. 'Do you have a picture of Luke?'

Gloria sniffed. 'I dare say you'll find a ton of them easily enough online. Luke isn't one to shun publicity.'

Alexi almost choked on the hypocrisy. She pulled her phone from her pocket and googled Luke's name. Sure enough, there were dozens of hits. Alexi chose a picture of the handsome, middle-aged man at random and showed it to Gloria.

'That's him,' she said dismissively. 'Although he has a lot less hair than that nowadays. That's either an old picture or it's been photoshopped.'

And you've been botoxed to within an inch of your life.

'I thought you hadn't seen him,' Jack remarked.

'I said that I'd had nothing to do with him. We don't speak but I was in Winchester the other day and he was there gladhanding with the mayor who'd just cut the ribbon to the show house on one of his building projects. We nodded to one another when we passed on the street but that was it.'

Alexi would bet a hundred quid that Gloria had gone to Winchester with the express purpose of bumping into her ex.

'Right, leave it with me,' Jack said, standing to indicate to Gloria that he'd run out of questions, time and patience. 'I have Vickery's ear and he will tell me what he can. Crystabel's lawyer will tell me everything. I'm betting that she will be interviewed under caution and released on police bail, pending further investigations. We'll know more later today.'

'But he arrested her!'

'Arrested but didn't charge and I very much doubt whether he will, unless he finds a motive.'

'How does Crystabel get on with her cousins and co-workers, her bridesmaids?' Alexi asked casually.

Gloria looked surprised by the question, which implied either that she knew nothing about Jenny and Giles or that she'd missed her vocation and ought to have been an actress. 'Absolutely fine,' she replied without hesitation. 'The girls were all feeling grateful to be included in the wedding. Well, all except Jenny, who seemed a little too envious of Crystabel's situation. Why do you ask?'

'No reason.' Alexi shrugged. 'Just curious.'

'Thank you,' Gloria said, standing. 'I'll be upstairs. Do let me know as soon as you have more information.'

'Will do,' Jack replied, opening the door for her.
'But keep off the internet. And no talking to journal-
ists. If you do, you'll make matters worse. You've
asked for our help and we'll do what we can. But if
you work against us then you're on your own.'

Gloria nodded. 'I hear you,' she said ungraciously, walking through the door.

Jack closed it behind her, sat down again and
wiped imaginary perspiration from his brow. 'What
a force of nature,' he said, shaking his head.
'Imagine having her for a mother.'

'I think you're probably the first man in a very
long time to tell her what to do without getting an
earbashing,' Alexi said with feeling.

Jack chuckled. 'Yeah, very likely.'

'She doesn't like men much, does she,' Drew
remarked.

'But she still carries a torch for Luke Farrington,'
Alexi said. 'I assume you picked up on that, Jack.'

'I did.' He shifted his position on his chair, threw
back his head and closed his eyes. 'We need to do a
ton of things and we need to do them fast, whilst we
still have all the players here at the hotel.'

'We need to speak to the staff who were on duty, don't forget,' Alexi said. 'We told Vickery that we would.'

'I haven't forgotten. Anton's our man. He was mixing it with the stags once he finished with his kitchen duties.'

'Did he actually know any of them?' Drew asked.

'Doesn't matter,' Alexi replied. 'Since he gained notoriety in the cookery contest, everyone wants to be his friend. But he's so laid back that he takes the acclaim in his stride and doesn't let it go to his head.'

'Marcel didn't show his face, far as I can recall,' Jack said, rolling his eyes.

'He's more likely to have entertained the hens,' Alexi said. Drew and Jack both laughed and nodded, well aware of the chef's reputation as a lady's man.

'Vickery's constables are here now,' Drew said. 'That's what I came to tell you. Two are in the annex and two upstairs with the ladies.'

'Should be interesting,' Alexi said.

'Whilst they're doing their thing, we need to talk to the staff and then Simon, once he's made his statement. We need to know if he did see Crystabel just before the body was found. It could be crucial.'

'There's a lot of animosity on Simon's part towards Crystabel,' Alexi pointed out. 'He might not tell the truth, Jack, just to drop her in it.'

'Yeah, he might not; you're right about that.' Jack stood and paced the length of the kitchen, cupping his chin with one hand. 'He's really cut up about Giles's death and thinks Crystabel's the guilty party. If he'd been with her shortly before he was killed then it would cast doubt upon her involvement so yeah, he might well keep shtum. After all, it would be his word against hers and right now Crystabel's word doesn't count for much; not after that tacky YouTube stunt which won't have won her many friends in places that matter.'

Drew looked dismayed. 'Fame comes at a high price,' he muttered.

'We also need to talk to Giles's father, if he's willing,' Jack said. 'But more importantly, we need to speak with Luke Farrington. Shawford isn't far from here. Less than an hour in the car.'

'I can't see him bumping off his estranged daughter's intended,' Drew said dubiously.

'No, but his coming back into his daughter's life at such a time is significant. Not sure how but Gloria told us about him for a reason.'

'Like we can believe a word that comes out of her

conniving mouth,' Alexi said, twitching her nose indignantly.

'Exactly why we need to speak with him. It could be that Crystabel was meeting someone else and Gloria threw her ex's name into the ring in order to protect that person.'

Alexi shared a bewildered glance with Drew. 'Why would she meet someone whose identity she wouldn't want us to know about?' she asked.

'Well, there's the question. We'll ask Crystabel when she gets back but I'd dearly love to know what's going on between her and her father, if anything is.' Jack grinned. 'My copper's nose is twitching.'

Alexi rolled her eyes. 'Stand well back, Drew,' she quipped.

'Okay,' Jack said, 'let's get started. We'll track Anton down in the kitchen before he gets too busy to talk to us. How about Brendan? He was serving behind the bar last night. Is he on today?'

Drew glanced at the clock and nodded. 'Yeah. He'll be here any time soon.'

'Fair enough.'

'How's Verity?' Alexi asked. 'With all the excitement, I forget to ask.'

'She's absolutely fine.' Drew's smile was wide and infectious. 'She already knows how to get her mum and dad's attention. She only has to sneeze and we're both reduced to the status of quivering wrecks, convinced that she's got some terminal childhood disease.'

'That's parenthood for you, mate,' Jack replied, slapping Drew's shoulder and grinning broadly. 'But they don't sell that aspect of the job along with the hype.'

'It would be a good way to curtail the population explosion if they did,' Drew said. 'I swear this latest scare has aged me ten years. God alone knows how I'll be when she's old enough to date.'

'A pleasure to look forward to,' Alexi said, standing on her toes and kissing Drew's cheek. 'Anyway, we'd best get on.'

Alexi and Drew tracked Anton down to the hotel's kitchen where he was getting stuck into the prep. Unlike Marcel, he wasn't afraid to get involved with the grunt work and did so with a perpetual smile on his face.

'Hey, guys.' He looked up when Alexi and Drew stopped at his bench, put his knife aside and wiped his hands on a cloth. 'Me you come to see?'

'Sorry about what's happened,' Marcel said from

the other side of the room. 'But I won't pretend it isn't a relief not to be a suspect.'

'Well then, you'd better hope we run the culprit to ground quickly or the hotel might not survive the scandal,' Alexi said with feeling. 'Who'd want to risk staying at a place associated with three murders?'

'Christ!' Marcel ran a hand through his hair. 'We assumed Crystabel was the guilty party and that you guys were just getting all your ducks in a row.' He grinned. 'I know the pair of you can't help involving yourselves.'

'Some people have short memories,' Jack said.

'No, mate.' Marcel shuddered. 'I still have nightmares in which I'm being carted off in handcuffs and it would have happened if it hadn't been for you guys. I'll never forget that it was you who got me off the hook. You own me.'

'Now there's a delightful prospect,' Alexi said, grinning at the handsome chef and earning herself a scowl of disapproval from Jack for her trouble.

'You joined the stags at last knockings, Anton,' Jack said. 'Did you notice anything unusual?'

'Other than the tension and the fact that everyone was wasted, mon, not a thing.'

'Did any of the women show their faces?' Alexi asked.

'Not once. Giles had refused them permission to crash the stag.' It was Marcel who responded. 'They crept down the stairs at one point and a few of the guys flirted with them but they didn't linger when it was made clear that their presence was unwelcome. After that, if any of them so much as put their faces round the bar door... well, let's just say that drunken men on a mission should not be messed with and they had the good sense to know it. I didn't join the party at the end of service but I was in the kitchen and I could see and hear what was going on.' He paused. 'I think the pretty little brunette bridesmaid crossed the hall at one point. She didn't enter the bar though. I can see both areas through the kitchen door windows.'

'That would have been Jenny,' Alexi said. 'About what time was it?'

Marcel shrugged. 'About an hour before Giles's body was found, I guess.'

Alexi nodded, glad that Marcel's account tied in with Jenny's. 'Where was Giles at that time?'

Marcel and Anton exchanged a look. 'I can't be certain but I think he sent a text or something just before that. I noticed him walk away from the others, punching something into his phone. And then...' Anton paused. 'I didn't see him again after that.' His expression sobered. 'It's funny, you think about what you would have done if you'd known you were seeing someone for the last time. But then, if I'd known he was in danger, I wouldn't have let him out of my sight.'

'Hindsight can be sodding annoying,' Jack said quietly. 'But look at it this way: if someone wanted to kill Giles that badly then they would have found a way to get to him sooner or later.'

'Not if Crystabel did it in the heat of the moment,' Marcel replied. 'They argued all the time, you know. I heard them several times when they were here before this, making arrangements for the wedding. It should have been a happy time but they were always sniping at one another.'

'Do you know why?' Alexi asked.

'The TV cameras, I think.' It was Anton who answered. 'Well, I know how that feels, living your life under a microscope and I signed up for it when I entered the contest. Not sure Giles knew what he was letting himself in for until he actually got a taste of it.'

'Did either of you see Crystabel before she discovered the body?' Jack asked.

'Nope.' The two chefs shook their heads in unison.

'I did.' Brendon appeared from the stockroom, tying on his apron.

'What time would that have been?'

Brendon shrugged. 'It had been manic in here. Me and Sally struggled to keep pace with demand. Drew helped us out until business started to tail off. I sent Sally home at about eleven and I saw Crystabel pass the bar door just after that. I assumed she'd coming looking for Giles. He'd disappeared a bit before but had come back. Like I say though, the party was winding down and I don't think any of the stags were seeing straight. They'd all sunk more than a few. Anyway, Crystabel didn't come into the bar.'

'Did you see where she went?' Alexi asked.

'I can only tell you that she headed towards the front door. I didn't see her again after that until all hell broke loose.'

'She got from the front of the hotel to the courtyard without you seeing her?' Jack asked.

'Yeah, she must have done. Things had slowed down but I was on my own by then so still kept busy. She could easily have come back again without my noticing.'

'Was Simon, the best man, in the bar during that time?'

Brendon thought for a moment and then shook his head. 'I don't think so but don't quote me on that. He could easily have been. Like I say, it was bedlam.'

'Did you see Simon and Crystabel talking in private at any time during the latter part of the evening?' Alexi asked.

Brendon shook his head. 'If they did then it wasn't in here. They wouldn't have got any privacy in the bar. Besides, like I say, it was a female-free zone and she would have stood out. We had not just the stags but a load of local men in here too. It was rammed.'

'Okay, thanks guys,' Jack said, indicating to Alexi that they should leave the bar.

'At least we know Jenny told the truth about meeting Giles,' she said as they walked away.

'We know they probably met. Jenny's text messages will prove that one way or another anyway and the contents of Giles's phone will confirm their relationship. Hopefully, Jenny will get a chance to admit to it before Vickery's techies look at the victim's phone. It will look bad for her if she doesn't. Bear in mind that we also don't know what they talked about when they met. Giles could just as easily have told her that he'd decided to go through with the wedding, but for...'

'That passionate kiss I saw,' Alexi finished for him.

'Right.' Jack paused midway across the entrance hall, mulling matters over. 'But significantly, we now know that Crystabel came downstairs a bit after Jenny. We can't be sure how closely she followed behind her cousin but just supposing, for the sake of argument, that she saw Jenny and Giles disappear into the staff corridor...'

'Except she headed for the front of the hotel, so she couldn't have.'

'Depends on the timing. We don't know how long she was out the front. She might have gone for a quick smoke for all we know, come back and seen Jenny and Giles emerging from the corridor, put two and two together and lost her rag.'

'And just happened to have a dagger about her person? Alexi added.

'Yeah, I'm still working on that part.'

'We should have asked Marcel and Anton to have another look at the picture of it. They say it wasn't a kitchen knife but in the cold light of day, they might have some ideas as to its provenance that will point us in the right direction.'

'Yeah, let's do that now,' Jack said.

They both turned when the front door to the

hotel opened. The police were still outside, stopping anyone who didn't have legitimate business from entering. And more specifically, keeping the marauding press pack at bay.

'Anthony,' Jack said, nodding sombrely at the bereaved father, who looked haggard and who had obviously not slept. 'Just the man I was hoping to have a word with.'

11

Jack examined Anthony Preston-Smythe as he walked towards him. He'd aged ten years overnight. His shoulders were stooped, as though struggling to bear the weight of his grief, and the fight appeared to have drained out of the formidable trainer. He had with him a younger woman, presumably the partner whose presence Giles had resented. The lady, probably in her late forties, was attractive in a no-nonsense sort of way and looked suitably desolate in her role as Anthony's supporter. Jack wondered if she actually saw the benefits to having had Giles removed from the scene. He had created problems for his father, for her and for their business and had been a general pain in his father's side. She wouldn't be human if she didn't feel a modicum of relief to have had the problem permanently eradicated.

The lady clutched Anthony's arm, almost as though she feared he would collapse if she didn't hold him upright. Alexi caught her gaze, some sort of unspoken communication passed between the two ladies and Jack suspected that Alexi had taken an instinctive liking to her. Jack could sense no malice in her and very much doubted if she'd entered the hotel and thrust a knife into Giles's heart. Apart from anything else, it had been a woman-free zone that evening and the two females who had dared to infiltrate it, albeit on the periphery of the action, had been noticed.

'This is Sarah Bishop,' Anthony said.

Jack and Alexi shook hands with them both.

'I'm surprised that you know who I am, Anthony,' Alexi said, when he introduced her by name. 'I can call you Anthony?' The man nodded impatiently. 'I don't think we've been properly introduced before now.'

'Your reputation precedes you,' he said impatiently, 'both as a journalist and investor in this establishment. Lambourn is a small place.'

Alexi dipped her head. 'That much is true.'

'Look, I was hoping to catch you. I've come to collect my son's things but I've just been told that I can't have them until the police investigation is completed.' He threw up his hands. 'What more investigating there is to do defeats me. The damned woman was caught standing over my son with the bloody murder weapon in her hand.' He paused to dash the back of his hand beneath his eyes. 'What more do they need?'

'I hear they have arrested Crystabel,' Sarah said in a soft, melodious voice, squeezing Anthony's arm as she spoke.

'Hope they throw away the damned key,' Anthony said.

'If you want to talk to us,' Alexi said, 'shall we go somewhere more private?'

Anthony nodded and Jack led the way back to Cheryl's kitchen. Cosmo and Toby were its sole occupants. Jack waited to see how Cosmo would react to strangers invading what he considered to be his personal territory. Depending on a cat's judgement would make Jack a candidate for the funny farm if word got out and his reputation as a hard-boiled detective would never recover.

Be that as it may, Cosmo had proven himself to be an astute judge of character and Jack was more than willing to take his impressions into account. He didn't possess a friendly disposition, it was true, but never left Jack in any doubt if he mistrusted a person. Every little helped, especially in a case such as this one when they were up against the clock. They had a day to satisfy themselves that Crystabel really was the murderer. After that, the rest of the wedding party would go their separate ways and Jack and Alexi would lose the opportunity to trawl for answers. Crystabel would be charged and the future of the hotel would remain questionable.

Jack held his breath as the cat got up, sniffed the air and growled. He then arched his back and settled back down again, as though giving Jack permission to carry on.

'I think he likes you,' Alexi said.

'Goodness, what does he do when he dislikes a person?' Sarah asked.

Alexi smiled. 'Trust me, you don't want to know.'

'I've wanted to meet Cosmo ever since the cookery contest aired and he stole the show,' Sarah said. 'I just wish this meeting could have come about under different circumstances.'

'We all wish that,' Alexi replied with feeling. 'Please sit down. Can I get you some coffee?'

Anthony and Sarah both declined so Jack and

Alexi sat across from them and Jack got right down to business.

'You argued with Giles last night,' he said without preamble.

Anthony glowered at Jack, who remained impervious to the implied intimidation. 'Your sympathy is noted,' Anthony said, a cynical edge to his voice.

'You wouldn't be here talking to us if you didn't want to know the whys and wherefores,' Alexi said softly.

Anthony deflated, presumably because he realised that throwing his weight around would cut no ice. 'I don't have any doubt that Crystabel killed my son. Good God, she was caught red-handed. What more do you need? Besides, she's been arrested.'

'But not charged,' Jack replied. 'In order to be sure of a successful prosecution, the police require a motive.'

'My understanding is that you issued Giles with an ultimatum,' Alexi said. 'Marry Crystabel and he would be disinherited.'

'I did say that several times in the weeks leading up to last night and came here yesterday to have one last go at him. The dumbest of people could see that it wouldn't have worked.'

'There is such a thing as divorce,' Alexi pointed out.

Anthony sighed and ran a hand through his thick, silver hair. 'What you have to understand is that my son was a quitter. He never stayed the course. The moment the going got tough, he was history. Don't get me wrong, I loved my only child unconditionally but that doesn't mean I was blind to his faults.' Jack noticed Sarah give his arm a reassuring squeeze when Anthony's words stalled. 'He blamed me for his mother's death. We had a terrible row about it. Things were said on both sides that were regretted but couldn't be taken back.'

'I'm sorry,' Alexi said and Jack knew that she was being sincere. There was a dignity about the grieving man that struck a chord with Jack. Besides, what little Jack so far knew about Giles indicated that he did indeed flit from project to project, woman to woman, whereas Anthony had built up a successful training yard in a highly competitive business through his own endeavours. Jack was starting to understand why Anthony might have been reluctant to pass on his life's work to a son who would likely either sell up or run it down.

'The fact of the matter is, I knew his mother was ill. Of course I damned well knew. I saw the deterioration in her and moved heaven and earth to try and find a doctor who could offer alternative treatment after she'd been told by three different specialists that the cancer was too far advanced; there was no hope. Giles was in his final year at Durham and Jess insisted he not be told. No one was to be told and she carried on as normal, helping me until she was too weak to stand.' Anthony dashed at his eyes with the back of his hand. Jack looked away, giving him a moment to compose himself.

'Did you try to explain that to Giles?' Alexi asked.

Anthony threw up his hands. 'For all the good it did me. He wanted someone to blame, an excuse to take himself off rather than knuckle down to working in the yard, and I was his scapegoat. Then I took Sarah on to run the admin, our relationship became personal and Giles accused me of replacing his mother before her body was cold. In actual fact, it was over two years before Sarah and I became romantically involved.'

'If you repeated your threat to disinherit Giles last night and if Crystabel knew about it then there's the motive the police need,' Alexi pointed out. 'All well and good if she actually did it, but despite all the evidence and despite the fact that she isn't a likeable person, we both remain to be convinced.' She paused, fixing Anthony with a piercing look that Cosmo couldn't have bettered. 'And I think, despite everything, you share our doubts.'

Anthony sighed, splayed his legs and focused his gaze on the floor beneath them. 'Who else could it have been?' he asked.

'Well, there's the question we all want answers to.' Jack paused to gather his thoughts. 'Who would have suffered if Giles did come back and run the yard?'

'That's just the point. He's working for me right now but it was never going to last. I knew that and it's one of the reasons why I didn't immediately put him into a position of authority. He had some hairy-fairy idea about doing Crystabel's promotion on-line.' He blew air through his lips. 'She wanted to produce her own TV shows. And star in them, obviously. But even if it had happened, he wouldn't have stuck at it. He never did. Despite his wanderlust, Giles was a country boy at heart and would have hated life in London, which is where Crystabel intended that they should base themselves.'

'Even so, had he decided to give training a go, which is the impression that I got, then your current assistant, Martin Hall, would have been out of a job.'

'It wouldn't have come to that.' Anthony waved the suggestion aside. 'And even if Giles had proven me wrong, Martin is incapable of killing a fly, if that's what you're implying, *and* a man with his impeccable track record would have got a job elsewhere in no time flat. Reliable and experienced assistant trainers are in short supply.'

'I'm simply considering all angles, which is what a decent defence barrister will do. If Crystabel's team want to convince a jury that she didn't do it, they need to come up with a plausible alternative suspect and on paper Martin fits the bill.' Jack gave an apologetic little shake of his head. 'Sorry.'

'I didn't make a statement to the police last night,' Anthony said, his expression hardening, 'I was too distraught. Besides, I didn't see any pressing need. They had their woman.' He scowled at Jack. 'Or so I thought. But you can be sure that I'll talk to them today and make it clear that I was serious in my intention to disinherit Giles if he married the damned woman.' Anthony's voice had risen but a gentle tap on the back of his hand from Sarah, who had yet to say very much, and he moderated his tone. 'That will give them more motive than enough.'

'If they can prove that Crystabel knew of your

intentions,' Alexi said into the ensuing silence. 'Besides, our understanding is that Crystabel's estranged father, a very wealthy man, intended to give her the funds she needed to start up her production company. So if you think that she wanted to marry Giles to get at your money then I'd say you're on the wrong track.'

'Then why was she so determined to have him?' Sarah asked. 'I've watched them together on several occasions. Crystabel was very possessive but not in love.' She smiled up at Anthony. 'If she had been then the signs would have been impossible to miss. Take it from one who knows.'

Anthony grunted. 'The only person that woman loves is herself.'

'She was in love with the romantic idea of a training yard but had no idea about the realities. The long cold winters, the mud. The impossible expectations of owners. The list goes on. As for Giles, his feelings for Crystabel were...' Sarah waggled a hand from side to side. 'At best affectionate but no more than that.'

'I want to see justice done,' Anthony said, 'and am fully conversant with the flaws in the legal system in this country, which appear to be slanted in favour of the accused. So I do understand what you're saying. Without a solid motive and with others who might have benefited from Giles's death, there's every opportunity that a slick barrister will get the charges dropped. So, if you want to talk to Martin and assure yourselves that he had nothing to do with Giles's death, then I'll have him come over here tonight, after evening stables.'

'Thank you,' Jack said. 'You realise, of course, that we have no authority and it's the police who will decide whether Crystabel, or anyone else for that matter, is prosecuted for the murder of your son.'

'I think the pair of you have more reasons than most for wanting to get to the truth, and to get there quickly.' Anthony shared a shrewd glance between them. 'And I also don't want there to be any shadows cast over my assistant trainer's character. He's a man who is dependable, knows his stuff and whom I trust absolutely.'

'And even a suggestion of his involvement would have a detrimental effect upon your business, I would imagine. Owners wouldn't want their precious nags stabled with a murder suspect,' Alexi said, not mincing her words. 'I understand because the owners and investors in this hotel are in the same position.'

Anthony inclined his head. 'Well then...'

Alexi passed her card to Sarah. 'Give me a heads-up when Martin is on his way over and we'll make sure we're here,' she said.

Sarah assured her that they would do so and the pair left the kitchen.

'Well, well, the plot thickens,' Jack said, leaning back in his chair and linking his hands behind his head as the door closed behind them.

'He isn't absolutely convinced that Crystabel did it and came here with the express purpose of speaking to us. We simply made it easy for them by raising our doubts.'

'I didn't tell him anything he didn't already know about Crystabel's defence pointing the finger at alternative suspects with compelling motives. He wouldn't lose any sleep if she was convicted, guilty or not. He's simply protecting his own back and needs someone to blame. The poor bloke has lost his wife and now his only child. You have to feel for him.'

'I do,' Alexi replied. 'It's just annoying that everyone's an expert on the law nowadays,' she added, rolling her eyes.

'Right. But at least we'll get to speak with Martin, which wouldn't have been possible otherwise. And bear in mind, by the end of the day, Vickery will know about Jenny. We will have to tell him that Brendan saw Crystabel downstairs at around the time Giles and Jenny were meeting up, which in itself will provide him with not just the missing motive but with opportunity too.'

'We should point out Anthony's threat to disinherit Giles to your former colleague too, if we're being thorough.'

Jack waggled a hand from side to side. 'That one, not so much. I find it hard to imagine that Anthony didn't make his intentions in that regard abundantly clear to Crystabel.'

'Thinking she was a gold-digger and hoping it would put her off.'

'Right. But if Giles really had decided to break it off with Crystabel and transferred his affections to horse-loving Jenny, that *would* potentially give Martin a motive as well.'

'I hear you, but I don't think his father knew about Jenny so how could Martin have found out?'

Jack shrugged. 'Jenny's into horses. It's a small world. She knows Martin. Perhaps she confided in him.'

Alexi fell momentarily silent. 'Will Vickery ignore the horse angle and charge Crystabel on the basis that she was riven with jealousy when she saw Giles and Jenny together, acting impulsively on the spur of the moment? A crime of passion, in other words.'

'The Vickery I once knew wouldn't but having said that, he does have a compelling case against Crystabel and will be under pressure to wrap this one up quickly. So, I wouldn't bet against it. Don't frown, sweetheart.' Jack stood and pulled Alexi to her feet and into his arms for a comforting hug. 'I don't like the thought of it any more than you do but don't forget that it will work in the interests of the hotel if the case is put to bed lickety-spit.'

'I know, but it doesn't mean that I have to like it.' She sighed and leaned the side of her face against his shoulder. 'Having a conscience is damnably inconvenient.'

'We're not finished yet. Come on, let's see if we can run Simon to ground, then we'll go to Shawford and see if Crystabel's father will see us. Damn, I wish Gloria had given us his number.'

'She says she doesn't have it.'

Jack sent Alexi a *seriously?* look, took her hand and headed for the back door. Cosmo and Toby got up to join them and Jack saw no reason to keep them out of things. If all else failed, he'd depend on Cosmo's judgement to identify the killer. He'd gotten results on an even flimsier basis in the past.

The stags were congregated in the annex lounge but there was no longer a police presence.

'We've all been roasted by the rozzers,' one of them said, sending Jack and Alexi a bleary-eyed look. 'Hey, keep that beast away from me!'

The others laughed when Cosmo stalked up the man, arched his back and hissed at him.

'Afraid of a harmless little pussycat?' one of them asked.

'I need a livener,' the guy replied, clearly attempting to regain his dignity when Cosmo showed no further interest in him.

'The bar's just opened,' Alexi told them, which was all it took to create a stampede.

'We've been told we can go home but we're booked into the hotel until tomorrow,' Simon told them, 'so we'll probably hang around, see what happens. Make sure there's justice for our friend. It's the least we can do for him now.'

'Talking of which, got a minute?' Jack asked.

'Sure.' He waved to the others. 'See you in a bit. What is it that I can help with?' he asked, returning his attention to Alexi and Jack.

'We're told that you and Crystabel met up just

before Giles's body was found,' Jack said, cutting to the chase.

Simon, lounging against the door jamb, straightened himself up and scowled. 'You've been misinformed,' he said calmly, 'and the other guys will vouch for that. I didn't leave them for long enough to do anything other than visit the gents. Besides, I have absolutely nothing to say to Crystabel that she'd want to hear and go out of my way to avoid her whenever I can.' He frowned. 'Anyway, who told you that?'

'I heard you arguing with her upstairs earlier in the evening,' Alexi said, pinioning Simon with a look.

'Oh, that.' He shrugged. 'Yeah, sure but I don't see how that's relevant. That was hours before Giles's death. She sent me a text, asking to see me. I didn't want to see her but knew she wouldn't give up, so I went upstairs. Less chance of being seen or heard that way.' He sent Alexi an ironic look. 'Or so I thought. She wanted to put the past behind us and be "friends" again.' He made quote marks with his fingers around the 'friends' part. 'Like that would be possible. I told her that we'd get through the wedding and be civil for Giles's sake, but that would be that.'

'Why were you so bitter?' Alexi asked.

'Ancient history.' There was finality in his tone. 'Nothing to do with last night.'

'Did you at least see Crystabel around the time that Giles was found?' Alexi asked.

'Nope. I've already told you that I didn't.' Simon's voice had taken on a hard edge.

'But Giles did leave the party several times,' Jack suggested.

'Yeah, like I told you before, he was hardly the life and soul so it all fell a bit flat.' Simon folded his arms defensively across his chest. 'Look, if I'd known that the vicious bitch intended to take a knife to him, I wouldn't have let him out of my sight. It was my responsibility as best man to look out for him but, then again, he was a grown man with his own agenda and I couldn't watch him the entire time.'

'What do you mean by his own agenda?' Alexi asked.

'I don't know.' Simon frowned with the effort of recollection. 'All I can tell you is that when I tried one last time to talk him out of marrying Crystabel, he said that he had it covered and that I had nothing to worry about.'

Jack and Alexi exchanged a look. 'What do you

suppose he meant by that?' Jack rubbed his jaw. 'Do you think he planned to call it off?'

Simon spread his hands. 'I don't know what his plans were; he was being uncharacteristically reticent. Ordinarily he was easily influenced, which is why my heart sank when I heard that Crystabel had got her talons into him. He would have been putty in her hands. But, and I hate to criticise the newly departed. I mean, it's not good form, is it? But the fact is that Giles never stuck to anything for long, that's why I knew that if he married the barracuda, it wouldn't last. That said, he was under a hell of a lot of pressure from his father to call it off, and as much pressure from her mother to see it through.' Simon sighed. 'The poor guy was getting it from all angles.'

'Do you think Gloria sensed his change of heart, if that's what he was having?' Alexi asked.

Simon shrugged. 'Perhaps. Who knows? It wouldn't surprise me. Not much gets past that one.'

'What happened to break up your engagement to Crystabel?' Alexi asked.

'And that's relevant to Giles's death, how?' A wary edge had entered Simon's voice.

Alexi smiled. 'Curiosity, I guess.'

'Let's just say that you get to see the real person beneath the façade when you spend so-called

quality time with them on holiday. It can be re-
vealing and I had a lucky escape. But Crystabel
doesn't take rejection well and she made life difficult
for me for a while, until she transferred her affections to Giles.'

'What did she do?'

'It doesn't matter.' Simon had clearly said all that
he intended to on the subject. 'But now, if there's
nothing else, I could do with a livener so I'll join the
guys in the bar.' He raised a hand as he opened the
door to leave. 'You know where to find me.'

'What do you think?' Alexi asked, as they
watched him through the window, his long legs
eating up the ground as he strode across the
courtyard.

'I think he told us the truth, at least insofar as he
didn't see or speak to Crystabel. But it's interesting
that he didn't want to explain his breakup with her,
or the reason for his continued antagonism towards
her.'

'So, either Gloria deliberately misled us when
she said that her daughter had gone downstairs to
talk to Simon, or else she...'

'Told us what Crystabel had told her,' Jack finished for her. 'And she'd actually gone downstairs to
see her father.'

Jack pulled his phone from his pocket.

'What are you doing?'

'Calling Vickery.'

Vickery picked up and Jack put the call on speaker. 'We'll be releasing her on police bail shortly,' he said by way of greeting. 'She will be back with you in a couple of hours, you lucky devils.'

Jack smiled at the cynicism in Vickery's voice. 'You remain to be convinced of her guilt,' he said.

'Oh, I'm pretty sure she did it.'

'"Pretty sure" won't cut it.'

'I'm aware of that, which is the only reason why she's not still in a cell. Just as soon as I gather enough evidence to make our case watertight... Anyway, what can I do for you?'

'You looked at her phone?'

'Duh, thanks for telling me how to do my job.'

Jack laughed. 'Just keeping you on your toes.' His expression sobered. 'Did she get a message late on the night in question?'

'She got several. Care to be more specific?'

Jack smiled, aware that Vickery wanted to know what Jack thought he knew. 'Was one of them from her estranged father, by any chance?'

'Damn, you're good!'

Jack chuckled. 'Have you spoken with him yet?'

'On the phone. We know he was there on the night in question but he has no obvious motive. Crystabel says he was there for less than five minutes, so we know what time to look for him and are checking the motorway cameras. If she told us the truth then his car will be picked up on CCTV and he'll be in the clear. It's doubtful that he would have entered the hotel anyway. Crystabel seems more concerned about upsetting her mother than she does about being accused of murder. And I get the impression that her mother would have had a hissy fit if her ex-nearest-and-dearest had anything to do with the wedding of the century. There's a lot of animosity there.'

'Farrington met his daughter outside the hotel shortly before midnight. Did Crystabel say why or what they talked about?'

'He wanted to meet Giles before his only child tied the knot. He'd been abroad for a while so there hadn't been an opportunity. It was, as you're aware, a whirlwind romance. They'd only been dating for a few months before they decided to make it official. According to Crystabel, who'd originally suggested that her father come over, she'd phoned to put him off.'

'Then why did he come over?'

'She says that conversation took place during the course of the afternoon and so she wasn't expecting him. When he texted to say he was there, she ran down to send him away again. The thing is, we can't see from her call log that she made or received a call to him that day.'

'Well, if you give me his number, I'll speak to him and perhaps go and see him.' There was a long pause. 'I know where he lives and I'll just turn up on his doorstep if you don't give me his number. You know I want to get to the truth as much as you do, even if Crystabel proves to be the murderer. Alexi and I are in damage limitation mode. I'm guessing you're under pressure to get a result too. Let's work together.'

Vickery's sigh echoed down the line. 'Don't make me regret this,' he said, reeling off the number that Jack needed.

12

Alexi smiled at Jack.

'Without wishing to inflate your ego, Vickery's got it right. You are sometimes scarily good at what you do.'

Jack squeezed her arm. 'We're a good team. Anyway,' he added, glancing at his watch. 'Let's see if Mr Farrington is at home and more to the point, if he'll agree to talk to us.'

'What if he puts the phone down on you?'

'Then we'll draw our own conclusions. But I'm guessing that he'll know Crystabel's been arrested and will be anxious to find out what they have on her. It's not as if he can ask Gloria.'

'That's silly. Surely they'll put aside their animosity for their daughter's sake.'

Jack chuckled. 'You heard Gloria earlier. Did she sound like a woman with a forgiving nature?'

'Perhaps not but there's no doubting her investment in Crystabel, both emotionally and professionally. If Crystabel goes down, so too do Gloria's ambitions. She knows that Farrington can buy Crystabel the very best defence team, which might be the mother and daughter's only chance of survival.' Alexi nodded emphatically. 'My money's on Gloria putting pressure on Farrington to step up to the plate.'

'Yeah, I guess I can see that happening, so let's see if we can gauge how willing Farrington will be to deliver.'

Jack dialled the number that Vickery had given him and put the call on speaker.

'Yes.' A deep, impatient voice answered. 'Who is this?'

'Mr Farrington, my name is Jack Maddox, I'm a private investigator.'

A long pause. 'I know who you are. I read the papers. How did you get my number? Is this about my daughter?'

'It is. My associate, Alexi Ellis, and I would like

to come over and speak with you about the situation, if it's convenient.'

'How's Crystabel?' Genuine-sounding anxiety had entered his voice. 'I heard she's been taken into custody. I'll arrange a lawyer for her.'

'She's being released on police bail. She already has legal representation but, of course, if you want to instruct someone else, that's your prerogative.'

'Can I speak with her?'

'When she gets back to Hopgood House, she'll be available on her mobile, but that probably won't be for another couple of hours. In the meantime, can we come over and discuss the situation?'

'Certainly.' There was no hesitation. 'I want to know what's going on; the police won't tell me anything and I can't phone Gloria. I'll text you the address.'

'We'll be there within the hour,' Jack replied, cutting the connection.

Alexi raised a brow at Jack. 'He does sound like he cares.'

'He does, but we'll know for sure once we see him face to face. Ready?'

Cosmo responded before Alexi could. He trotted to the door, then looked round at Jack, twitching his tail as though defying him to leave him behind.

'Okay, big guy,' Jack said, bending to tug gently at one of his ears. 'You can be security.'

Alexi laughed. 'He'll want to be on the payroll soon.'

Jack unlocked his car and opened the passenger door for Alexi. She slid onto the seat and winced when Cosmo landed on her lap with a soft thud. Jack programmed Farrington's address into his satnav and negotiated his way slowly through the massed thong of press. Cosmo hissed at them, earning himself yet another photo opportunity.

'Have you heard from Patrick again?' Jack asked casually as he cleared the congested lane and put his foot down.

'No, but I will.' She rolled her eyes. 'Never doubt it.'

'Just so long as he doesn't turn up in person, which he has a habit of doing.' Jack paused at a junction, waiting to turn left. 'He does know that you and I are now together, doesn't he?'

'He does,' Alexi replied without hesitation, re-living in her mind the tirade she'd had to endure when she'd broken news that couldn't have come as a complete surprise to Patrick. She had spared Jack the lurid details. He didn't need to know that Patrick, in all probability, was delving deep into Jack's past, attempting to dig up more dirt. His disclosure that Jack had been driven out of the Met under a cloud wasn't news to Alexi, which she knew had both disappointed and frustrated Patrick.

Alexi hadn't recovered from Patrick's treachery, his willingness to have her dismissed from a position that she'd worked night and day to establish herself in and was good at, without giving her so much as a word of warning. She had been completely blindsided, disillusioned and very, very angry. That being the case, if she had to compare the two men's integrity, Jack would win hands down.

'What are you so deep in thought about?' Jack asked when they hit the motorway and Alexi hadn't spoken another word.

'Just comparing you to Patrick and wondering what I see in you,' she quipped.

'Do you miss him and your previous life?' Jack spoke lightly but Alexi could detect the anxiety he'd been unable to completely conceal. Her answer clearly meant a lot to him but he was attempting not to make a big deal about it. His sensitivity caused Alexi to fall a little more in love with him. 'The countryside can be quiet.'

'Quiet? Ha! I'd settle for quiet right now and no, surprisingly enough, I don't miss it at all. Patrick did me a favour by forcing me to leave the capital, despite the fact that he didn't do it for that reason.'

'Then I won't kill him if he comes sniffing around again.'

'Please don't kill anyone. I've had quite enough murders to last me a lifetime, thank you very much. Besides, Vickery would resent all that paperwork.'

Jack laughed. 'In that case, I'll simply be exceedingly smug the next time the creep comes down here.' He took one hand from the wheel and placed it on Alexi's thigh, or tried to. Cosmo was occupying her entire lap and Alexi knew he had no intention of moving. 'I shall not be a gracious winner.'

Alexi dozed for the rest of the journey. She hadn't slept well, which was hardly surprising given the circumstances, and always found the hypnotic sound of wheels on tarmac soporific. She woke with a jolt when she felt the car slowing to a crawl.

'Sorry,' she said, sitting up in her seat and yawning behind her hand. Cosmo had remained on her lap for the duration of the journey, his weight almost causing Alexi to lose all feeling in her thighs. He stirred himself too, stood up on her lap and shook himself. 'Have we arrived?'

'We have.'

Alexi peered through the window as Jack turned

the car into a driveway protected by tall, wrought-iron gates. 'Blimey,' she muttered.

Jack lowered his window and pressed a button on a brick pillar. A camera swivelled on its turret, arrowing in on Jack's face. 'Jack Maddox and Alexi Ellis to see Luke Farrington,' he said.

The gates swung open and Jack drove his car slowly along a pristine gravel driveway, flanked by manicured lawns and well-tended flower beds in full bloom: a glorious riot of colour that looked as though it had sprung up naturally. Alexi knew that it must have taken someone hours of planning and careful nurturing to achieve. The house was a modern mansion: an enormous edifice of smooth lines, wide balconies and an abundance of glass. The nearest neighbours were a flock of sheep in a distant field and aquatic fowl populating a lake.

'One of his creations, do you suppose?' Alexi speculated, glancing up at the building.

'Probably. It's not so bad. I expected something more ostentatious.' He parked close to the front door and cut the engine. 'Shall we?'

Alexi pressed the button to open a window a few inches. Cosmo sent her an arch look, leapt over her shoulder and settled down on the back seat. Jack shook his head but refrained from comment.

Before they could reach the front door, it was opened by a tall man who looked every inch the successful entrepreneur. He was also incredibly handsome still.

'Gloria got it wrong about his hair,' she said to Jack in an undertone before they reached him. 'He still has it in abundance.'

'Can't say as I noticed,' Jack replied, scowling.

Alexi laughed and punched his arm. 'Liar!'

'Mr Maddox. Ms Ellis. Luke Farrington.' He extended a hand and shook each of theirs in turn firmly. 'Thanks so much for coming. I appreciate it. Please come in.'

He stood back as Alexi walked into a marble-tiled foyer with a sweeping staircase that led to a galleried landing. Full-length windows at the back of the house looked out onto a swimming pool and there was an unimpeded view of the countryside beyond.

'Wow!' she said, because she couldn't help herself.

'Glad you like it,' Farrington replied with an easy smile. 'It's not what you were expecting, I take it. You assumed gaudy.'

Alexi laughed, having taken an immediate liking

to the man's self-deprecating style. 'Something like that,' she replied.

'Please, come through.'

He led the way into a sun lounge, the doors of which were thrown open to a decked terrace and the swimming pool. What breeze there was gently agitated the surface of the turquoise water. Overheating, Alexi felt like diving in.

'Sit over here. There's a cooler. Don't often need it in this country but it's earning its keep for once.'

The cooler turned out to be a full air conditioning system, working to maximum capacity because the doors were open. Alexi didn't want to think about how much such a wasteful approach must be costing, both the man and the environment.

'Can I offer you something to drink?'

They both accepted soft drinks and sat back to savour them when they were delivered, not by the servant that Alexi had expected to material but by their host himself.

'Now then.' Farrington sat across from them and draped one long leg casually across its twin. It was, Alexi suspected, a relaxed pose he'd perfected over the years when entering into complex business negotiations with sharp rivals. In this case, it wasn't working and genuine anxiety for his daughter's plight evaded his best efforts to conceal it. 'How can I help you prove my daughter's innocence?'

'Excuse me for my bluntness,' Jack replied, 'but we have time constraints and so let's not waste precious minutes by tip-toeing around one another.'

'Fine by me.' Farrington leaned forward, not appearing to have taken offence. 'I prefer a man who speaks his mind.' He smiled as he transferred his attention to Alexi. 'And a woman too.'

'Then we will get along just fine, Mr Farrington,' Jack replied.

'Call me Luke.'

'The thing is, Luke, you say your daughter is innocent. Well, of course you would think so but it's my understanding that you've only recently established contact and that you barely know her, so how can you be so sure?'

'A very good question.' Luke paused, as though it had only just occurred to him, but Alexi suspected that his reaction was a pretence. A successful, self-made man would have anticipated the question and have an answer prepared. 'Of course, I can't know, not for sure. But what I can tell you is that my daughter was infatuated with Giles Preston-Smythe and had their future together as a married couple already mapped out. She's like her mother in that respect: a long-term planner.' A slight frown marred his features at the mention of his ex. 'Anyway, she was also looking forward to her wedding being televised so tell me, why would she kill the man who would have helped her to achieve the fame she craved?'

'Any number of reasons,' Alexi replied crisply. 'Giles was under considerable pressure from his father and his closest friends not to go through with it.'

'Crystabel told me about that.' Luke breathed more easily, apparently relieved that they were the only reasons she'd come up with. What else did he know, she wondered, glancing at Jack to see if he'd picked up on Luke's reaction. His expression gave nothing away; it seldom did when he was interviewing a person of interest. 'But she also assured me that Giles was committed to the wedding and wouldn't give way to pressure. Significantly, she also told me that he had no intention of assuming his father's role as a trainer so didn't much care if he was cut off. As far as he was concerned, his father could leave his business to whoever he liked. He wasn't the sort of man who assumed he had a natural right to inherit.'

'I see.' Alexi wondered if that was the actual

truth, or Crystabel's version of it. All the evidence they'd accrued pointed to the latter. 'You never met Giles, I understand.'

'No, sadly not.' He sighed. 'And now I never will.'

'Surely you could have made time,' Jack said.

'Their romance was a bit of a whirlwind. Crystabel admits that she leaned on Giles after she ended her previous engagement to Simon and that reliance developed into a passion.' He allowed himself a brief smile. 'Her words. But you're right, I don't know my daughter well and I understand that her abrasive nature and fierce determination doesn't always earn her friends. But underneath that tough exterior, she's really quite sensitive, you know.'

Alexi didn't, so would have to take Luke's word for it. 'You're right in that she doesn't always do herself any favours,' she said diplomatically.

'I blame myself for that. I'm afraid I didn't behave very well when Gloria told me she was pregnant. We had a firm understanding that we wouldn't have kids until I was better established, you see.'

'Ah.'

'I'm guessing from your reaction, that isn't the way Gloria told it.'

'Not precisely.' Jack fixed Luke with a direct look.

'Not to put too fine a point on it, she says you ran out on her and left her to cope alone.'

'I did.' He paused. 'But did she tell you why?' He shook his head, not waiting for Jack to respond. 'No, I'm absolutely sure that she didn't.' He flapped a wrist, a slight look of irritation disturbing his features. 'For what it's worth, I'll tell you what actually happened and you can decide for yourselves which of us is being truthful.'

Luke paused to take a sip of his drink. The ice clinked against the crystal as he returned the glass to the coaster on the table beside him, but apart from that, there wasn't a sound in the room, discounting the soft whir of the air conditioning and the distant indignant quacking of a duck. Luke took a deep breath and momentarily closed his eyes. Alexi and Jack waited him out, comfortable with the silence. For her part, Alexi was already half-way convinced that they would get a truthful account from him, then adjured herself not to pre-judge.

'Gloria was the one for me,' he said. 'I didn't doubt it from the moment I set eyes on her. She was a stunner, enormous fun, willing to push the boundaries, and popular with the opposite sex. Very popular. But I chose to believe that she settled for me for reasons other than the fact that I'd started to make money at an early age.' He gave a cynical little laugh. 'More fool me but then I probably wasn't thinking with my brain at the time.'

'What happened to open your eyes?' Alexi asked softly.

'I had a business partner, a charismatic guy who flirted outrageously with Gloria. But he never took things further than that. He had a wife and two kids and doted on them but I saw how he struggled to juggle his work/home commitments, which is one of the reasons why I didn't want a family getting in the way. Selfish?' He shrugged. 'Perhaps, but then I've always thought that it's even more selfish to have children simply for the sake of procreating. You see it all the time. Kids are an expensive and sometimes inconvenient luxury and the world's already over-populated.'

'True,' Jack said mildly when Luke paused to reflect. Alexi had no way of knowing if Jack agreed with Luke's assessment. They'd never discussed having children; their relationship was still too new. Besides, Alexi wasn't sure herself how she felt about the prospect. She enjoyed spending time with little Verity but had no qualms about handing her back to her parents either. What did that say about her maternal instincts?

'Anyway, long story short, Brian, my partner, came to me one evening and admitted that Gloria had gone to him in floods of tears.' Luke's words jolted Alexi out of her reverie and she concentrated her entire attention on Luke. 'She'd told Brian that I was neglecting her, blah, blah. One thing led to another and they finished up doing the deed.'

'Ah.' Alexi nodded pensively.

'Brian was riddled with guilt but instead of living with it, he chose to tell me. To open my eyes, as he put it, to Gloria's true character. I forgave him. Despite his flirtatious ways, I knew who was responsible. I had been away a lot for a few months, negotiating a building contract in Spain. Gloria had wanted to come with me but, contrary to what she thought, it was all work and she would have slowed me down. I'd already realised by then that she was high maintenance and had a low threshold for boredom. She didn't like her own company and found it hard to make female friends.' His chuckle owed little to humour. 'She didn't like the competition. She also didn't trust me away on my own but was mistaking my character for her own. I have never played away when in a relationship, married or otherwise.'

Alexi believed him. 'Go on,' she said.

'I'd started to see Gloria's spiteful nature by that

point. It came to the fore when she didn't get her own way and she deliberately turned to Brian as an act of petty revenge, not imagining for one minute that he'd tell me about it.'

'You confronted her?' Jack asked.

'What would you have done?'

Jack nodded. 'Yeah, I hear you. I assume she denied it.'

'You assume correctly. She placed all the blame on Brian. Said he pursued her relentlessly whenever I was away and that because she'd rejected him, he was attempting to get his revenge by saying that something had happened when it hadn't, driving a wedge between us.' Luke shook his head at the memory. 'She was so convincing that I almost believed her.' He paused. 'Almost.'

'You threw her out?' Alexi asked.

'No. She told me she was pregnant but, of course, I knew there was a very real possibility that the child wasn't mine. If she'd cheated with Brian then who else had she had her jollies with when I was away and she was sulking? I told her in no uncertain terms that I wasn't ready to be a father, that we'd agreed. We were living in one of the show houses on a development of ours. I let her stay there until the building work was completed. She agreed, thinking I'd come back but I didn't want to know.'

'No wonder she's bitter,' Alexi muttered, almost to herself.

'Well anyway, the rest, as they say, is history. I gave her a generous settlement, more than she deserved, and arranged through my lawyers for a DNA test when Crystabel was born. The results proved that she was mine, so I provided financially for her.'

'You didn't attempt to see her?' Alexi asked.

'I did, but how do you think that went down? Like I already told you, Gloria does not take rejection well.'

'When did Crystabel first get in touch?'

'After her engagement to Simon ended. It was by chance really. I'm not in this country all that much but one particular day, I was around when we broke ground on a new building project. She was there. Told me she'd seen something about it online and had come in the hope of meeting me. I was delighted but, of course, we had to keep it from Gloria. Her animosity towards me has not diminished over the course of the years and she doesn't know to this day that Crystabel and I are talking to one another.'

'Actually, she does,' Alexi replied.

'Really?' Luke quirked a brow. 'First I've heard of

it. I'm surprised Crystabel told her. Gloria goes into a rage at the mere mention of my name, apparently. All these years on and she still bears a grudge when she only has herself to blame for the way things turned out and she knows it. A transference of blame can't be healthy.'

'Crystabel didn't tell her,' Alexi said. 'Gloria guessed when your daughter made excuses to go places that didn't ring true. So she checked Crystabel's phone and found some of your messages.'

'Then I'm even more surprised that Gloria hasn't warned me to back off,' Luke replied, with a careless flap of one hand.

'She knows that Crystabel will do whatever Crystabel wants to do. But all the time she thinks Gloria doesn't know she will protect her feelings, and Gloria probably realises it,' Jack said.

'I suppose.'

'Why did you go to Hopgood Hall last night?' Alexi asked.

'Because Crystabel asked me to. She wanted me to meet Giles before the big day because she knows her mother would have busted a gut if she'd insisted upon me being there.'

'Crystabel told the police that she called you yesterday afternoon and cancelled.'

'Did she?' Luke pulled his phone from his pocket and scrolled through it. 'No missed calls,' he said, handing it to Jack. 'See for yourself.'

'The police already know that she lied, at least about that, because they checked her phone and she hadn't made any calls to you.' Jack handed the phone back to Luke. 'Why she would lie about something that's so easy to disprove has got me baffled.'

'I have absolutely no idea,' Luke replied, 'but if I had to guess I'd say that she wasn't thinking straight. Being arrested is, I'm sure, a pretty traumatic experience. Anyway, I reckon she was attempting to keep my name out of things.'

'Why?' Alexi asked. 'What reason would you have to kill her fiancé?'

'Not for that reason but because she wouldn't want her mother to know that I was there.'

Jack nodded. 'That sounds more like it. How long were you at the hotel?'

'No more than five minutes.'

'You didn't text Crystabel to say you'd arrived.'

'Yes. I told her when I'd get there and she knows me well enough by now to be aware that I'm always punctual, so she would have been expecting to hear from me. Time's money in my game and early on, I realised that it couldn't be wasted.' He shrugged. 'Old habits die hard. Anyway, I met my daughter in the car park. She apologised for my wasted journey. She said she couldn't find Giles and that she couldn't crash the stag party to look for him so we'd have to rearrange. I was irritated, but I wasn't about to make an issue out of it.'

Alexi thought about what they'd just learned. If Crystabel really couldn't find Giles, and the likelihood was that she couldn't because he was with Jenny at the time, then her excuse rang true.

'Can you recall approximately what time you arrived and what time you left again?' Jack asked.

'I can.'

Luke reeled off his arrival and departure times. Jack wrote them down. 'I'll give these to the police, although I think they already have them. I gather they're attempting to pick your car up on the motorway cameras and once they do you'll be exonerated.'

Luke offered up a half-smile. 'Good to know,' he said. 'Can I see Crystabel when she's released?'

'That's between you and her. And Gloria.' Jack stood and offered Luke his hand. 'Good luck with that one.'

Luke stood too and shuddered. 'I'll need it but

given the circumstances, I think it's time I stopped pussyfooting around my former wife's feelings.'

Alexi smiled when he turned to shake her hand. As she moved towards the door, she noticed an array of framed photos on a table that had been behind her. She paused to look at them.

'Is that your wife?' she asked, pointing to one of them, in which a fresh-face woman some years younger than Luke smiled at the camera, a puppy in her arms.

'Yes.' His smile was uncontrived. 'That's Petra, the love of my life. We've been married for five years now and not a cross word.'

'Is she here now?' Alexi asked. 'I'd like to meet her.'

'No, she's been in London for a few days chasing down a new commission.' He paused, pride radiating from his core. 'She's an up-and-coming portraitist of some renown.' He pointed to a decent portrait of himself hanging in pride of place in the vast entrance hall. 'That's her work.'

'She's very talented,' Alexi replied. She rummaged in her bag, produced one of her cards and handed it to Luke. 'If you think of anything else that might shed light on the murder, any chance remark that Crystabel made about problems Giles might have had with anyone, please give me a call.'

'I will.' Luke placed Alexi's card on a side table. 'Believe me, if I can make this go away for my daughter without a stain on her character, it will go some way to making up for my neglect of her for all these years.' He sighed. 'I should have fought Gloria harder, insisted upon seeing Crystabel, but I knew she would oppose me every step of the way. Perhaps I deserved to be cut out of my daughter's life, if only because I took the easy option.'

Jack and Alexi shook Luke's hand once again and left the property. They were greeted by Cosmo who went to the trouble of opening one eye when they got in the car and then went straight back to sleep again.

'Did you believe him?' Alexi asked.

'For the most part.' Jack paused with his hands on the wheel. 'Wish I knew why he lied about his first meeting with Crystabel though.'

Alexi arched a brow. 'Was that a lie? I didn't pick up on it. What gave him away?'

'It was too full of unnecessary detail, like it had been rehearsed.'

'I guess so but...'

'I've conducted too many interviews to be fooled, even by a slick performance.' He started the engine and turned the car in a tight circle. 'Still, perhaps his reasons are personal and nothing to do with this enquiry.'

'Yes, now you've drawn it to my attention, it did seem like he'd rehearsed his answer to that particular question.'

'I'm not the only one who picked up on details, I'm thinking. What was it about Luke's wife that got you so agitated?' Jack asked.

'Petra isn't in London, or wasn't yesterday.' Alexi focused her worried gaze on Jack as he steered the car along the gravel driveway. 'She was a guest at Hopgood Hall.'

13

Jack slammed his foot on the brake and stared at Alexi. 'You sure?' he asked.

'Positive. The stags didn't take all the rooms. There were long-standing bookings for a couple of them that we honoured.'

'Why would Petra have booked a long way in advance and not told the man who clearly adores her?'

'That I couldn't say, but I do know that there was a last-minute cancellation and presumably Cheryl accepted Petra's booking because she had the space. We'll ask her. Petra wouldn't have known that the hens would crash the party and demand accommodation themselves.' Alexi tapped her fingers on her thigh. 'Luke won't like it if we get his daughter off the hook by placing his wife on it. If he had to choose to save one of them, I reckon he'd have a tough time deciding which way to swing.'

Jack removed his foot from the brake and drove slowly through the gates that swung open as he approached them. 'Why on earth would Luke's wife want to involve herself with the stag party?'

'Presumably she wanted to speak with Giles for some reason without Luke knowing.'

Jack nodded. 'More to the point, did Crystabel see her?'

'We'll ask her,' Alexi replied. 'I only caught a brief glimpse of Petra when she checked in. I happened to be there at the time but she is very distinctive looking and I recognised her immediately in that picture shrine of Luke's. I'm good with faces, as you know. Anyway, she definitely needs to explain herself to Vickery, if not to us.'

'She would have had to leave a contact number when she checked in,' Jack said, as he indicated and moved out to pass a slow-moving van. 'If it was a genuine number, we'll be able to ring her.'

'I'd rather look her in the eye when we speak to her.'

'Me too but we're up against it timewise, don't forget.'

'As if I could.' Alexi pondered for a moment. 'I wonder if she registered under her real name? She would have had to show some form of ID but that can be easily faked.'

'We'll know soon enough.'

'What did you make of Luke, contrived answers notwithstanding?' Alexi asked.

'I think he was being honest with us for the most part.' Jack frowned at the road ahead, even though there were no impediments to irritate him. 'He was holding something back I'm sure, but hell if I know what.'

'I found his explanation about his breakup with Gloria more plausible than hers.'

Jack nodded. 'Me too, which is perhaps one of the reasons why Gloria didn't want Crystabel to get to know him. If he told her the truth then she would have to question the account that Gloria's fed to her all these years. Gloria is a bitter and resentful ball-breaker and she's raised Crystabel in her own image. Lies have a way of coming back and biting a person on the arse though and that might just be what's happening to Gloria.'

'Yeah, I believed him as well. He's very plausible but probably not the saint that he made himself out to be.' Alexi paused. 'I do think that he genuinely wants to help his daughter though.'

'Everyone has skeletons.'

Alexi grinned. 'Even you.'

Jack winked at her. 'Especially me.'

'Now I'm intrigued.'

They drove the rest of the way in companiable silence. Jack spent the time trying to fit the pieces together. There was something he was missing, a lead that he ought to be giving priority to, but it remained elusively just out of his reach. He was no nearer deciding what it was by the time they'd reached Hopgood Hall.

'I must be losing my edge,' he muttered.

'The press pack has grown,' Alexi said, groaning.

'Word of Crystabel's arrest and subsequent release has doubtless leaked out, as these things have a habit of doing,' Jack replied, pulling his car into a space and cutting the engine. 'What's the betting that she poses for them when Ben drives her back?'

Alexi rolled her eyes. 'You won't get many takers.'

The two of them exited the car. Cosmo took a detour as far as the barrier where a policemen prevented anyone without legitimate business in the hotel from entering it. That included the press.

Cosmo arched his back and hissed at them. The cameras lapped the performance up.

'Something to fill their next local news slots with,' Jack said, laughing.

'Cosmo, you know better than that.' Cosmo meekly trotted over to Alexi's side and rubbed his big head against her shins. 'I swear he just showed them his better profile,' she added, exasperated yet trying not to laugh herself.

They entered the hotel and found Drew and Cheryl in their kitchen. They accepted an offer of coffee and filled their friends in on the progress they'd made thus far.

'You still think she didn't do it?' Drew asked when they ran out of words.

'I think Vickery will find it hard to get the case to stick, until Jenny's statement is drawn to his attention.' Jack's expression remained grim. 'That will be a game-changer: the motive he needs to firm up the charges.'

'Well, at least it will take the spotlight off us,' Drew said. 'The hotel can't be held responsible for a lover's tiff that got out of hand.'

'You know how suspicious people can be,' Cheryl replied, clearly not convinced. 'Some locals still blame us for Graham Fuller's conviction, even though he was guilty as sin. He was a local man and a successful trainer and that's all they care about.'

'Fuller's victim had nothing to do with the hotel,' Jack reminded them.

'No, but you and Alexi brought him to justice and Alexi almost lost her life at his hands. That much is public knowledge but holds no sway with the locals.'

'Locals don't book our rooms, love,' Drew reminded his wife.

'They can start rumours and speculation though, locally and online.'

'Let's hope it doesn't come to that,' Alexi said. 'Speaking of which, you had a lady called Petra Farrington staying here this weekend. Has she checked out yet? She's Luke Farrington's new wife.'

Cheryl, who handled the bookings and had a good memory for names, looked blank. 'I don't think we had anyone staying called Farrington,' she shook her head and sent her husband a bemused look. 'I can check.'

She pulled up the laptop that said permanently on the kitchen counter and looked up their bookings.

'This is the single woman who stayed with us last night but she checked out this morning.'

Jack and Alexi looked over her shoulder.

'Petra Horton.' They shared a look. 'That has to be her,' Alexi said. 'And she left a mobile number which is probably a dud.'

'She showed a passport when she checked in.' Cheryl pulled up the picture.

'It's definitely her,' Alexi and Jack said together.

'The plot thickens,' Jack said, peering more closely at the passport. 'That document is current, so presumably Horton is her maiden name and she didn't take Luke Farrington's name when they married.'

'If she was an artist building a name for herself before she got hitched, she probably didn't want to change it,' Alexi said. 'A lot of women don't nowadays.'

'What do you intend to do about her?' Drew asked. 'Time's running out.'

Before Jack could answer, the door opened and Ben ushered a very subdued Crystabel through it.

'Welcome back,' Cheryl said. 'Would you like coffee?'

Crystabel looked as though she would like something considerably stronger but shook her head and took a seat at the table. Jack was surprised. He had assumed that her first port of call would be to her mother. He examined her face. Without makeup, she looked younger and he caught a glimpse of the vulnerability that her father had insisted was there if one delved deeply enough. She looked confused, and worried, as well she should; especially if she was as innocent as she claimed to be.

Ben accepted coffee and sat beside Crystabel. 'It isn't looking good as things stand,' he said. Jack knew he would be repeating what he'd already told Crystabel on the drive back. Her resigned expression confirmed that supposition. 'Vickery only lacks a motive.'

'Which doesn't exist.' Crystabel had been focusing her gaze on the surface of the table but looked up now, a defiant spark illuminating her dull eyes.

'Unless they can prove that Giles was having a change of heart,' Alexi said briskly, not one iota of sympathy in her tone. Jack knew that she would be feeling sympathy for Crystabel, even though she didn't like her but that she had gauged, probably rightly, that it would be better for all concerned if they kept emotion out of the discussion.

'But he wasn't!'

'Are you sure about that?' Jack asked. 'Not to put too fine a point on it, he was under considerable pressure from his father to call off the wedding or risk being disinherited and he—'

'He didn't care about the stupid training yard!' Crystabel's voice turned shrill as she tugged at the ends of her hair. 'He said he'd had more than enough of flighty horses and their demanding owners to last him a lifetime. We were going to work together on my production company.'

'Simon put pressure on him to call it off too,' Alexi pointed out.

'Ha! Simon is jealous because I broke off our engagement.'

Jack stood. 'Come on, Alexi, we have things to do.'

'Where are you going?' Crystabel wailed. 'Ben said you'd help to find the real murderer.'

'Which I can only do if you tell me the truth,' Jack shot back at her.

'You didn't call off the engagement,' Alexi added in a more moderate tone, 'Simon did. And it's obvious to anyone with eyes in their head that you still care deeply for him. If we noticed, you can be sure that Giles did. What man would marry knowing that his bride would prefer to be saying "I do" to the best man?'

Crystabel wiped away a tear. 'That's harsh,' she

said. 'I've been grilled at a police station for hours and now you're throwing accusations my way when you're supposed to be on my side. No one seems to remember that I'm in shock. Grieving.'

'You can grieve as much as you like once the murderer has been captured,' Jack said. 'And for the record, I'm not completely convinced that it isn't you.'

'You desperately wanted to keep tabs on Giles and make sure that none of the stags talked him out of marrying you,' Alexi added. 'You knew this would be their last opportunity to make him see sense, which is why you moved the hen party here. You thought you could manipulate Giles and didn't expect him to throw you all out of his stag. You came here because you wanted to be close to Simon too. There was something you wanted to talk to him about. Care to share?'

She shrugged. 'I just wanted to clear the air between us. I didn't want any antagonism spoiling our big day.'

Jack allowed the lie to past uncontested. For now. 'You came downstairs supposedly to talk to Simon. That's what you told your mother. Did you run him to ground?'

She shook her head. 'No,' she said shortly. 'He

was in the bar and I wouldn't have been able to get him alone.'

'Why did you really come down?' Jack pinioned her with a stony look.

She let out a protracted sigh. 'I met my father, Luke Farrington,' she said. 'And I didn't want Mum to know we were in contact. It would have upset her needlessly.'

'I'm struggling to get my mind round the fact that an independent woman as forthright as you are, feels unable to tell her own mother that she's in contact with her father,' Alexi said.

'Their history is complicated.' She spread her hands and Jack noticed that her nail varnish was chipped: an unimaginable situation twenty-four hours previously. 'Mum still feels badly done by. He abandoned her when she was pregnant with me.'

'Not the way he tells it,' Alexi replied.

'Yes well, I expect there's some truth on both sides.'

'Why did you tell the police you'd called him that afternoon, telling him not to come over?' Jack asked. 'You must have known they'd check your call log and discover that you hadn't been in touch.'

'Isn't it obvious?' she asked, a modicum of impatience underlying the words.

Jack fixed her with a look that implied he was rapidly running out of patience himself. 'We are trying to help you, in case it had escaped your notice and aren't asking questions that the police themselves won't get around to sooner rather than later.'

'My first thought was keeping the truth from Mum, just like always,' she replied on a note of bitterness. 'Old habits are hard to break, even in the scariest situations, I now have reason to know.' She puffed out her chest. 'It's pretty daunting, being dragged into a police station and thinking you're about to be charged with a crime that you didn't commit. So excuse me if I didn't think straight when questions were fired at me. I naïvely believed that my account of my actions would be... well, believed. That said, Luke was at the hotel for less than five minutes, he'd never laid eyes on Giles and had no reason to kill him. He didn't enter the hotel either so he, at least, is above suspicion which is more, apparently, than can be said for me.'

'Who did you see when you returned to the foyer?' Jack asked. 'Think very carefully. It could be vital. Was Giles anywhere in sight?'

'No, I didn't see him.' She closed her mouth and stretched her lips into a tight line that implied she'd said all she had to say on that particular subject.

'Who did you see?' Alexi asked.

'There was a lot of noise coming from the bar. I did poke my head round the door, which is why I know Giles wasn't in there. I wondered if he'd gone outside to get some air. It was still very hot. So, I went out there too...' She covered her mouth with her hand and choked on a sob that seemed genuine. Her eyes flooded with tears. 'And that's... that's when I found Giles. His eyes were open and staring and blood oozed from his chest. I knew he wasn't alive and now that I'm thinking more rationally, I also know that I shouldn't have pulled that dagger out. Instead, I should have called for help, even though I knew he was beyond help.'

'Did you check for a pulse?' Jack asked.

Crystabel shook her head. 'No. I just screamed and then everyone poured outside to see what was happening and... well, you know the rest.'

'You didn't see anyone in the courtyard?' Alexi asked. 'We're all agreed that Giles had only been dead a matter of minutes, if that. So you might well have disturbed the killer before he or she had time to escape.'

'The detective asked me the same question and obviously, I've had time to think about it. But no, I don't remember seeing anyone. Not that I looked and anyway, there are loads of large planters and stuff that someone could have hidden behind. Then that person could just have emerged and mingled with everyone else.' She shrugged. 'That seems plausible to me.'

'It could have happened that way,' Alexi agreed.

'Look, my marriage to Giles was going to be the making of my career. Despite what you might have heard, we understood one another and Giles was fully committed to it. He didn't care about his father's threats so what reason would I have to kill him? I asked the detectives that and they didn't have an answer.'

'I'm afraid they do now,' Jack said.

'What?' Crystabel opened her eyes very wide and focused her attention exclusively on Jack. 'What have people been saying?'

'We have it on very good authority that Giles had transferred his affections elsewhere,' Alexi said softly.

Crystabel blinked several times, then a look of relief flooded her features as she smiled and shook her head. 'Nonsense!' she said briskly. 'We were committed to one another.'

'Alexi's right,' Jack said. 'Giles and your cousin Jenny were—'

'Jenny?' Crystabel made a disparaging sound and waved the suggestion aside. 'Don't be so ridiculous! Giles wouldn't have thrown me over in favour of her.'

'We've seen the text messages they exchanged and the police will have too. In fact, I'm surprised they didn't mention them,' Jack said.

Ben, who had remained silent yet alert, hadn't appeared too concerned about the speculative nature of their conversation. Jack knew they hadn't raised any issues that the police didn't already know about. Until now. At this latest revelation, his expression turned severe.

'That surprises me as well,' he said, tilting his head in a considering fashion. 'They must have not known what they implied.'

'Possibly not,' Alexi said. 'They were short and mostly just referred to times and places. No expressions of affection. I know because Jenny showed me her phone earlier.'

'Which could mean anything and nothing,' Crystabel said. 'I'm sure that horrible detective who clearly didn't like me would have made some mention of the messages if he thought they meant anything at all.'

Jack knew that Alexi could contradict that argument. She opened her mouth to speak but at a warning look from him, she closed it again without uttering a word. Crystabel was vindictive and Jack couldn't rule out the possibility of her taking physical revenge against Jenny when she could no longer deny the mortifying truth. Her reaction to the suggestion had confirmed to Jack's satisfaction that she'd had no idea about Jenny's involvement with her intended. Crystabel's incredulous response would have eluded the most professional of actresses.

And so, unless she had confronted Giles and he'd told her that he planned to call the wedding off without making any mention of Jenny, then Crystabel was in the clear, at least insofar as Jack was concerned. Vickery and his superiors would doubtless have other ideas.

Jack glanced at Ben, a look passed between them and they both knew that Crystabel's name was now more firmly in the frame than ever.

'Then we have a problem,' Ben said tersely. 'It's the motive that Vickery was looking for.'

'I'll talk sense into Jenny,' Crystabel said. 'She's a fantasist and has clearly got a crush... had a crush on Giles. Those messages between them can, I'm sure, be explained away. She only had to tell him that she needed to speak to him on my behalf about wedding arrangements...' She spread her hands. 'I dare say it's nothing more than that and that she doesn't realise the damage her statement will do to me.'

'Jenny isn't stupid,' Alexi said.

'Nor does she have any reason to harm me,' Crystabel shot back. 'I'll talk to her.'

'No!' Alexi, Jack and Ben all said together.

'Steer well clear of her,' Ben added.

'But I...'

'No buts.' Ben held up his hands to prevent another interruption. 'You will make matters ten times worse for yourself if you attempt to intimidate a witness. Leave it to us to have your best interests at heart.'

'And in the meantime, I have to go upstairs, see her and pretend I don't know how vindictive she's being?' She rippled her shoulders. 'I had no idea she was quite so envious. It's always the quiet ones.'

'You can avoid her easily enough,' Alexi said. 'Besides, the only other option is a jail cell, which is where you will end up if you take matters into your own hands, to say nothing of making yourself look even guiltier than you already do.'

Crystabel let out a protracted sigh. 'Very well.

Have it your way.' Her phone buzzed and she glanced at the display. 'My mother. Again. I haven't taken her calls because I don't know what to say to her.'

Jack was surprised that she hadn't seen Crystabel return from her window and demanded to be included in this debrief. It would only be a matter of time, he knew, and right now he couldn't deal with the woman.

'Go up to your room now and tell her everything, including about your father, since she already knows anyway. But make it clear that she's to steer well clear of Jenny as well.'

'Where was Jenny at the time of the murder?' Crystabel asked, a malicious glint in her eye. 'If she was fixated on Giles, confronted him and he rejected her, well...'

'She is not a suspect,' Jack replied.

Crystabel folded her arms, but her expression implied that she remained to be convinced on that score.

'How do you get along with your stepmother?' Alexi asked.

A scowl briefly graced Crystabel's features but was as quickly eradicated. Ah, Jack thought, so there's antagonism there. Rivalry for Luke's affections. 'I barely know her,' she said, dismissively.

'Right, that's it for now.' Jack's expression remained set in stone. 'Stay upstairs until we need you. But know this, if you put anything else online about the case, or if you or your mother try to talk to Jenny, then Alexi and I will no longer help you. Is that clear?'

'It is,' she said ungraciously, standing and heading for the door.

Ben got up as well and opened it for her. 'Leave it to me,' he said. 'I'll be in touch very soon.'

14

'Do you think she actually did it, Ben?' Alexi asked as soon as the door closed behind Crystabel.

'What I think doesn't matter,' Ben replied. 'She's a stroppy little madam, that much isn't up for debate. Her answers to Vickery's questions were confrontational. She seems to think that she's above suspicion and that being arrested was an infringement upon her human rights, or some such nonsense.' He shook his head. 'I've seen a whole spectrum of reactions to being arrested but hers was in a class of its own.'

'She isn't that naïve,' Jack said. 'She was attempting to play him. "Poor little me. I'm grieving and these horrible men are trying to say that I killed the love of my life." She's used to bulldozing her way through life and getting what she wants but I can't see Vickery falling for that one.'

'He wasn't taken in for a moment,' Ben replied.

'Her performance either implies genuine innocence or an astonishing degree of arrogance,' Drew remarked. 'But I'm still not sure which.'

'Giles and Jenny were definitely an item,' Alexi said. 'I saw them together not long before Giles was killed and they sure as hell weren't discussing wedding plans. Well, maybe they were but Crystabel wouldn't have been the bride.'

'Ah,' Ben said, looking grave. 'Was this around the time that Crystabel came down to see her father?'

'Just before,' Alexi replied. 'But the thing is, we don't know how long Jenny and Giles were together and, more to the point, if Crystabel saw them when she returned to the hotel. The chances are that Jenny and Giles would have been emerging from the staff corridor where I saw them at about that time.'

'It fits with the time that Giles was found,' Jack added. 'Can you imagine the temper on that one if she saw the two of them together?' He pointed with a thumb to the floor above for emphasis but it was unnecessary because they all knew he was referring to Crystabel.

For her part, Alexi had seen flashes of that temper when minor hitches had occurred in the wedding preparations and, more particularly, in the filming of them. If a person could fly off the handle over the positioning of a table for the wedding gifts, what else would she be capable of if she'd seen her future husband and cousin getting up close and personal, shattering her illusions of a dream wedding. Simon had got shot of her and Crystabel hadn't recovered from the humiliation. Now history was about to repeat itself, only this time it would be worse because she's publicised her wedding to the world at large, and social media in particular.

She would have seen the career that she'd planned to launch on the back of the sparkling ceremony, all her hopes and aspirations, shattering before her very eyes.

'She would have been fuming and more than capable of retaliating in the heat of the moment,' Cheryl, who'd remained silent throughout the discussion, spoke almost in a whisper.

'I think we're all agreed about that much,' Drew replied, covering his wife's small hand with his much larger one and giving it a reassuring squeeze.

'Christ!' Ben ran a hand through his red hair, leaving it standing on end, making it look as though he'd just been on the receiving end of a cattle prod.

'That's not all,' Alexi said, going on to explain about Petra's mysterious presence in the hotel.

'We haven't told Vickery about that yet. I thought you might like to do the honours,' Jack said.

'Can't think off the top of my head why Farrington's second wife would want to kill anyone other than perhaps Crystabel, who'd be more than capable of monopolising a father whose conscience bothers him.'

Jack snapped his fingers. 'That could be it! Petra killing Crystabel would be too obvious but killing Giles and framing Crystabel would be the answer to her problems.'

'A bit of a stretch,' Drew said, frowning. 'How did she know that Crystabel would find the body?'

'I'm working on that part, but there could be any number of explanations.'

'Except Petra wouldn't have known that the hens would crash the stag,' Drew pointed out.

'True.' Jack shrugged. 'Perhaps she came here to persuade Giles to think again. Without the big wedding, Crystabel wouldn't need funding for her production company.'

'Why not?' Alexi asked. 'She could have gone it alone, if Luke backed her.'

'Luke adores Petra, that much was obvious to Alexi and me when we went to see him earlier. But if Crystabel was in danger of spoiling the party by demanding Luke's time and money, distracting his attention away from her, well...'

'She obviously came here for a specific reason and we won't know what that is until we speak with her,' Alexi said, permitting her frustration to show.

'Well, we have the number that she gave us when she registered,' Drew said. 'It has to be worth a try.'

'Even if it's a genuine number, will she talk to us?' Alexi asked.

'She obviously didn't want Luke to know she came here,' Jack replied, 'so yes, if we make it clear that we've spoken to him but haven't yet mentioned her presence here, then my guess is that she will see us.'

Drew reeled off the number and Jack dialled it. The room felt silent as they all listened to it ringing. On the point of giving up, a breathless voice answered.

'Yes. Who is this?'

'Petra Horton? Mrs Luke Farrington?'

'Yesss,' Petra sounded hesitant. 'Who is this?'

'My name is Jack Maddox. I'm a private investigator attached to Hopgood Hall. My associate, Alexi Ellis, and I spoke with your husband this morning regarding the death of his daughter's fiancé.'

A prolonged pause, so long that Alexi thought she'd cut the connection. 'I know nothing about that.'

'Even so, we're aware that you were a guest at Hopgood Hall on the night of the murder. The police will want to talk to you about that.'

'There's nothing I can tell them.'

'Perhaps not but they will still have to be told. That being the case, I wondered if you would care to speak with us first.'

Another prolonged pause. 'Very well. But I am not coming to the hotel if Crystabel's still there.' She named a local pub, which implied she still hadn't returned home. 'Meet me there in an hour.'

And this time, the line did go dead.

'Interesting,' Ben mused. 'What did she do whilst she was here?'

'It was only for the one night,' Cheryl said. 'Drew just checked with the kitchen. She ordered room service on the fateful night. She didn't come down for breakfast this morning and no one I've spoken to saw her in the public areas of the hotel. Doesn't mean she didn't show her face, of course, but if her reason for being here was to corner Giles then the arrival of the hens would have scuppered her plans.'

'And she wouldn't have wanted Crystabel to see her,' Alexi pointed out. 'We already know from her reaction when I asked her how she got along with Petra that there's a ton of antagonism, at least on Crystabel's side. She's finally linked up with her father and doesn't want to share his affections.'

'Well, we'll have some answers soon enough,' Jack said, 'and once we've spoken to her, we'll let Vickery know what she has to say for herself. He won't be best pleased that we haven't told him about her being here on the night in question but, then again, if his team had done their job right then they would have asked to see a full list of residents.'

'They probably assumed that the entire hotel had been taken over by the wedding party, which it more or less had,' Drew pointed out.

'And we're attempting to keep the hotel's reputation intact,' Jack said, 'not do Vickery's job for him.'

'Don't forget that we're seeing Martin Hall later,' Alexi said.

Jack explained about the assistant trainer's unlikely involvement.

'People have killed for less,' Ben said gravely. 'Positions like his in a successful training yard are highly sought after.'

Jack nodded. 'And I gather Martin's been with Preston-Smythe since leaving school, working his way up and proving his loyalty. I don't suppose he was too happy when the prodigal returned, threatening to usurp him, especially since he seemed less than dedicated.' He shrugged. 'People have indeed killed for less.'

'Well anyway, we have time to see Petra. It's only mid-afternoon, even though the day feels as though it's gone on forever.' Alexi yawned behind her hand. 'Martin won't be available until after evening stables.'

Jack glanced at his watch. 'Come on, Alexi,' he said standing. 'Let's get ourselves into town. I want to get there ahead of Petra. It will be interesting to see if she arrives alone.'

'Or if she comes at all.'

'She'll come,' Jack replied confidently. 'She won't want to risk us telling Farrington where she was on the night the murder occurred.'

Cosmo stirred, ready to accompany them. He arched his back and growled when Alexi told him he wasn't coming this time. Toby yapped in disapproving support of his feline friend, making everyone smile.

Jack and Alexi spoke little as Jack drove the short distance to The George, the eighteenth century pub where they'd agreed to meet Petra. The car park was only half full.

'Late lunchers,' Alexi speculated.

'Very likely.'

They parked up and entered the bar. Jack bought drinks for them both and they took a table close to a window that overlooked the car park. Ten minutes later, a flash blue Mercedes convertible took a space close to Jack's BMW.

'Ten quid that's her,' he said.

'I wouldn't bet against it.'

Jack raised a hand when an elegantly understated female with a waterfall of brunette hair entered the bar and glanced around. She too closely resembled the picture of Petra they'd seen in Farrington's house for there to be any doubt about her identity. She walked over to them, her expression impossible to read as Jack made the introductions and they shook hands.

'Thanks for meeting with us,' he said. 'What can I get you to drink?'

Jack went to the bar to purchase the desired soft

drink, leaving Alexi and Petra to size one another up.

'What do you make of Crystabel?' Alexi asked.

'Like I told Jack on the phone, I barely know her. Luke likes to keep her to himself, so tends to see her while I'm working.' She paused. 'He told you that I'm an artist?'

'He did.' It was Jack who responded as he returned to the table and placed her drink in front of her. 'He pointed out the portrait of him that you painted. You have talent.'

'Thank you.' The compliment appeared to erase some of her wariness and Alexi could sense that she'd relaxed her guard, just a little. 'You asked about my relationship with Crystabel. Well, I didn't really have one. We haven't met more than a handful of times but I did sense some resentment on her part. I didn't want to get into a contest with her. I'm confident of Luke's affections and don't feel threatened by her.'

Alexi nodded, believing what she'd just heard. She glanced at Jack and could see that he was halfway to being convinced as well. This lady knew her own worth and was not possessive. 'Then why check into Hopgood Hall when you knew the stag party would be there? And why did Luke think you were in London?'

'I was in London but came back early.' She paused, avoiding eye contact with them both. Alexi suppressed a sigh, aware that she was trying to decide how much of the truth she planned to tell them.

'We haven't mentioned to the police that you were there.' Jack paused. 'Yet. But they will need to know.'

'Why?' She blinked at Jack.

'Don't be so naïve,' Alexi said. 'Of course they will need to know but we're trying to control the damage to the hotel's reputation. This murder being committed in its grounds, so soon after the contestant in the cooking contest lost her life under similar circumstances, is bound to have an adverse effect. That being the case, we need to get to the bottom of things quickly and prove that it wasn't neglect on the management's part that resulted in two murders.'

'Surely you don't think that I...' She pointed to her own chest for emphasis. Alexi thought she was being deliberately disingenuous. Of course, she would realise how suspicious her presence must look to an outsider. If Crystabel knew she'd been in the hotel, she'd jump at the chance to point an accusatory finger her way, if only to put a spanner in the works of her father's second marriage.

'We won't know what to think until you tell us why you were there,' Jack pointed out mildly.

'Just for the record, neither Luke nor I had met Giles and for my part, I was happy that she was marrying.'

'Even if it meant that she'd sponge off Luke in order to get her production company off the ground?' Jack asked.

Petra waved that assertion aside. 'Luke is a very wealthy man and I have independent funds. I didn't marry Luke so that I could spend his money, if that's what you're thinking. My paintings sell well and I am financially secure in my own right.'

Alexi nodded, aware that it was true. She'd googled Petra's name on the drive to the pub and had raised a brow when she saw how well and how much her work sold for.

'Then what possible reason did you have to crash his stag?' Jack asked.

Petra took a long sip of her drink and failed to make eye contact with either of them. Alexi recognised procrastination when confronted with it but, like Jack, also understood the value of silence. They both remained quiet, watching Petra closely as she

appeared to conduct an inner battle with her conscience, and the tactic worked. Alexi had taken a
liking to the woman and really hoped that she
wouldn't attempt to lie to them. Jack would see
through her in a heartbeat.

'You are aware just how much trouble Luke had
with Gloria in the early days of their marriage? The
reason why he didn't acknowledge Crystabel as his
own at first?'

Alexi and Jack nodded in unison. 'He mentioned
the problems,' Jack said.

'Since you've also met him, you're aware that not
only is he wealthy, in itself more reason than enough
for him to be targeted by gold-diggers, but also
handsome and charismatic too. It hardly seems fair
that one man has so much and I never for a moment
considered that he would take a serious interest
in me.'

Petra paused to take a sip of her drink and once
again, Alexi and Jack remained silent.

'He'd avoided live-in relationships since getting
his fingers burned with Gloria and there didn't seem
to be the remotest possibility of him marrying for a
second time,' Petra said, returning her glass to the
table. 'What we had was a coming together of minds
and a physical passion. A fling, in other words. Ex-

cept it turned out to be more than just sex. He took an interest in my work, which is how we met. He bought two of my paintings and wanted to encourage what he described as my exceptional talent.'

Petra again paused but Alexi didn't think she'd done so in order to come up with a plausible explanation for her presence at Hopgood Hall. What she had told them thus far was, she was almost certain, the unvarnished truth.

'Go on,' Jack invited.

'He came to one of my exhibitions, more than five years ago, bought the works I just mentioned and invited me for a drink. We got along well, really well, and I fell for him hard; I won't deny it. He told me after the event that he'd felt the exact same way. We talked about our respective pasts and I learned just how badly Gloria had hurt him, so I couldn't admit to him that I'd been seeing someone else at the same time that we started dating.'

'One of the stags,' Alexi said, as the pieces fell into place.

Petra inclined her head. 'I didn't think that anything would come of my friendship with Luke. I got lonely in my downtime in those days and so didn't want to cut off my other relationship. It sounds pathetic, but I needed a shoulder. Besides, Luke had

made his feelings regarding forever relationships apparent from the word go. He simply didn't trust
women to be faithful.' She spread her hands. 'So
how could I tell him that I was pregnant with another man's baby? A baby that had been conceived
after we started dating. It would have destroyed
him.'

'Ah,' Jack said, nodding. 'What happened to the
baby?'

'I miscarried in the third month but by then, I
had broken it off with Will and have never looked at
another man other than Luke since that day.'

'Was the father aware that you were pregnant?'
Alexi asked. 'Presumably he was, which is why you
were at the hotel. You wanted to talk to him. Persuade him not to mention your past to Luke.'

Petra nodded emphatically. 'Precisely. But Crystabel moved her party to the hotel so I had to keep a
low profile and never had an opportunity to talk to
Will.'

'Will Ashworth?' Alexi recalled the tall, handsome member of Giles's wedding party and could
understand why Petra had been attracted to him.

'Could you not have called him?' Jack asked.

Petra shook her head. 'I no longer had his number. I didn't even know he would be at the wedding

until I saw a list of ushers that Crystabel had given to her father. Despite Gloria's opposition, she was determined that Luke would be at the ceremony, you see. And he was equally determined that I would be there with him. Will and I separated without any animosity but I had no way of knowing how he would react when he saw me again. One spontaneous word about our shared history would have destroyed Luke's faith in me and I couldn't let that happen.'

'I hear you,' Alexi said, impulsively reaching across to squeeze the artist's hand.

'We will talk with Will discreetly to corroborate your account,' Jack said, 'but for what it's worth, I believe you. We will then have to inform the inspector in charge of the investigation.'

Fear flitted through her eyes. 'But why, if you believe me?'

'Because it's the right thing to do. If a thorough defence lawyer did his job properly and realised you were at the hotel that night, it would be a lot worse for you.'

'In your position, I'd explain everything to your husband,' Alexi said softly. 'It was clear to us that he loves you unconditionally, so I'm sure he will forgive you. He's likely to find out anyway so it will be better if it comes from you.'

Petra nodded. 'I know.' She expelled a long sigh. 'I just hope that you're right about the depth of his feelings for me.'

They left the pub and went their separate ways.

'I feel sorry for her,' Alexi said. 'She told us the truth, didn't she?'

'I'll find another profession if she didn't,' Jack replied.

They arrived back at the hotel to find the stags in occupation of the bar, most of them the worse for wear.

'We're sinking a few in memory of Giles,' Simon explained when Alexi and Jack entered the bar. 'Any news? I gather Crystabel's been released.'

'Pending further enquiries. The police need a solid motive,' Jack replied.

'Drink?' Simon asked.

They both accepted. It would give them a valid reason to remain in the bar and attempt to get Will alone. Alexi hoped that Jack wouldn't draw unnecessary attention to the man by asking for a word. He did not. Instead, he waited until about ten minutes later when Will moved away from the rest of the party to answer his phone. The moment he pocketed it, Jack and Alexi casually joined him at the quiet table he'd sat at whilst taking his call.

'A quick word,' Jack said.

'Getting the thumbscrews out, are you?' Will looked bleary-eyed, which wasn't to be wondered at. The stags had been knocking back the booze like they were on a mission the night before and had carried on where they'd left off that morning, albeit for different reasons. 'Giles was a good guy. Good but misguided. He'll be missed.'

'Misguided?' Alexi asked.

'Too easily influenced by a pretty face.'

'You don't like Crystabel?' Jack asked.

'None of us do. We could also see that Giles was making a monumental mistake, and all because he didn't want to train racehorses for the rest of his days.' He took a long swallow of his drink: whisky by the smell of it. 'Well, he won't have to worry about career choices any more, will he.'

Alexi allowed a moment's respectful silence before speaking. 'I gather you and Petra Horton used to be an item.'

'Yeah, we did,' Will replied without hesitation. 'I was pretty cut up when she broke it off, but she'd fallen for Luke and I couldn't compete with him.'

Jack took up the questioning. 'She was pregnant with your child?'

'She was and she intended to tell Luke. She

thought he'd not want to know her after that but she also said that she wasn't going to have an abortion just so that she could be with the man she loved.' Will took another swallow of his drink and then stared at the bottom of the glass, as though surprised to find it empty. 'Then she was knocked down in the street by a courier riding his bike on the pavement. The fall left her with a broken wrist and the shock caused her to miscarry.'

Alexi hadn't known the cause of the miscarriage but had no reason to doubt Will's account. It would be easy enough to check if it came to it.

'Have you seen Petra since your split?' Jack asked.

Will shook his head. 'I've thought about her a lot though. I did half hope I'd see her at the wedding and have a chance to catch up but I also knew there was no possibility of that happening. According to Giles, the mother-in-law-from-hell was determined that Crystabel's father wouldn't be at the ceremony and she is about the only person who's views Crystabel takes into account.'

'You weren't aware that Petra stayed at this hotel last night?' Alexi asked.

'Did she?' Will widened his eyes. 'I had absolutely no idea. Why would she have done that?'

'You didn't see her?'

'Nope. And trust me, if I had, I would remember. As you know, we checked in, dumped our bags then went to the races. As soon as we got back, we started seriously drinking. I didn't see anyone other than members of the wedding party.'

'She saw that you were an usher and panicked. She didn't know how you would react to seeing her. So she came here, hoping to see you and persuade you not to speak about your past. Before she could, the hens turned up and she had to stay out of sight in her room.'

'Is she still here?'

'No, she checked out first thing.'

Will looked disappointed. 'I still don't get it. Farrington wasn't on the guest list,' he said, running a hand abstractedly through his hair. 'So Petra had nothing to worry about.'

'Seems Luke was determined to come to the wedding, which meant she would have been with him. A man like Farrington, what he wants, he usually gets. Crystabel needed his financial backing in order to fulfil her ambitions so she would probably have found a way to make her mother agree to his being there.'

'I wouldn't have said a word, she needn't have

worried about that. We all have skeletons that are best left in the cupboard.'

'I will have to tell the police that she was here, so they will want to talk to you again, I dare say,' Jack warned.

'No problem. I have nothing to hide and will tell them what I just told you.' He stood up, his legs a little unsteady. 'Christ, what a mess!'

Jack slapped his shoulder. 'We'll get to the truth and find out who killed Giles. It's all we can do for him now.'

'I hope you do but I don't have any doubt in my mind that Crystabel is the guilty party. I get that the police have to have a solid case against her though. You're aware, I take it, that she has one hell of a temper on her? Gets it from her mother, if you ask me, which you didn't, but there you have it.'

'Was Giles aware that you and his future step-mother-in-law were once an item?'

Will shrugged. 'Not as far as I know. I'm five years older than Giles. We both played rugby for the local club which is how we met when he came back from a holiday in Greece that he described as a disaster. My point is, we didn't mix in the same social circles. He was still at school doing A levels when I dated Petra.'

'Okay,' Jack said. 'Thanks for your time.'

As they walked away Alexi noticed that Anton had put out a tempting array of nibbles in the probably vain hope that they would soak up some of the alcohol that the stags had consumed. They were becoming increasingly rowdy, their maudlin mood replaced with raucous accounts of Giles's activities that had them roaring with laughter. Alexi's stomach gave an embarrassing rumble at the sight of the food, reminding her that they hadn't eaten. It was a testament to Jack's concerns over the identity of the murderer that he hadn't insisted upon feeding them both. He didn't ordinarily allow anything to stand in the way of him and his stomach.

'Grab a plate,' he said, laughing at Alexi's mortification. 'I intend to.'

Alexi didn't need telling twice. She helped herself and sat at the nearest table to consume her makeshift lunch.

'What do we do now?' she asked.

'We give Petra a few hours to get home and make her confession to Luke. Then we tell Vickery.'

'Seems a shame, given that neither Petra or Will are murderers, but I do understand why it has to be done.'

'Right.' Jack wiped his fingers on a napkin. 'You done?'

'Just about.' Alexi popped a final bite of quiche in her mouth and stood up. 'Let's update Cheryl and Drew, then wait for a call from Martin. But after that, unless he comes up with something insightful, we're no further forward.'

15

Jack followed Alexi into Cheryl's kitchen. Both she and Drew were there, fussing over baby Verity. Cosmo and Toby were still curled up in the same position in Toby's basket. Cosmo was using the little dog's body as a pillow but got up immediately he saw Alexi and wound his way round her legs, demanding food.

'He's blackmailing you,' Jack said, laughing at the cat's antics. 'Playing on your guilt because we left him behind.'

'I know.' Alexi rolled her eyes. 'And I fall for it every time.'

With the cat fed and happy again, Alexi told her

friends what they had learned from Petra. 'Will backed up her account and insists that Giles knew nothing about their relationship.'

'We believed him but just supposing for the sake of argument that Will had confided in Giles in a drunken moment. It seems odd that he'd say nothing when he knew of the connection between Giles's intended and his old flame,' Jack said pensively.

'Even if he mentioned they'd dated, I very much doubt it he would say anything about Petra's miscarriage,' Alexi replied. 'Men generally don't talk about that sort of stuff.'

'Even if Giles did know and planned to tell Luke when they met, what reason would Will have to kill his friend?' Drew asked. 'It makes no sense.'

'Unless Giles told Crystabel,' Cheryl added. 'Only imagine what she could have done with that enticing nugget to cause a rift in her father's marriage.'

Jack and Alexi nodded in unison. 'It's not something we can ask her,' Jack replied. 'She'd hardly tell us the truth. And worse, if she didn't know and we enlighten her, you can bet your life that she'd find a way to use it against Petra.'

'Too late for her to do any damage,' Alexi

pointed out. 'Petra will have confessed all to Luke by now. He will either have forgiven her or sent her packing.'

'True enough,' Jack said.

'I believed Will when he said that he hadn't wanted to split from Petra but that it had been her decision,' Alexi remarked. 'I reckon he'd have taken her back in a heartbeat if her marriage fell apart.'

'A good reason to put a spoke in the wheel of said marriage?' Drew suggested.

'Not if he wanted her back. She loves Farrington and would hardly rush into the arms of the man who'd caused the breakup,' Jack said.

'If she knew he was the guilty party.' Drew nodded his acknowledgement of Jack's point as he bounced his daughter on his lap. 'Just trying to think in the same way as your ex-colleagues will,' he said cheerfully.

'Except I doubt whether they will,' Jack replied. 'Not when they know about Jenny and Giles. That's a far more plausible motive for murder and one that reinforces Crystabel's guilt. They will talk with Jenny but at the end of the day, she will be saying that Giles intended to break off his engagement to be with her, and Crystabel will say the opposite. The police have the generic texts that Giles and Jenny shared, but they could be interpreted in any number of ways and are by no means conclusive. Alexi's confirmation that she saw Jenny and Giles romantically entangled will be the ace that Vickery needs to pursue a conviction.'

'Great!' Alexi mumbled, burying her face in her hands.

Jack extracted his phone from his pocket, called Ben and updated him on their findings, insisting that he not repeat anything to Crystabel.

'I'll not say a word, especially since Petra had a valid reason for being at the hotel.' Ben's voice sounded tinny and depressed as it echoed through the phone's speaker. 'One less alternative suspect to distract Vickery with.'

'Yeah well, we can't manufacture suspects. Alexi and I hope to talk with Martin Hall shortly but don't get your hopes up.'

'I hear you.'

Jack cut the connection, leaned back in his chair and laced his hands behind his head. 'The stags are making severe inroads into your bar's stock.'

Drew smiled. 'The more they drink, the happier I'll be. We've lost an entire day's service in the restaurant because the police want to keep the wedding party away from the press. Hopefully, we'll be able to open for a Sunday lunch service tomorrow. We have two full sittings so your ex-colleagues, inventive buggers that they are when it comes to poking their noses in where they don't belong, won't get beyond the bar. No offence, Alexi.'

'None taken. I wrote the book on inventive journalism but, obviously, I'm a reformed character now. I have a cat to worry about and who'll feed him if I get carted off on a trespassing charge?'

Cosmo growled indignantly, making them all smile.

'That damned feline is a law unto himself,' Drew said. 'I'm sure he was human in a previous life.'

'But has a much better time of it now,' Alexi pointed out, blowing her cat a kiss. 'He can do what he likes and *he* doesn't have to worry about breaking the law. In fact, it amuses him to flout the system.'

'The wedding party will be allowed to leave in the morning anyway,' Cheryl said, 'or that's our understanding. They're champing at the bit to be gone, now that the shock's worn off and I suppose you can't blame them for that.'

Verity wriggled on her father's lap. Drew put her on the floor and she shuffled on her bottom until she reached Toby's basket. Jack tensed, never sure how Cosmo would react when confronted with human interference, but Alexi seemed perfectly relaxed and smiled indulgently at the little girl's curiosity. Jack realised why when Cosmo sniffed at the baby, and then allowed pudgy fingers to dig into his thick coat.

'Remarkable,' Jack said, shaking his head.

'He knows he'll be the dish of the day in Marcel's kitchen if he harms a hair on that precious baby's head,' Alexi replied, beaming with pride.

Cosmo sent Alexi a wounded look and continued to submit himself to Verity's attentions.

'He'll let her know when he's had enough but he won't hurt her,' Alexi predicted.

Sure enough, a few moments later, Cosmo got up, turned in tight circles and settled down again with his back to Verity. Alexi swooped the baby into her arms and bounced her on her knee, making her giggle.

Jack watched them together and just for one short moment, he wondered how he would feel if they had a baby of their own. He chased the rogue thought away. Now wasn't the right time. Perhaps there never would be one. Jack was unsure how he felt about fatherhood. It wasn't a subject that he had previously dwelt upon because the prospect of having responsibility for another human being had scared him shitless. Now that he'd found the right woman, that possibility didn't seem nearly so daunting, but there were a ton of other considerations standing in the way of such a monumental decision. In Jack's view, people produced kids far too casually, without stopping to consider the restrictions that the huge responsibility for a child would bring to their lives, financially, emotionally and practically.

Kids were most definitely not a fashion statement.

Besides, Jack's work took him all over the county and beyond, sometimes for days at a time. Would it be fair to expect Alexi to do all the heavy lifting if they had a child? She had a career too.

Alexi smiled up at him as she kissed the top of Verity's head and handed her back to her mother. 'I think she needs changing,' she said, wrinkling her nose.

Cheryl laughed. 'Very likely. She eats almost as much as her father and it has to go somewhere.'

Jack's phone rang. He answered it, conducted a short conversation and hung up. 'Martin's on his way over,' he said.

'Then we'll attend to our daughter's needs,' Drew said, standing up and taking Verity from

Cheryl, 'and give you our kitchen to do your interrogating in.'

'How are we going to play this?' Alexi asked when she and Jack were alone.

'By ear. I don't suspect Martin, and yet I also suspect everyone. Let's see what he has to say for himself and react accordingly.'

'Fair enough. He'll be here any minute. I'll meet him in the hall.'

* * *

The hallway was deserted but the sound of the increasingly drunken stags that echoed from the bar, causing Alexi's spirits to sink. Poor Giles, she thought. He'd been inoffensive enough, even if he had been easily led. Well, he had to have been, she reasoned, otherwise he would never have fallen for Crystabel's toxic charm. Why Crystabel was so determined to have Giles though was another matter entirely and one that Alexi had yet to get her head round. They were opposites in every respect.

Her thoughts drifted towards the expression on Jack's face, almost envious, as he'd watched her earlier with Verity. Did he want children? She wondered for the second time in the same day, surprised that a subject she'd never before dwelt upon seemed determined to play on her mind. Alexi loved Verity and sometimes felt broody as a consequence but she was also pretty sure that she didn't want a child of her own. At least not now. If Jack did then she couldn't see how their relationship would endure. It was such a big step and although she did most of her work from home nowadays, she still enjoyed the freedom of travelling if she needed to chase down a story.

Or for any reason at all.

Having a child would change all of that. She had seen how Cheryl and Drew managed, but also saw what was involved and how exhausted they both perpetually were. She wasn't sure that she was up for that right now.

Her introspective thoughts were interrupted by the arrival of an individual whom she immediately recognised from the previous night as Martin, even though they hadn't been introduced.

'Thanks for coming over,' she said, shaking the man's hand as she sized him up. 'I'm, Alexi Ellis, investor in Hopgood House.'

'Good to meet you,' Martin replied. 'Wish it could have been under better circumstances. Hell of a thing to have happened,' he added. 'The guvnor's putting on a brave face but he's actually in pieces.'

Martin was short, shorter than her, and although she'd been told that he was only in his late thirties, his hair was already in full retreat. Alexi reckoned that he might once have aspired to be a jockey, a fact borne out by his slender build. He looked as though a strong gust of wind would blow him over but he was wiry, with the ruddy complexion of a man who worked outside in all weathers, and Alexi reckoned that he was a lot stronger than he looked.

'Come through to the private kitchen and meet my partner.'

'I think we already did, last night. Hard to remember. I'd sank a few. Don't often let myself go. Horses equate to ridiculously early mornings but... well, it was Giles's stag so I thought why the hell not.' He chuckled, then appeared to recall why he was there and quickly schooled his features into a more appropriate expression. 'Hangovers are for wimps,' he added, but upon examining him more closely, Alexi could see that he was suffering from the aftereffects of over-imbibing.

Alexi smiled. 'So I've been told.'

Jack stood when they entered the kitchen and shook Martin's hand. Cosmo lifted his head, hissed because it was what he did, even if he didn't detect any threat from newcomers, and then settled back to sleep again: the feline seal of approval.

'Have a seat,' Jack said. 'Can I get you anything?'

'I'm good, thanks.' He rested his elbows on the table and focused his attention on Jack, seated across from him. 'How can I help to clear this mess up? Not that there appears to be much doubt about who did it, but I understand the police lack a motive.'

'How did you get along with Giles?' Jack asked.

'Honest truth?'

Jack nodded. 'Always best.'

'Not to speak ill of the dead but he'd had everything too easy. His mother overindulged him, which is why he failed to knuckle down to a career, in my humble opinion.' Martin rubbed his nose abstractedly. 'He was an ace horseman; did you know that?'

Alexi and Jack both shook their heads.

'Could get them to dance for him. Of course, he grew up around them and could ride before he could walk, but he always hankered after that elusive something. The bright lights. The high life. Being involved in the excitement of horseracing was never enough for him.' Martin shrugged his bony shoulders. 'Hell if I know what he thought was missing from his life but I do know for a fact that Crystabel wasn't the answer. She was trouble with a capital T but he was the only one who couldn't see it. Broke his father's heart to see them together, so it did.'

'But if Anthony had persuaded Giles to call the wedding off and decided to stay here, your position would have been under threat, wouldn't it?'

If Martin was offended by the implied accusation, he reacted by throwing back his head and laughing. 'Not for a second. Giles wouldn't have stayed the course. It simply wasn't in his nature. He had a lot of issues with his father following his mother's death, you know that? Giles couldn't be what his father expected him to be, even if they'd wanted the same things. It was almost a matter of pride with Giles to go against his father's wishes in a misguided effort to get revenge on his mother's behalf. Like I say, that boy and his mother were devoted to one another.'

'Anthony mentioned that there were problems which they were working through. Giles also had issues with his father's new partner, Sarah, I gather,' Alexi said.

'Right, and Sarah is a lovely person. So was Giles's mum but the big C got her in the end and there was nothing that could be done to save her. Tragic, but there you have it. I was one of the few people who knew the full extent of her illness and that it was terminal but she was insistent that Giles not be told. I thought he deserved to know, to have a chance to spend quality time with her whilst she was still lucid, but it wasn't my call.'

'I gather you know Jenny Blake, Crystabel's cousin.'

Martin's face lit up. 'Have done for years. She's a talented horsewoman and as different from her cousin as it's possible for any two people to be. We're very good friends which is why you could have knocked me down with a feather when I found out that she and Crystabel are related. Jenny has never said anything about her "famous" cousin. I don't think she approved of her methods.'

'They're very different people,' Alexi remarked diplomatically.

Martin guffawed. 'You can say that again. For all her looks and style, I wouldn't give Crystabel the time of day. No depth. Everything is about her.'

'How did you meet Jenny?' Jack asked. 'She's into eventing and you're with the horseracing set.'

'Yeah, but the horsy world is a small one, especially in this neck of the woods. Jenny kept her two eventers with Anthony when I first went to work with him. We keep a few saddle and driving horses as well as the racers. Her dad had two good chasers in training so Anthony was happy to help him out when Jenny was stuck for stabling. I was an apprentice jockey at the time. I became Anthony's stable jockey, we got along well, and when I got too heavy to ride competitively, I fell into what I do now.'

If Martin was too heavy to be a jockey, Alexi wondered how much smaller the successful ones actually were.

'Anyway, Jenny and I became friends and I helped her out by riding out with her every so often. She told me that she'd dreamed of becoming a professional eventer, much as I'd dreamed of becoming a top jockey; we had that much in common. Thwarted ambitions.'

'Did you and she date?' Alexi asked. 'You're obviously very fond of her.'

'Sadly not. We'd go out in a crowd with the stable lads from time to time but I never got up the courage to ask her out on a *date* date. She wasn't giving me encouraging signs and I'd prefer to have her as a friend rather than being rebuffed and making things awkward between us.' Martin sniffed. 'Of course, we don't see as much of each other now that she's moved her horses but we chat on the phone occasionally.'

'Did you speak to Jenny last night?'

'Nah, no opportunity. Giles put his foot down for once and barred the ladies from mixing with us.'

Alexi knew they were no further forward. Martin appeared to be open and honest, answering their questions without hesitation. But he had also confirmed that he and Jenny were more than good friends, or he would have liked them to be. If she'd confided in him about her relationship with Giles then it would give Martin a strong motive to do away with what he would consider to be unsuitable opposition, both for his position at the training yard and more especially in Jenny's bed. Martin was not one of Giles's fans and wouldn't have wanted to see the woman he lusted after throwing herself away on a man who didn't know his own mind.

Alexi had run out of questions and glanced at Jack. The elephant in the room had yet to be raised and she wasn't about to do it. But as she had known would be the case, Jack seamlessly picked up the questioning.

'When did Anthony last see Giles, prior to last night?' he asked.

'A couple of days ago. Him, Crystabel and her

mother called in so that her majesty could issue orders about the wedding. Apparently, they took a
look at the carriage horses and wandered around
the yard before Sarah invited them into the house
for coffee. Anthony was out on the gallops, so was I.'
Martin rubbed the side of his nose; a habit of his
Alexi had noticed when he was discussing a subject
that distressed him. People gave a lot away about
their inner feelings through subconscious tells, she
had discovered during the course of interviews she'd
conducted on the *Sentinel*. 'Now it would be hard to
find a more easy-going person than Sarah but even
she has her limits and took exception to Crystabel's
high-handed manner.'

'What happened?' Alexi asked.

'I wasn't there but Molly, who does the catering,
was in the kitchen and heard every word. Sarah
made some mild comment about the horses Crystabel wanted to pull the carriage taking her to the
church. She wanted matching greys but Sarah told
her that the only greys in the yard weren't broken to
harness. I don't think Crystabel even knew what she
meant by that. The only horses we had who could
be trusted to behave themselves between the shafts
weren't matching colours, you see, and Crystabel
wasn't having any of it. She simply flew off the han-

dle, saying some spiteful things to Sarah about her being jealous because Anthony hadn't actually married her.'

'Ouch!' Alexi muttered, well able to imagine it.

'Poor Sarah was too gobsmacked to respond but Crystabel tore into her, saying that she'd ruined Giles's life by taking his mother's place even before she'd died, which is total crap by the way. She made a load of other hurtful accusations too.'

'Didn't Giles try to rein her in?' Jack asked. 'Or her mother, for that matter.'

'Nope. He just stood there like a rabbit caught in the headlights apparently and her mother appeared to enjoy the confrontation. I know that because Anthony and I came in on the tail end of her tirade. Anthony sent Giles a look of deep condemnation, then told Crystabel to get off his property, only not quite so politely. I've never seen him so angry. The mother tried to smooth things over, told Anthony to put it down to pre-wedding jitters, but her intervention came far too late to be effective.'

'Anthony assumed that Giles had been feeding Crystabel his account of his mother's death, I imagine,' Alexi said.

'Very likely. Anthony adores Sarah and woe betide anyone who attacks her. Not that anyone ever

has before as far as I'm aware. She is the most inoffensive person I know, caring and considerate.
Mindful of the feelings of others.'

'Giles knew that but didn't stop Crystabel?' Alexi
asked, wondering if he hadn't bothered because he'd
already decided to leave her for Jenny. Crystabel behaving badly towards his family would have given
him the excuse he needed to break things off. And
yet he'd gone ahead with the stag and hadn't actually backed out.

Or hadn't had a chance to before he was killed.

'So Anthony's last words to his son, before last
night, had been spoken in anger,' Alexi said. 'I dare
say that bothers him now.'

'Anthony doesn't wear his heart on his sleeve but
yeah, I imagine that it does. He and Giles were at odds
with one another but Anthony had hoped for a recon-
ciliation once he returned from wandering the globe.
They were some of the way to achieving that ambition
before Crystabel got her hooks into Giles. She'd been
around for a bit after that Greek holiday and Anthony
was mighty relieved when their friendship waned.'

'Only to be resurrected sometime later,' Alexi
said.

'Right.'

'And Anthony would have done just about any-thing to break them up again,' Jack idly speculated. But Alexi knew that it was a far from idle specula-tion. He was testing Martin's loyalty towards An-thony, wondering if it would hold firm if he himself was the guilty party.

'Whoa! Hold on there.' Martin's face flushed even redder than it already was. 'Anthony didn't like Crystabel and made no secret of the fact. He thought their marriage would be a massive mistake but he also thought it wouldn't last. As we've already estab-lished, Giles doesn't stick at anything for long and tends to bail when the going gets tough. So Anthony most definitely didn't kill him.'

'You were with Anthony the entire time last night?' Alexi asked.

'We're not joined at the hip so no, I circulated and so did he.'

'Did either of you come out onto the terrace prior to Giles being found?' Jack asked.

Martin shrugged. 'I didn't but I can't speak for Anthony.'

'What Giles saw in Crystabel, other than a pretty face, is a mystery to me,' Jack said. 'You don't need to be in her company for long to assess her true manipulative character. Did she have some sort of hold over Giles?'

'Not that I'm aware.'

'Do you have any idea what went wrong on that Greek holiday?' Alexi asked. 'Something did but no one's saying. Crystabel went away engaged to Simon but came back single again.'

'I know nothing about that but I do know that Anthony thought Giles selecting Crystabel was an act of rebellion.'

'A bit extreme,' Jack remarked.

'Giles wasn't terribly mature, still bore a massive grudge against Anthony and was given to sulking. Despite all of that, like I already said, Anthony thought they were working through their problems. Then Crystabel came on the scene. Anthony actually said to me that Giles had taken up with her just to spite him and that he'd never marry her.' Martin shrugged. 'Well, he won't now, will he?'

'You share the general view that Crystabel's the guilty party?'

Martin raised a brow in evident surprise. 'Don't you?'

'Possibly.' Jack waggled a hand from side to side. 'Probably.'

'She was standing over him with the murder

weapon in her hand. Not sure what more evidence you need.'

'Have you ever seen the dagger that was used before?' Jack asked. 'We're struggling to decide where she got it from.'

'I wasn't close enough to see it. Everyone was screaming and crowding round. It was bedlam. Besides, I was at the back and am not very tall. Couldn't see much of anything.'

Jack pulled up the picture of the dagger on his phone and showed it to Martin. 'It's pretty unusual and doesn't belong to the hotel.'

'Bloody hell!' The heightened colour drained from Martin's face. 'That's not unusual around these parts. It's not a dagger though. That's a farrier's hoof knife.'

'Are you sure?' Alexi asked, sharing a look with Jack.

'Course I'm sure. See that hook on the end?'

Jack and Alexi both nodded. 'We'd been wondering about that,' he said.

'Sharp as buggery, they are. They have to be to cut through overgrown hoofs, a bit like a horsy pedicure.'

Jack scratched his head. 'Where the hell did Crystabel...'

'They have ergonomic handles,' Martin explained, looking more closely at the picture on Jack's phone. 'And that one is for a left-hander.'

'You have them at your yard? Is it one of yours?' Alexi asked.

Martin shrugged. 'No idea. I can check to see if one's missing but I'm not sure how many we had in the first place. We tend to deal with little hoof problems ourselves rather than calling out the farrier. Most trainers do. You have to be a bit of a Jack-of-all-trades in the horsy world.'

'Anyone lefthanded in your yard?' Alexi asked.

'Even if they are, since only three of us with a vested interest were present last night, that won't mean anything.' He paused. 'And we're all right-handed.'

It became clear to Alexi that Martin had nothing more of value to tell them, if one discounted the identification of the knife, and that he was getting agitated by their implications. Jack must have reached the same conclusion because he thanked Martin for calling in and sent him on his way.

'Phew!' Alexi fanned her face with her hand when the door closed behind Martin. 'The plot thickens. How the hell did Crystabel get hold of a farrier's knife?'

'Vickery will say that it proves premeditation. I mean, it's not as though any were left lying around for her to pick up so whoever killed Giles brought it with him or her with the express purpose of threatening him at the very least.' Jack tapped his fingers restlessly on the table top. 'What had you got yourself involved with, Giles?'

'We need to find out which of our suspects are left-handed,' Alexi said.

'We also need to tell Vickery what the knife is, if he hasn't already found out, which is unlikely. This is horse country but regular punters wouldn't get to see that knife. It's obviously very significant though.'

'Crystabel's left-handed,' Alexi said, after a prolonged pause. 'She was writing something in the bar the other day and I noticed.'

'I would imagine it's important to have a knife to suit your preferred hand if you're about to cut into a horse's hoof,' Jack said in a reflective tone, 'but I don't suppose it makes much difference if you simply want to thrust a hooked knife into the soft flesh of a man's chest.'

Alexi shuddered. 'It would take some force though. Remember that hook. That wouldn't go directly through flesh. It would have to be twisted.

Even so, a fit and angry woman could do it, I'm absolutely sure.'

'Yep. I agree. Vickery will say that following her
argument with Anthony and being unceremoniously evicted from the training yard, Crystabel was
mortified. She picked up a dagger but did she do so
with the intention of killing Giles? It seems a bit
extreme.'

'So does taking it downstairs to meet her father?'
Alexi shook her head. 'I don't buy it. Jenny is more
likely to have one, or know where to get hold of one,
given that she's an equestrian. That's a fact that
Crystabel's defence team will grasp if they decide to
blame Jenny for the murder. Giles had broken up
with her and she wanted her revenge.'

'It would be enough to create reasonable doubt,'
Jack agreed.

Cosmo stirred himself, walked across to the table
and leapt onto Alexi's lap. 'It's not food time yet,' she
told her cat, smoothing his back with long sweeps of
one hand. 'You do realise that Martin is in love with
Jenny,' she said, switching her attention back to Jack.

Jack's head shot up. 'Is he?'

Alexi laughed. 'You men don't see what's under
your noses when it comes to affairs of the heart.
They're good friends but Martin would like it to be

more than that. Just suppose that Jenny confided in him about Giles. She knew it would make Anthony happy if he broke up with Crystabel. I'm guessing she needed to tell someone she thought she could trust and satisfy herself that Anthony would be happy to see *her* engaged to his son.'

'It would give Martin a motive,' Jack said, looking sombre. 'Shame, because I believed him. But he did say that he and Anthony weren't together all the time last night. Perhaps he saw Jenny and Giles emerge from that passageway and lost his temper.'

'The knife?'

'Yeah.' Jack sighed and stretched his arms above his head. 'It always comes back to the knife. I'm sick of that damned knife spoiling my theories.' He lowered his arms again and glanced at his watch. 'Anyway, we've given Petra enough time to bare her soul to Farrington.' He pulled his phone from his pocket and dialled Vickery's number. 'I need to tell him about her presence at the hotel last night, and about the identity of the murder weapon, if he doesn't already know.'

'Then what?' Alexi asked.

'And then, my darling, I'm all out of ideas and Crystabel will just have to take her chances. I can't think of anything else we can do to protect her and

I'm not sure I even want to. The more I hear about her character, the more convinced I become that she actually did it anyway.'

Alexi gave a glum nod. 'Me too,' she said. 'Me too.'

16

Jack felt frustrated and deeply disturbed by the direction the case had taken. He mulled things over as he waited for Vickery to answer his call. But instead of picking up, the man himself entered the kitchen with the faithful Constable Hogan in his wake.

'We can't keep meeting like this,' Jack said, pointing to the coffee pot. Both detectives accepted and Alexi got up to pour for them.

'I came over as soon as I read Jenny Blake's statement,' Vickery said, seating himself opposite Jack.

'I guessed you would.'

'It would have saved time if you'd told me,'

Vickery said on a note of mild censure. 'I thought you wanted this case wrapped up quickly.'

'Giles has been dead for less than twenty-four hours,' Alexi pointed out as she handed round the coffee and placed a plate of Cheryl's homemade biscuits in the middle of the table. Both men helped themselves. Alexi and Hogan declined.

'We want it cleared up, of course we do,' Jack said, 'but we also want to be sure that the right person is charged. And if you thought you had enough evidence to charge Crystabel, you'd have stopped looking and she'd be back in custody by now.'

'Now we do have enough,' Hogan said, making a rare contribution to the conversation. Ordinarily, she demurred to Vickery who had told Jack that the woman was a probationary DC, still earning her stripes. Vickery had advised her very strongly to keep her eyes wide open and her mouth firmly closed whilst she learned her trade.

'But for the knife,' Alexi pointed out. 'Where did it come from and why would she have it with her?'

This time Hogan remembered to remain quiet and it was Vickery who answered. 'We're working on that,' he said.

'Let me help you out,' Jack replied. 'It's a farrier's knife.'

'Is it indeed?' Vickery took a moment to absorb information that was obviously new to him. 'Crystabel was engaged to a horseman, so that more or less clears things up.' He offered Jack his hand in a high-five gesture. 'Thanks very much.'

'Still doesn't explain why Crystabel would have such a knife or, more specifically, why she had it with her when she went in search of Giles,' Jack said. 'If she did.'

'Did she take a bag with her when she went downstairs?' Alexi asked. 'Did you think to ask her that question?'

'We did and she said not. All she had with her was her phone.'

'Well then, where did she hide the knife when she came downstairs?' Jack asked. 'It was a warm night and she wasn't wearing much. Certainly not enough to hide a sodding great knife. Besides, although no one saw her, if she came down intent upon murdering her fiancé and had the weapon with her, she couldn't be sure that her arrival would go undetected.'

'And it still begs the question: where did Crystabel get the knife in the first place?' Alexi said. 'She was engaged to a trainer's son and had been to the yard a couple of times but she wasn't welcome there. Anthony Preston-Smythe disliked her intently and I think it very unlikely that she would have set foot in the tack rooms where, presumably, such items were stored. And even if she had, why on earth would she filch one? No one will convince me that she planned to deliberately stab her fiancé with some sort of symbolic weapon during the course of his stag night.'

'You're forgetting that she was about to be thrown over in favour of a cousin whom she didn't consider to be any sort of threat.' Vickery shook his head. 'To be dumped so unceremoniously when she'd gone to so much trouble to publicise her wedding. That must have been galling.' Vickery paused. 'Of course, she'll no doubt insist that Giles wasn't interested in Jenny and the messages between them are pretty ambivalent, open to misinterpretation, far from the smoking gun we need, in other words, in order to make the case against her rock solid.'

'Ah.' Alexi looked sheepish. 'I should have mentioned that I saw Giles and Jenny together just before Giles was killed.'

Vickery scowled. 'You should indeed have mentioned that not insignificant fact. Anyone would think that you want Crystabel to be innocent.' Vickery emitted a long-suffering sigh. 'What, when and where did you see them?'

Alexi explained. 'I was going to tell you but thought it would be better if Jenny got in first.' She leaned towards Vickery. 'I didn't want you to pre-judge anything she said to you on the basis of my evidence.'

'And Alexi, I think we can all agree, is someone whose word you can accept,' Jack said, his voice silk on steel.

'Without question,' Vickery replied. 'Pray continue, Alexi.'

'I walked past them whilst they were getting up close and personal, making no effort to do so quietly, and yet they remained totally focused on one another. They were kissing very passionately; oblivious to anything and anyone else. Trust me, Giles and Jenny were besotted. Crystabel might try to imply that he was breaking it off with her but I'd swear under oath that what I saw gave the exact opposite impression.'

'Good enough for me,' Vickery said, nodding emphatically.

'I can buy that Crystabel saw Jenny and Giles emerge from that corridor when she returned to the hotel after speaking with her father,' Jack said. 'She put two and two together, lost her rag and confronted Giles. He told her then that the wedding was off and she lost it. Everyone says she has a temper that she can't always control. If she thought Giles was cheating on her with Jenny of all people *and* intended to throw her over in Jenny's favour then she really would have let rip. But...'

'It all comes back to that knife.' Vickery finished for him. 'Bugger! Even so, I think we have enough evidence to charge her. Whether the CPS will actually prosecute if we can't find a plausible way to put that knife in her hand before she pulled it out of his chest is another matter.'

'Perhaps one of the other horsy set had it in his coat pocket,' Hogan suggested.

Jack shook his head. 'It was a warm night. No one was wearing a coat, or even a jacket. Besides, I doubt if anyone would bring the tools of their trade to a stag.'

'If your people checked the hotel's register, they might have noticed that someone else involved with Crystabel was a guest last night,' Alexi said.

'Care to enlighten me?' Vickery asked, sipping at his coffee.

'Petra Horton.' Alexi paused when Vickery looked at her blankly. 'Mrs Luke Farrington.'

'Did we know that fact, Constable?' he asked, drilling poor Hogan with a look.

Hogan looked flustered and blushed as she consulted her notebook. 'I don't believe we did, sir.'

'Right. I'll be having a word with the uniforms who checked the guest list.' Vickery discarded his coffee and sat a little straighter. 'And what, may I ask, brought her to this fine establishment?'

'She's coming in to see you to tell you herself. All I'll say is that she had a previous friendship with one of the stags and wanted to make sure that he wouldn't speak out of turn in front of Luke about said relationship,' Alexi explained. 'She hadn't thought that she and Luke would be attending but he was determined to do so. When she realised that Will Ashworth was an usher, she decided to have a quiet word on her way back from time spent on business in London. She's an artist.'

'Right.' Vickery's expression implied that was all he needed but what the inspector had against artists, Jack was at a loss to know.

'When the hens crashed the party,' Alexi added, 'Petra knew she wouldn't get an opportunity to speak with Will simply because she couldn't risk

Crystabel seeing her. Luke thought she was in London until today, you see, and Crystabel would have had a field day stirring up trouble for Petra.'

'Trouble is that woman's middle name,' Vickery said, sighing. 'But if I arrested everyone who annoys me without just cause then I'd be out of a job.'

'We've spoken to Petra and Will,' Jack said, 'and I'd stake my reputation on neither of them having anything to do with the murder. Neither one of them has a motive.'

'Bloody motives are overestimated,' Vickery complained, crumbling the remains of his biscuit on a plate.

'Let her come to you. She was going to confess all to Luke first,' Alexi explained. 'Give her time, she's a genuinely nice lady attempting to deal with the step-daughter-from-hell being thrust upon her.'

'I'll give her until the morning, then go looking for her. Can't have any loopholes in our case.'

Jack wanted to point out that it already had more holes than a Swiss cheese but refrained. 'Thanks,' he contented himself with saying.

'Well, you two have been busy.' Vickery closed his eyes, threw his head back and pinched the bridge of his nose. He looked exhausted, much the same way that Jack used to feel when he was in the job. Too many cases, not enough trained detectives, too much paperwork, too much abuse, too much pressure. He sometimes wondered why people were drawn to the career. He frequently wondered why he had been. 'I'm going to have to follow up on...'

Banging and loud voices coming from above their heads caused all four of them to jump to their feet. Jack opened the door but Cosmo, who had been sound asleep a few moments previously, beat them all to it. He sprang through the opening and emitted a sound that was a cross between a growl and a mewl. The stags tumbled from the bar, all of them decidedly the worse for wear, but Cosmo in combative mood stopped them all in their tracks.

'You conniving little bitch.' Crystabel's voice was shrill with anger. 'After all I've done for you, you try to swipe my fiancé from beneath my nose.'

Jenny's voice was quiet and controlled. 'I didn't have to try, Crystabel, but he'd probably already told you that. Is that why you killed him?'

They were all now halfway up the stairs and could see the ladies squaring up to one another. The rest of the hens and Gloria were watching on, transfixed. Jack could tell from their expressions that it was the first any of the bridesmaids had heard about Jenny's relationship with Giles and they appeared to be enjoying Crystabel's humiliation. None of them attempted to calm the situation down at any rate. Gloria ought to have done so but it didn't surprise Jack when she remained rooted to the spot, her expression set in stone.

'Take that back, you vicious cow!'

Crystabel screamed and gave Jenny a hefty push. She fell backwards, hit her head on the banister and cried out as she landed on the rug with a heavy thud. She didn't move and had clearly passed out. Crystabel covered her mouth with her hand in a "what-the-hell-have-I-done" gesture. Before Vickery could reach her though, Cosmo tore up to her, flying off the top step and landing softly on all four feet in front of her. He hissed louder than a full-grown snake in a bad mood. Crystabel gave a little shriek and backed away. She didn't appear to care that she had injured Jenny, possibly badly. Jack wondered if she realised that she'd assaulted her cousin in front of a large audience, including a senior policeman. She definitely hadn't noticed that in the absence of the cameraman, Abby had recorded the entire episode on her phone.

Alexi crouched down beside Jenny, who was regaining consciousness and groaning.

'Sit up slowly,' Alexi said. 'Let me help you. Where does it hurt?'

'Everywhere but especially here.' Jenny covered her heart with her hand. 'And that pain was unendurable even before she started in on me.' She pointed a wavering finger at Crystabel.

'You didn't confront her?'

'No. I've been keeping a low profile. That's what you told me to do.'

'We told her the same thing, for all the good it did us.' Alexi examined Jenny's scalp. 'You're going to have a big lump but there's no blood, which is a good thing. Even so, we need to get you to the hospital and have you checked over.'

'I don't need to—'

'Yes you do,' Alexi replied firmly. 'You might be concussed.'

Vickery grasped Crystabel's arm. 'I'm arresting you for grievous bodily harm,' he said sternly. Jack knew that would enable him to keep her locked up while he looked for the last piece of evidence required to charge her with murder.

'Don't be ridiculous!' Gloria stepped forward, her ever-present, oversized bag swinging from her shoulder. Cosmo prowled towards her hissing, and she hastily stepped back again. 'It was simply a discussion that got out of hand. Emotions are running high. Crystabel didn't mean to hurt Jenny. It was an accident and Jenny will confirm that.'

'You might like to ask me before assuming you can speak for me, Gloria,' Jenny said in what for her was a forceful manner.

'The very least you can do after all the trouble you've caused is to see Crystabel's side,' Gloria snapped.

Jenny flashed a smile that owed little to humour. 'I will give evidence when the case comes to court, Inspector,' she said calmly. 'I saw Abby recording the entire incident on her phone before Crystabel attacked me so she can't lie her way out of this one.'

17

Alexi shuddered at the turn events had taken, wondering why she hadn't anticipated something of that nature and why she hadn't suggested separating Crystabel and Gloria from the rest of her party. It transpired that one of the stags was a paramedic. He checked Jenny over in a competent manner, despite being slightly the worse for wear himself. He did a few basic tests and said he was satisfied that she wasn't concussed.

'Put some ice on that lump at the back of your head and get some rest,' he advised. 'That will do you more good than hanging around for ages in A&E.'

'We'll take care of her,' Abby said, grasping Jenny's arm as she helped her to her feet, simultaneously sending Gloria a glower.

Crystabel had been led away by DC Hogan and now appeared to be as meek as a lamb. Significantly, she didn't express remorse. Her features were set in a grim mask and she didn't utter a single word. Wearily, Jack pulled his phone from his pocket and summoned Ben. Alexi stood beside Jack and heard Ben at the other end of the line, issuing a few choice expletives directed at clients who were too stupid to live before agreeing to meet Crystabel at Reading nick.

'That's all we can do for her and more than she deserves,' Jack told Alexi, loud enough for Gloria to hear them.

'Look, Jack,' Gloria said, her tone placatory. 'I know she was stupid but for goodness sake, she'd just learned that her fiancé was carrying on with her cousin. She was grieving, accused of murdering Giles, and now this. How did you expect her to react?'

'With more consideration for her own situation,' Jack replied curtly.

'Why didn't you prevent her?' Alexi asked.

'I... she took me by surprise. I thought she'd just

want to vent, which is hardly surprising. I had no idea it would get physical.'

Of course you didn't!

Cosmo arched his back and hissed at Gloria, almost disdainfully.

'You didn't try to intervene even when it got out of hand.' Alexi shook her head and walked away with Jack, Cosmo at their heels. The cat turned to offer Gloria one final hiss and descended the stairs with twitching tail aloft. The stags, now somewhat subdued, followed after them, muttering amongst themselves. The bridesmaids had jointly taken responsibility for Jenny, no doubt gagging for more information about her relationship with Giles. Only Gloria was left standing on the landing, looking if anything pleased with herself.

'I don't believe her,' Alexi said, wanting to follow Cosmo's example and hiss at the woman too. 'She's something else.'

'You do realise that the brawl was deliberate,' Jack replied as they entered the kitchen and Cosmo returned to Toby's basket as though nothing had happened.

'I just heard.' Drew burst into the room. 'What was that all about?'

Jack gave him an abbreviated account.

'Christ!' he replied, rubbing the back of his neck. 'What else is going to happen? How could Crystabel be so stupid? I thought she was more savvy than that.'

'Jack says it was contrived but he has yet to explain why,' Alexi replied.

'Vickery now has his motive, based on the premise that Crystabel already knew about Giles and Jenny. He will say that Giles told her, she lost her rag and stabbed him.' He flapped a hand. 'We'll gloss over the question of the knife for now. But...'

'But, if in a state of shock,' Alexi said, nodding her understanding, 'she confronted Jenny about the affair, it could reasonably be argued by a decent defence brief that she hadn't known about it before being told by Vickery. She felt shocked, humiliated, and could hardly be expected to sit back and say nothing to Jenny.'

'That would make sense.' Drew looked tired and tense. 'Vickery's car is outside. Gloria and Crystabel would have been able to see it from their window, knew they had their audience and took the opportunity.'

'It would explain why Gloria looked smug rather than distraught when Crystabel was carted off,' Jack remarked.

'We should have anticipated something of this nature and moved the bridesmaids into the annex,' Alexi said. 'This is all our fault.'

'Nonsense!' Drew's tone was brisk. 'All you're trying to do is to help the woman. Well, as far as I'm concerned, enough is enough. She threw your help back in your faces so she's on her own.'

Alexi blinked. She had never seen easy-going Drew half so angry before. She reminded herself that this hotel was not only his livelihood but had also been his family's home for generations. He was financially and emotionally attached to the place but its future was now in jeopardy, all thanks to the antics of a would-be influencer and her ambitious mother. Alexi reached out to touch Drew's hand and he flashed an absent smile.

'It will be all right,' she said in a softly reassuring voice, even though she couldn't be sure of any such thing. 'We'll get through this.'

'I hope Vickery throws the book at her,' Drew said, a little less belligerently, 'regardless of whether or not she's actually guilty.'

'It will make the whole murder business go away that much faster,' Jack agreed.

'Come on,' Drew said, 'none of us has eaten properly today. Everything will seem better on full stomachs. The restaurant's just about to open. We'll eat in there and put on brave faces.'

'Sure,' Alexi agreed. 'But where's Cheryl?'

'She's with Verity. I'll eat and change places with her.'

'Bring the baby into the restaurant,' Alexi said. 'I know the owner. I'll put in a good word for Verity.'

Drew smiled. 'Good plan.'

'He doesn't like to have Verity in the public part of the hotel,' Alexi explained as they waited for him to return. 'He says some punters don't like babies, if you can believe that, especially if they cry and disturb their meal.'

'He has a point, insofar as people spend a lot of money to sample Marcel's food, often waiting weeks to get a booking.'

'I know that but these are exceptional circumstances.'

Jack smiled and kissed the end of her nose. 'Indeed they are.'

'Are we really going to abandon Crystabel to her fate?' Alexi asked as she decanted a packet of food into Cosmo's bowl.

Jack shrugged. 'I don't see that we have much choice. We've run down all the leads available to us and nothing new has popped. Drew's right. Crystabel's just forfeited any rights she might have had to our help with that little fiasco upstairs. We'll let the professionals take it from here.'

Alexi wiped her hands, then walked up to Jack and wrapped her arms round his neck. 'But in spite of everything, including the fact that Crystabel is highly unlikeable, you're still not convinced that she did it and it will eat away at you unless you get to the truth.'

Jack pulled her close and kissed her. 'Can't win 'em all,' he said.

'Get a room, you two!'

Drew seemed more like his old self again as he entered the kitchen with Cheryl, and with Verity in a carrycot. She was sleeping peacefully.

'After we've eaten,' Jack quipped as he released Alexi.

The stags were already in the restaurant but the incident upstairs appeared to have sobered them up and they were disproportionately quiet. They nodded at Jack and his party and then returned their attention to the menus placed in front of them.

'Don't think we can depend upon their repeat custom,' Drew said gloomily.

'Oh, I don't know,' Alexi replied. 'Once the dust's settled, morbid though it sounds, they'll dine out on the story about the stag party to top all stag parties.' She raised a hand to cut off Cheryl's protest. 'Sorry, but that's the way of the world. I learned at least that much as a reporter. The more macabre, the greater the interest.'

'And,' Jack added, clearly picking up on Drew and Cheryl's depression and doing his bit to cheer them up, 'if Crystabel is charged with murder, the trial will be extensively covered. If her defence team cast sufficient doubt upon her guilt, the world and his wife will want to visit the scene in order to make their own judgement.'

Cheryl shuddered. 'Not my preferred means of filling rooms but I'll take what I can get.'

'That's the spirit.'

They placed their orders and Alexi felt herself relaxing a little when a large glass of wine was placed in front of her and she took a healthy sip. The food, naturally, was delicious and she was able to ignore the curious glances sent their way by other diners as the restaurant filled up.

'Whew!' Alexi leaned back in her chair and patted her stomach. 'That's better.'

Verity agreed by letting out a loud wail.

'That's our cue to leave you to it,' Cheryl said, as she and Drew stood and Drew picked up Verity's carrycot. 'No, don't rush your coffee. We'll see you in a bit.'

'It feels like midnight,' Alexi said as she watched them leave, acknowledging people they knew as they went, 'but it's only eight o'clock.'

'It's been quite a day,' Jack agreed. 'You okay?'

'Your standards are rubbing off on me, I guess. I shouldn't care about Crystabel's fate and should leave it to Vickery to get things right but... well, I'm just not convinced that she did it.'

'Me neither.' Jack took Alexi's hand and ran his fingers down the length of hers. 'But we always knew this one was going to be time sensitive. The entire wedding party will scarper tomorrow and we will lose the opportunity to ask questions.'

'Yeah, I know.'

'We did all we could, Alexi. Not that it would make much difference if the guests stayed. Once the shock wears off, they will worry about being suspect and speak more guardedly. If we were to focus our suspicions on one of them, you can bet your last penny that person would tell us to take a hike since we have no authority to ask them anything.'

'If we had grounds for suspicion, we could take them to Vickery.' Alexi sighed. 'Even so, I hear you.' Alexi pushed her chair back. 'Come on. Let's go and collect his highness and head for home. There's nothing more we can do here tonight.'

Hand in hand, they crossed the hotel's foyer and were about to enter Cheryl's private kitchen when someone called Jack's name. They both turned and were confronted by a stranger: a tall man with wispy, red hair and gangly limbs.

'Hi,' he said, holding out a hand to Jack. 'I'm guessing you must be the man I'm looking for. Jack Maddox?'

Jack nodded slowly. 'And you are?'

'Paul Makin. We're in the same profession, I believe.'

Jack shook his outstretched hand. 'And what profession would that be?'

'I recognise Ms Ellis,' Makin added, 'from her byline.' He offered Alexi his hand and she instinctively shook it. 'I'm a great admirer of your work.'

'Thank you.'

'What can we do for you?' Jack asked.

'It's more a question of what I can do for you.' The stags had emerged from the restaurant and were watching the exchange with varying degrees of interest. 'Is there somewhere private that we can talk?' Makin asked, glancing at their audience.

Alexi and Jack exchanged a look and simultaneously nodded. 'Sure,' Jack said, shrugging. 'Follow us.'

Alexi felt her heartrate quicken. Whatever this stranger had to say to them, she instinctively sensed that it would help to clear up the mystery of Giles's murder. She had experienced that feeling more times than enough whilst chasing down stories for the *Sentinel*. It had never let her down and she had learned to trust her instincts.

Cosmo reacted with mild disinterest to Makin's appearance and gave only a perfunctory hiss before turning his back on him.

'The famous Cosmo, one assumes,' Makin said.

'You've heard of him?' Alexi smiled and shook her head. 'For goodness sake, don't tell him that. His head is already quite big enough.'

Makin smiled as he took a seat at the table when invited to do so by Jack. 'I did some research on the hotel overnight, after I heard about the murder.'

'Excuse me,' Jack said, 'but what's your interest?'

'I should explain that I've been hired by representatives in this country of a Greek family to try and get to the bottom of their son's death.'

Alexi's mouth fell open. 'The Crete holiday,' she breathed.

Makin nodded. 'Constantine Drakos was heir to the Drakos shipping empire.'

'Never heard of it,' Jack replied.

'When I say empire, it's more of a company, definitely not on the Onassis scale, but still a profitable business.'

'How did Constantine die?' Alexi asked, a chill running down her spine.

'He was a playboy. Had his father's yacht moored off Crete during the time that Crystabel Hennessy and her party were holidaying on the island. Constantine had an eye for the beautiful people and my understanding is that despite being engaged to Simon Morton at the time, Crystabel took one look at Constantine when he came ashore with his friends and was all over him like a rash.'

Alexi shared a look with Jake and nodded. They both had no trouble believing it.

'And,' Alexi said, 'let me guess, Crystabel and her friends were invited to join Constantine onboard in order to carry on partying.'

'Right. The party went on for the next three days and got out of hand. Everyone was pissed as parrots on the night that Constantine fell overboard. He drowned.'

'Damn!' Jack muttered.

'Right. The boat was underway, moving on to another location overnight. The two crew members were intent upon their duties. Most of the others were down below, sleeping off their excesses, but Constantine and Crystabel were on the aft deck, still drinking and dancing and… well, whatever else they got up to under the stars. There's a camera for security and safety reasons on that deck but Constantine must have turned it off so I guess they were joining the maritime equivalent of the mile-high club. Except that the crew heard raised voices.'

'Did they go to see what was wrong?' Alexi asked.

Makin shook his head. 'Not their business. They knew better than to interrupt the boss's son when he was entertaining. No one quite knows what the argument was about. The only person awake at the time was Giles Preston-Smythe and the family are convinced that he must have seen what happened. What caused Constantine to fall.'

'Shit!' Alexi said.

'What was his account?' Jack asked.

'He *says* he didn't see, he'd just got up to use the head and was drawn to the voices but by the time he got there, Constantine was in the drink and Crystabel was screaming her head off.'

'That sounds familiar,' Alexi muttered.

'The Drakos family have never bought Giles's explanation. The crew were on the flybridge, driving the boat and minding their own business, which is what they were paid to do. Crystabel said the boat hit a surge, rocked to one side, Constantine lost his balance and fell. The crew did their emergency drill the moment he was missed but it was dark, it took a while to find him and when they eventually did, he was already dead.'

'I assume he could swim,' Alexi said.

'Like a fish, but he'd received a bash on the head and was probably unconscious when he hit the water. No one could prove that he didn't hit his head on the bathing platform when he fell but Drakos senior has never bought that explanation either.'

'He thinks Crystabel hit him over the head?' Alexi frowned. 'I have no trouble believing that she'd latch onto a rich Greek but why hurt him? Presumably she wanted to make a lasting impression upon him but not by killing him.'

'Like I said, this was day three of Crystabel and her entourage tagging along with Constantine. Maybe she thought she'd be a permanent fixture in his life but he was due to return the boat and get back to work, so bye bye Crystabel, it's been fun knowing you.'

'In the meantime, she's burned her bridges with her fiancé for no reason. She would not have been happy about that,' Alexi said. 'I think she knows now what she didn't understand then insofar as she has genuine feelings for Simon.'

Jack grunted. 'She probably thought her ship had come in, no pun intended,' he said.

'And we know Crystabel has a vicious temper when she doesn't get her way,' Alexi added.

'No charges were brought against her?' Jack asked.

'Nope. She called in favours from her father, who contacted the British Embassy and had the entire party brought home. Constantine's death was ruled accidental and that was that.'

Alexi glanced at Jack, thinking that Crystabel had obviously been in touch with her father long before either of them had implied. It would explain Luke's over-elaborate explanation of his first meeting with Crystabel here in England.

'This was over a year ago,' Jack said. 'Excuse me, but why are you here bringing it all up again?'

'Constantine's father has considerable resources and won't rest until he knows the truth. He instructed me about six months ago to track down members of Crystabel's party and see if their recollections had altered in the interim.' He shrugged. 'It seemed like a waste of time to me but he was paying well so who was I to complain. Time has passed, the people who were there have had a chance to dwell upon events and possibly their consciences had gotten the better of them.' He shrugged. 'Tenuous, I know, but Drakos is a grieving father who can't move on with his life until he gets to the truth.'

'Did you actually speak to Crystabel?' Jack asked.

'No.' Makin shook his head. 'There would be no point without additional evidence. She would have run to her father and he would have found a way to close me down. I mean, if he had enough sway to get the entire party out of Greece then managing a nosy PI in this country would be child's play to a man of his stature. Besides, Drakos has asked me to keep the investigation low key.' Makin paused. 'I did however speak with Giles, and the guys and girls who'd claimed to be asleep at the time. Giles insisted that he hadn't seen anything untoward, but he seemed very uncomfortable when he trotted out the same old same old. Just for the record, the boat did hit a swell at the time Constantine fell, the crew confirmed it, but we're talking Greece in the summer. It wasn't a storm, just a freak wave.'

'Guardrails on yachts are high for that precise reason. It must have been some swell if it knocked a grown man off balance and sent him over the edge,' Jack said.

'I agree. It's highly suspicious and I can understand why Drakos can't let it rest. Constantine did have a massive amount of alcohol in his system, and traces of recreational drugs, and that's why the authorities ruled it an accident, lacking firm evidence to the contrary. But even so...'

'I see.' Alexi felt helpless. This latest evidence was vital but she was still unsure what it had to do with Giles's murder. If Crystabel hadn't been questioned herself but Claire had, perhaps she'd mentioned something about it to Crystabel, which would have panicked her cousin. 'If Giles and Crystabel were married, then he couldn't be made to give evidence against her,' she said in a speculative tone. 'That explains a lot.'

'But not why he agreed to marry her,' Jack replied.

'If I had to guess then I'd say that it was a penance. He probably did see what happened but was anxious to get out of Greece. He couldn't grass up his mate's fiancée and anyway, if he said what he'd seen, they might all have of been detained indefinitely. You hear about foreign nationals getting banged up abroad in such situations. Even so, he'd lied and it was eating away at him. Crystabel came on to him and convinced him that it hadn't been her fault; it was an accident. Giles felt that marrying her to protect them both was the price he had to pay to assuage his conscience, to say nothing of pissing his father off. Then he met Jenny, fell in love and decided to put himself first.'

'Yeah.' Jack nodded. 'That would work. We know that Giles was weak but he also had a grievance against his father and saw marrying Crystabel as a way to get back at him. I'm betting that he also got wind of Drakos's determination to pursue the matter, or perhaps Crystabel did. Either way, if they were married then they could protect each other.'

'That makes sense,' Makin said. 'When Drakos heard that she and Giles had enjoyed a whirlwind romance only after I'd spoken to Giles and the others, and that their marriage was to be televised whilst his own son would never get to marry or give him grandchildren, he got very interested.'

Alexi and Jack looked at one another. For her part, Alexi struggled to absorb all she'd just heard, also understanding that it explained a great deal. No least, the reason why Crystabel had settled for Giles when previously, she had set her sights considerably higher.

'Why have you come to us with this?' Jack asked. 'Surely the police ought to be your first port of call.'

Makin shook his head. 'I'm acting on my client's orders. He doesn't have a high opinion of the British police and wants this dealt with below the radar. I've been watching the hotel since the stags got here, saw you two and knew you had a connection to the place. I also read the papers and know about the previous two murders you solved.' Makin shared a glance between them. 'I don't have a single trace of doubt in my mind that Crystabel pushed Constantine overboard, perhaps deliberately. Possibly because they'd both had a few and their argument got out of hand.'

'Without being in possession of all the facts, I'm inclined to agree with you,' Jack said. 'Especially since the only person who actually witnessed the altercation is now dead. Murdered.'

'The fact of the matter is that I'm stumped,' Makin admitted. 'So I thought I'd fill you in and hopefully, you can do something with the information I've provided.'

'You realise that we will have to go to Vickery with this? I understand your client's desire for discretion but there's a very real possibility that the events in Crete are connected to Giles's murder. It can't be kept under wraps.'

'Do what you think is right.' He stood up and again shook each of their hands. 'Here's my card. I'm staying in Newbury. If you need me, please get in touch.'

They promised that they would and sent him on his way.

'Phew!' Alexi threw herself back into her chair. 'What the hell do we make of all that?'

'Well, for a start, we know why Simon broke up with Crystabel and is so disgusted by her behaviour. She was engaged to him but saw a better prospect in Constantine, which tells us all we need to know about her character.'

Alexi pouted. 'Like we weren't already aware.'

'It also tells us why she took up with Giles, only after she knew that Constantine's father had an investigator on the case.'

'It explains why she moved her hen party here too. With an investigator on the loose, she didn't want Giles talking out of turn. But how did she know he was loitering around these parts if he didn't speak to her?'

'No idea. Perhaps someone noticed him watching the hen party and remarked upon it. Claire doesn't like Crystabel but does have a conscience and I bet Constantine's death plays on that conscience, despite the fact that she was sleeping at the time and had nothing to do with it.'

Alexi nodded. 'The hens went to a spa yesterday and I'm betting that Makin followed them there, hung around outside and Claire saw him.'

'The people on that holiday appear to have sworn a pact of silence. Or then again, perhaps they all want to put it behind them.' Jack paused to contemplate. 'Not the sort of thing you want to shout about, is my guess. Being interviewed by foreign police, which they all would have been, would be a daunting experience.'

'So, if we're right then Claire noticed Makin outside the spa, pointed him out to Crystabel and that spooked Crystabel into moving her hen party here. She wanted to make sure that Makin didn't crash the stag and interrogate the guys when they were half cut and less likely to be discreet.'

Jack shrugged. 'But he didn't come anywhere near them. Crystabel would have known that, so

why would she have murdered Giles and drawn unnecessary attention to herself?'

Alexi probably looked as perplexed as she felt. 'It
makes no sense.'

'Makin would agree with you. That's why he
came to us and didn't go direct to Vickery. He knew
that we would, obviously, but he can assure his
paying client that he abided by his need for discretion.'

'This is the smoking gun that Vickery needs,
isn't it?'

'Yep.' Jack looked uncompromisingly grim.
'Doesn't look as though there's much doubt about
Crystabel's guilt now but at least we'll know that
Vickery has the right woman, so our consciences
will be clear.'

'She really is a piece of work, isn't she?'

'She really is.' Jack squeezed Alexi's hand. 'Run
up and ask Claire if she saw Makin and mentioned it
to Crystabel.'

'Good idea.'

Alexi jogged up the stairs with Cosmo at her
side, tapped at Claire's door and was greeted by a
soft voice inviting her to enter.

'Ah good, you're not Gloria,' Claire said, drawing
an audible sigh of relief and reaching out a hand to

touch Cosmo. Alexi held her breath, never sure how her taciturn cat would react to the attention of strangers. To her relief, he condescended to be petted. 'She's been in twice, ostensibly to check on Jenny but in reality to try and talk the issue down. If Jenny isn't willing to give evidence then there's less chance of charges being pressed. I tell you, emotional blackmail doesn't come into it.'

'I have no difficulty in believing it.' Jenny was in the room too, sitting with her feet up on a sofa. She looked pale.

'How do you feel?' Alexi asked.

'Numb,' Jenny replied. 'It's all too much to absorb.'

'Then I won't insult your intelligence by offering up platitudes. It will take time for you to recover from your loss. There's just one quick question I wanted to ask Claire.'

'Ask away,' Claire replied.

'Makin, the PI asking questions about Greece—'

Claire gasped as she exchanged a glance with Jenny. 'You know about that?'

'I do.' She allowed a significant pause. 'Now. And I'm guessing that you've confided in Jenny. Why didn't either of you say anything?'

'It didn't seem relevant,' Claire said feebly.

'Makin was here just now, updating Jack and me.'

'It was terrible,' Claire said. 'We were all impossibly drunk. I still don't know what happened. Giles saw more than he admitted to, he told me that much at the time but didn't elaborate. He wanted to put it behind him. We all did and so agreed to move on and never refer to it again.' She blinked up at Alexi. 'What has this got to do with Giles's death?'

'That's what Jack and I are attempting to establish.' Alexi paused. 'Tell me, do you think Crystabel pushed Constantine overboard?'

Claire opened her mouth to speak but Jenny got in first.

'Giles had no doubt,' she said. 'He told me about it last night. He said that he saw it but lied to the police. He'd agreed to marry Crystabel for that reason, you see. He felt responsible for the death, or more to the point, for Constantine's grieving family not having closure. I told him it wasn't his fault and he finally came to see things that way.'

'We spent three entire days on his yacht, living the high-life and Crystabel loved every second of it,' Jenny said, taking up the story. 'It was as though Simon no longer existed. And then, on that last night, something happened between her and Constantine. I don't know what, but I do know they argued and then... well, that was that. Constantine was gone.' She sighed. 'It was terrible, and I knew absolutely nothing about it until the hullabaloo woke me.'

'Tell me, Claire, and this is important,' Alexi said. 'Have you noticed Makin hanging around the hen party this weekend?'

'Actually yes, I noticed him when we came out of the spa yesterday. He was making no attempt to keep a low profile and I pointed him out to Crystabel.' She clasped a hand over her mouth. 'Do you think that's why she killed Giles?'

18

Jack grimaced when Alexi returned to the kitchen and told him that Claire now held herself responsible for Giles's death.

'Poor girl,' he said. 'I'm sure you did what you could to reassure her. If anyone's to blame then it's Giles himself for not having the courage of his convictions.'

'He shouldn't have let the wedding preparations progress so far if he didn't intend to go through with it.' Alexi nodded. 'I couldn't agree more but denigrating the memory of the man Jenny loved would not have made Claire feel better about herself. So I trotted out the usual platitudes. Claire probably feels that murder dogs her footsteps: first Constantine and now Giles.' Alexi shuddered. 'I know how she feels.'

'I'm guessing that Martin will take it upon himself to look out for Jenny,' Jack said. 'She'll get through this.'

'So, what now? We ring Vickery presumably.'

'Shortly. I want to see if I can run Simon to ground first and get his confirmation on what we just heard.'

Alexi widened her eyes. 'You doubt Makin's account?'

Jack winked at her. 'You know me, darling. I never take anything at face value and always double check my facts. Don't forget that Makin got what he told us from a grieving father. Drakos needs closure, someone to blame other than himself.'

'He wasn't even there so how can he be culpable?'

'He overindulged his son and gave him easy access to a floating gin palace. A recipe for the disaster that occurred.'

'You're probably right. I hadn't stopped to look at it in that light.'

'Right.' Jack stood and Alexi followed suit. So too did Cosmo, who indulged in a feline stretch before trotting to the door. 'Let's see what Simon has to say for himself.'

They found the stags in the annex half-heartedly playing darts. The desire to put Hopgood Hall and its horrors behind them was palpable, as attested by the guys' lacklustre attempts to entertain themselves.

'Here come the resident sleuths,' Will said, slurring his words as he offered them a mock salute. Cosmo growled at him, making all the guys laugh when Will stepped hastily backwards.

'How's it going?' Jack asked easily.

'We're debating how best to get a refund on the wedding gifts,' someone said.

Jack knew it was gallows humour, their way of coping with what had happened to their friend, so he simply smiled. 'Got a minute, Simon?' he asked.

'Hey up! Watch out, mate,' Will said. 'They'll get the thumbscrews out.'

'Not allowed to do that any more,' Jack replied. 'Shame, it saved a hell of a lot of effort when it came to extracting confessions.'

'If I'm not back in ten minutes, someone bail me out,' Simon requested. 'What's up, guys,' he added when they stepped out onto the terrace, instinctively avoiding the area where Giles had been killed. 'I gather Crystabel's been arrested. Again. Case closed as far as I'm concerned. Soon as we're sober enough to drive, we're out of here. No offence,' he added, smiling at Alexi.

'None taken,' she replied.

Cosmo, Jack noticed, hadn't growled or hissed at Simon and had contented himself with taking advantage of the day's heat still lingering in the flagstones. He stretched out but only closed one eye, clearly waiting to see if his services as head of security would be required after all.

'We just had a visit from a guy called Makin,' Jack said.

'Ah, is he still sniffing around?'

'You didn't think to tell us about him?' Alexi asked, her tone mildly accusatory.

Simon lifted one shoulder. 'Didn't think it was relevant.'

Jack closed his eyes and threw his head back. 'Think about it,' he said through gritted teeth.

'You really imagine that Giles was killed to stop him speaking about what he saw?' Simon scratched his head. 'Blimey! I suppose she might have gone that far. Frankly, nothing about Crystabel's behaviour would surprise me. Number one is all she cares about. She's ruthless in her determination to become "famous" and being suspected of tipping a guy overboard because he'd rejected her would put a spanner in her ambitions; I can quite see that.'

'She made a play for him?' Alexi asked.

'Oh, I'm pretty sure they finished up in the sack together, but for Constantine, it was just another conquest. Crystabel read more into it than was actually there. Why would a young rich guy like Constantine settle for a woman who was engaged to someone else and yet dropped her knickers for him at the first opportunity?'

'And now Makin is here, stirring it up again. How do you think she would have reacted to that?' Jack asked.

'Look, I don't know what happened to Constantine, other than he fell overboard and drowned. He was a decent guy and I had no beef with him.'

'Even though Crystabel had latched onto him when she was engaged to you?' Alexi asked.

'Yeah, about that: in many respects, it did me a favour. I'd begun to have doubts about her even before she set her cap at a rich stranger. She was an outrageous flirt and I was starting to wonder if she drew the line at just flirting. Well, seeing her with Constantine well and truly opened my eyes to her manipulative ways and I would have broken the engagement, even if that holiday hadn't ended in disaster.'

'It was obvious to me that she'd like to get back with you, even though she was engaged to Giles,' Alexi said.

Simon waved the suggestion aside. 'She was wasting her time. Far as I was concerned, I'd had a lucky escape.'

'Those of you on that holiday don't talk about it and have tried to put it behind you,' Jack said. 'I don't blame you for that but I do wonder what it is that Crystabel thinks Giles overheard on that fateful night. It might well have been something damning enough to get him killed. Did you not talk about it at all in the immediate aftermath?'

'Giles mentioned it just once after we got out of that awful Greek police station. I really thought they were gonna throw us in cells and leave us there to rot. Anyway, Crystabel's father used his clout to get us released.'

'What did Giles say?' Alexi asked.

'Only that Crystabel had been on at Constantine to let her stay with him. The discussion got out of hand, she finished up yelling at him, he stepped backwards and toppled overboard. But Giles had seen her give him a push.' Simon spread his hands.

'That's pretty much how I imagined it must have gone down. Crystabel does not take rejection well.'

'Did he tell the authorities that?' Jack asked.

'Of course not. That would have meant him being held in Greece as well as her. Perhaps all of us would have been.' Simon shook his head to emphasise his point. 'He said that he hadn't heard what they were saying. He'd seen them together but claimed that the noise of the engines drowned out their voices. I'm guessing that Constantine's father didn't buy that, hence Makin.'

'And his suspicions would have been on high alert when he discovered that Crystabel had gotten her claws into Giles,' Alexi said. 'What I don't get though is why did your friend agree to marry her, given what he knew about her behaviour when she didn't get her own way?'

'Well, that's what we all wanted to know. But Giles... well, he was immature, easily led and at war with his father. He probably saw the glamorous lifestyle she had mapped out for them as a better way forward than dealing with temperamental racehorses and their even more temperamental owners.' Simon shrugged. 'The grass is always greener and I never stopped trying to impress upon him the fact that he was making a monumental mistake, just because his conscience was troubling him, but Giles didn't want to hear it.'

'I'm starting to see why you had no doubts about Crystabel's guilt,' Alexi said.

'Whereas I've not stopped wondering why you two seemed to think she might not have done it. Trust me, that woman won't let anything stand in the way of her ambitions.'

'Right.' Jack paused, watching Cosmo as he rolled onto his back and exposed his belly to the evening's light breeze. 'What did you tell Makin?' he asked.

'I stuck to the script. Well, it was no script. We were all asleep when it happened. The first day on Constantine's yacht was fun, I won't deny it, but you can have too much of a good thing and the rest of us had had enough after two days. It was Crystabel who wanted to overstay our welcome. Bear in mind that we didn't know the chap from Adam before we met him in a bar. We'd all had a few, he invited us on board and... well, the rest as they say is history. But yeah, we were all asleep. Only Giles witnessed the confrontation between Constantine and Crystabel and since he never told me the precise details, I couldn't tell Makin. It wouldn't have counted for anything even if I had given him my views because

Giles is no longer with us and can't speak for himself.'

'Yeah, I get that,' Jack said. 'In your situation, I'd have kept quiet too.'

'I have absolutely no desire to see the inside of Greek police station again,' Simon said, shuddering. The conversation had clearly sobered him up. His words had been slightly slurred at the start but were now crystal clear. 'And that, I assume, is what might happen if Makin can pick up any definitive proof about what really happened. The fact that all of us, other than Crystabel and Giles, were asleep seems to have little or no bearing on the case. That is why we've kept quiet all this time.'

'I assume you warned Giles that Makin was poking around,' Alexi said.

'I did but it didn't seem to faze him.'

Jack glanced at Alexi, who shook her head. She had run out of questions and so too had Jack.

'Well, thanks for being so candid,' Jack said, slapping Simon's shoulder. 'It can't have been easy, stirring it all up again.'

'Well, if it gives Vickery the motive he needs then it was worth it.'

'We'll let you get back to your darts,' Alexi said.

'Safe trip home if we don't see you again before you leave.'

'Yeah, later.' Simon gave them a casual wave over his shoulder as sauntered back to the annex.

'Vickery?' Alexi asked as they walked back to Cheryl's kitchen. 'We can't leave him in the dark over this.'

'Yeah, I guess.' Cosmo joined them and wrapped himself around their legs. Jack absently bent to scratch his ears. 'What do you make of it, big guy?' he asked.

Cosmo mewled, which Jack knew was his not-so-subtle way of asking for food. Alexi laughed. 'He can't think straight on an empty stomach,' she explained.

Cheryl and Drew were in the kitchen and Jack took a few minutes to update them on developments whilst Alexi fed Cosmo.

'There's no doubt then?' Drew shook his head. 'I've met some conniving females in my time but Crystabel is in a class of her own. She'd really kill the man she supposedly loved and intended to spend the rest of her life with rather than risk him incriminating her? It's like something out of a horror movie.'

'The only person that one loves is herself,' Cheryl said, rippling her shoulders indignantly.

'At least it will all be over and done with now,' Drew said. 'And hopefully bookings won't suffer too much.'

'I've been thinking about that,' Alexi said. 'Instead of attempting to play down the hotel's reputation as murder central, why don't we exploit it?'

'What do you mean?' Cheryl asked.

'Murder mystery weekends,' Alexi replied with a mischievous smile.

Drew guffawed. 'You have to hand it to the girl...'

'No!' Cheryl said at the same time. 'We couldn't.' She shared a look between them all. 'Could we?'

'Don't see why not,' Jack said cheerfully. 'I'll be the resident detective if you like. Nothing like the real thing to lend authenticity to roleplay. We should certainly give it some serious thought.'

'Come to Hopgood Hall, if you dare!' Drew said, making spooky gestures with his fingers.

'We still have the issue of the knife to contend with,' Jack reminded them all when the laughter died down. 'Vickery can take his pick when it comes to Crystabel's motive insofar as she found out about Jenny, and then Makin stirring up the past, but he's no nearer to putting that knife in her hand.'

'Does it matter, given that she now has a very strong motive?' Alexi asked. 'We've ruled out all the other potential perpetrators. It has to be her. Convictions are secured on circumstantial evidence, aren't they?'

'They are and Vickery has more than enough of it to press charges.'

'Then what's stopping him?' Cheryl asked.

'Give him time,' Jack replied. 'It's only been a day. But to answer your question, if I had to guess, I'd say that he's getting pressure from Crystabel's rather formidable father.'

'He doesn't strike me as the sort to give in to peer pressure,' Alexi said.

'You know how the world works.' Jack smiled at her. 'If Crystabel's father was a local plumber, then his views would probably be disregarded but if you're a bastion of the local community, a generous contributor to charitable causes, probably including the police benevolent fund. If you play golf with the chief constable...'

'Does he?' Alexi asked.

Jack chuckled. 'No idea, but it wouldn't surprise me.' He stared off into the distance. 'That knife bothers me and I'm betting it bothers Vickery too.

Ah well, I guess I'd better make his life a little easier.'

Jack extracted his phone from his pocket but before he could call Vickery, it rang.

'Martin,' he said, glancing at the display and then at Alexi. 'Hi,' he said, taking the call and putting it on speaker. 'What can I do for you?'

'It's more a case of what I can do for you. I checked our supply of farrier's knives. We have three, which live in the tack room. Currently there's only two there. No one thought much of it when I asked. These things have a habit of being left in the wrong place and then turning up again. I conducted a thorough search this morning but it hasn't come to light. I asked the barn managers about it. They tell me that two of the three knives were for right-handers, and they're accounted for, but the left-hander is missing.'

'Ah.' Jack should have felt relieved when this last piece of the puzzle fell into place. Instead, he felt uneasy, without any clear indication of why that should be. 'Crystabel must have helped herself when she came round that last time.'

'Not exactly.'

'What do you mean?' Alexi asked before Jack could.

'We have CCTV in the yard. I checked it for the day in question and... look, I'll email you the link.'

'Thanks,' Jack said, cutting the connection.

They waited in uneasy silence until Jack's phone pinged to indicate the arrival of an email. He hesitated before opening the link, conscious of his friends looking over his shoulder.

'Bloody hell!' Drew said for them all when a blurry figure came into the camera's line of vision. The person walked into the tack room, took a furtive look around, pocketed the knife that so bothered Jack, and as quickly disappeared again.

19

Alexi shared a shocked look with the others. 'Premeditation, or what?' she asked.

'Absolutely,' Jack agreed.

'Do we call Vickery or tackle her ourselves?'

'Oh, I think we play this by the book.'

This time, Jack succeeded in putting his call through. He gave Vickery an abbreviated account of Makin's role and went on to explain about the knife.

'Send me the link?'

'Already did.'

There was a long pause. 'Right. It's her. No question. Hold fire. I'm on my way. Don't let anyone leave before I get there and don't talk to her until I arrive.'

'We're crowding you,' Drew said eventually, after

they had talked round in circles for some time. 'We'll make ourselves scarce and leave you to sort this mess out.'

Vickery arrived soon after that, with Hogan in tow. 'We've sent two uniforms upstairs to bring Gloria down for questioning,' he said by way of introduction.

'Shouldn't you do that formally at the police station?' Alexi asked.

'We should but since you cracked the case, it seems only fair that you should hear her explanation.' Vickery took a seat and sniffed. 'This is just an initial interview, of course, and the others will be conducted formally under caution but hopefully, with all the evidence we have against her, she'll save us a lot of trouble and taxpayers' money by confessing. But of course, if she decides to lawyer up then we're screwed.'

Cosmo stirred himself, arched his back and hissed, as though enjoying the prospect of extracting a confession from the guilty party.

'Yeah, don't go anywhere, big guy,' Vickery said, laughing. 'Your services might be required.'

'What is the meaning of this?' Gloria's imperious voice rang out as the uniforms ushered her into the kitchen. 'Isn't it enough that you've taken my daughter into custody with no obvious reason? Now you've had constables drag me down the stairs in front of everyone as though I was a common criminal.'

'Your daughter assaulted her cousin. A situation which I'm told you've done your best to talk down,' Vickery replied calmly.

'Rubbish!' Gloria sniffed indignantly. 'I merely reminded the ungrateful child that family should come first; a fact that seemed to have slipped her memory when she made cow's eyes at *my* daughter's future husband.'

Alexi rolled her own eyes, thinking that Gloria sounded like a character from a historical novel.

'Sit down, madam.' Vickery spoke quietly but imbued his voice with sufficient authority to see Gloria comply, albeit with a theatrical flounce. Watching her closely, Alexi admired her performance but could detect a modicum of unease beneath the haughty façade. Cosmo prowled up to her, batted her leg with one paw and remained crouched at her feet.

'Aw, get that feral creature away from me!'

Alexi called Cosmo off. It would make the sort of headlines Gloria would revel in under different circumstances if her prosecution failed because she'd been intimidated by a cat. Cosmo jumped onto Alexi's lap, a vantage point from which he could glower at Gloria from across the table. It was clear that he'd already made up his mind about Gloria's guilt, reinforcing Alexi's belief in his extraordinary talents.

'Now, why am I here?' Gloria asked, still maintaining her bluff. 'Is there news?'

'What do you know about your daughter's involvement in the death of a Greek national during a Crete holiday?' Vickery asked.

The question was clearly unexpected and completely wrong-footed Gloria, or that was the impression she wished to create, Alexi thought. If they were right and she had killed Giles in order to protect Crystabel then it couldn't have come as a complete surprise.

'It was a tragic accident and ruled as such. My poor girl still has nightmares about it.' Gloria sat a little straighter. 'What has that got to do with anything? My daughter is guilty of nothing more sinister than bad luck. Drakos was drunk and drugged to the eyeballs, I'm told, and lost his balance. Someone with a grudge against Giles killed him in a petty act of revenge and my money's on Jenny. Of course Giles didn't intend to pass my daughter over in favour of her. The very idea is laughable but when he put her straight, her feelings were hurt and she acted on the spur of the moment.'

'Giles was killed with a farrier's knife,' Vickery said.

'Well, there you are then. Jenny has horses.' Gloria gave a self-satisfied little nod but her performance was shallow and Alexi could sense her underlying anxiety. Hardly surprising, since she had just complained about being hauled from her room by two uniformed constables as opposed to being politely asked to join the inspector downstairs for an update. 'What more proof do you need?'

'Before we get into that, do you require legal representation?'

'Me?' She pointed at her chest for emphasis. 'Good heavens, why ever would I need a solicitor? Am I being accused of something?'

'Yes, madam,' Vickery replied in an urbane tone. 'I will very soon be charging you with the murder of Giles Preston-Smythe.'

'Murder?' The colour drained from her face, her shoulders slumped and she physically deflated. 'First my daughter did it, now I'm the guilty party.' She rallied again. 'Really, Inspector, perhaps you should take a little more time to get your facts straight before you go around charging people with crimes they didn't commit.'

'We know it was you,' Jack said. 'What we don't know is why? What damage could Giles possibly have done if he'd spoken about the events in Greece? Then again, perhaps he told Crystabel that he intended to call the wedding off. Simon had already jilted her and you weren't willing to let history repeat itself, given that you are achieving your own thwarted ambitions vicariously through your daughter. You'd probably gotten wind of Giles's preference for Jenny several weeks ago. You don't leave anything to chance and were not going to allow an ungrateful upstart to spoil your plans. So, thinking ahead, you stole that farrier's knife when you visited Giles's father's training yard, assuming that if you were forced to use it then it would be traced back to someone with connections to horses.'

'A very neat way of exacting revenge on Jenny and preventing Giles from speaking out about Greece. That was something you couldn't depend upon him not doing,' Alexi said, 'because unlike your daughter, his conscience bothered him.'

'You really do have the most vivid imaginations, both of you.' Gloria smiled but the gesture appeared strained. 'A wonderful theory but I have yet to see a shred of proof.'

'You allowed your daughter to be arrested without speaking out,' Jack said, 'because you knew they wouldn't be able to connect the murder weapon to her and without that connection, no prosecution was likely to succeed.'

'Why would I put Crystabel through that if I could prove she wasn't guilty?'

'Because you were thinking ahead to the interviews and circuit of chat shows; the poor victim wrongly accused of killing the man she adored. It would have been a sure-fire way to establish Crystabel in the public eye, which has always been your ambition,' Alexi said, wrinkling her nose disdainfully.

'You knew that your husband had got Crystabel and her party out of Greece and whilst you were relieved, you were also furious that he had stepped back into her life and bailed her out of trouble without breaking a sweat.' Jack fixed the woman with a blistering glare. 'You had to go one better and saw the way to secure Crystabel's loyalties as well as her fame, albeit for questionable reasons.'

'Your proof,' Gloria said, tapping her fingers restlessly on the tabletop. But her casual pose was spoiled by the tic beneath one eye that she was unable to control.

'Look,' Vickery said, 'this has gone on for quite long enough. You have not been arrested yet, or read your rights, Mrs Hennessy. I would strongly advise you not to say anything self-incriminating and to consult with a solicitor. We can continue this discussion at the police station under formal conditions.'

'I don't need a solicitor,' she reiterated, lifting her chin disdainfully. 'And unless you can show me some proof to back up these ridiculous allegations then the only way you will get me inside a police station is in handcuffs.'

Jack glanced at Vickery. Alexi knew he'd taken a big chance in talking to Gloria so informally. It showed a great deal of respect for her and Jack, which was appreciated and reciprocated. He had also covered his bases by twice suggesting that Gloria engage legal representation. But now was crunch time. Gloria clearly hadn't known that Giles's father's yard was covered by CCTV. A city dweller would be accustomed to cameras at every turn. It hadn't occurred to her that villages rich with horse-flesh made equally tempting targets for the unscrupulous.

Wordlessly, Vickery produced his phone and showed Gloria the clip that Martin had sent to Jack.

'What's this?'

She snatched the phone from Vickery's hand. It seemed as though everyone in the room held their breath whilst Gloria absorbed what she watched. The colour that had returned to her cheekbones abruptly faded and a hand involuntarily covered her mouth when a gasp escaped.

'It could be anything,' she said carelessly. 'Or anyone.'

'Your bag gives you away,' Alexi said, pointing to the overlarge satchel that Gloria always carried with her. Right now, the handle was looped over the back of her chair. 'Your size, build, your hair. It's you.'

'It's fine if you don't want to admit it,' Vickery said, pocketing his phone again. 'The only thing preventing me from charging your daughter with first degree premeditated murder up until now was that knife. I had no plausible way of putting it in her hand but this clip provides me with the final link in the puzzle.' He paused, watching Gloria intently as she absorbed his words. 'Preston-Smythe's yard is missing one farrier's knife and you are seen in that clip handling one.'

'I was curious to see what it was.' The excuse

sounded lame and when Gloria's eyes darted from side to side, it was clear that even she realised it. 'Besides, there must be dozens of them in this godforsaken village where there are more horses than people. You can't prove the one used to kill Giles is the one I briefly looked at and then put back.' She shot Vickery a defiant look. 'Nor can you categorically say that I helped myself to it.'

Vickery's smile was reptilian. 'You're not aware then that farrier's knifes are for both right and left-handed users? The handles are adapted accordingly. The vast majority in this village are, I'm told, for righthanders, which makes sense given that about 90 per cent of the country's population are righthanded. It's unfortunate for you that you stole a knife for a lefthander and that one is missing from Preston-Smythe's yard.'

'And your daughter is lefthanded,' Alexi added quietly, watching as Gloria's posture again slumped and she leaned heavily against the back of her chair.

'So, your daughter will be formally charged with murder when I get back to the station and even your ex-husband's wealth won't get her out of this one,' Vickery said, going in for the kill. 'But not to worry, you will be able to visit her inside and plan her reinvention when she gets out in twenty or thirty years' time.'

The silence that ensued was loaded with tension but no one broke it, leaving Gloria to contemplate her options, which were limited. Alexi considered that any woman with an ounce of maternal instinct wouldn't hesitate to confess in order to protect her only child, especially if she herself was guilty of the crime that the child in question was being charged with. With Gloria, there was no way of knowing which way she'd jump.

'Very well,' she said, letting out a long, slow breath. 'I took the knife.'

'To be clear, are you confessing to the murder of Giles Preston-Smythe, madam?' Vickery asked.

'Yes, of course I am! Isn't that what you wanted? You ought to be pleased with yourself. Let's get this over with.'

'We should continue this conversation at the station, under caution, and once again I would suggest that you consult a solicitor before saying anything more.'

Hogan had been making copious notes and underlined something in her notebook: hopefully the fact that Vickery had just offered Gloria the opportunity to consult a solicitor for the third time.

'I might as well get it all off my chest now,' Gloria replied with an impatient flap of one hand. 'There's not much a solicitor can do for me and I'm guessing that if I tell you what happened, how badly I was provoked, then things will be better for me. I knew about Giles and Jenny but I hadn't told Crystabel. I simply assumed that Giles was having last minute jitters and was using her as a distraction.'

'How did you know?' Alexi asked.

'I called at her flat a few weeks ago. She shares with Claire. Jenny was on the phone and didn't hear me arrive. I heard snippets of her end of the conversation. Claire said she had a new boyfriend but was very secretive about him. She wouldn't reveal his identity, not even to Claire. Well, that got my attention. Claire went off to work but I stayed to have coffee with Jenny. When she went to her bedroom to get her bridesmaid's dress to show me a flaw in the fabric she left her phone on the table. I took a look, saw Giles's number and put two and two together.'

'You didn't ask her about it?'

'God no! I didn't see how Giles could seriously prefer her to Crystabel. I intended to have a quiet word with him before the ceremony but all the time he seemed happy to go ahead with the wedding I assumed I was right about him and didn't see any reason to rock the boat. By the time the stag weekend came around and he was still on board, I decided that he and Jenny must be history and that no further action was necessary.'

'But still you took that knife,' Vickery said. 'Why?'

Gloria shrugged. 'If you must know, I planned to teach Jenny a lesson.'

'How?' Vickery asked.

'I'm not sure.' She looked away evasively.

Alexi assumed that the deranged woman had planned to harm someone with the knife and then plant it amongst Jenny's possessions. Nothing would surprise her.

'Putting that aside for a moment,' Vickery said, presumably because she couldn't be charged with planning a crime that she hadn't carried out and anyway, murder trumped everything else, 'what made you kill Giles?'

'I hadn't planned to. Crystabel made an excuse to go downstairs late last night.' Gloria ran a hand through her tangled hair. 'Was it only last night? I knew she was going to meet her father.'

'You checked her phone too, I suppose,' Hogan said, abruptly closing her mouth again when Vickery glared at her. It was probably bad form to interrupt a suspect when they were confessing to murder.

'I knew they had been in touch even before she went to Greece. I didn't like it but pretended not to know. Crystabel wouldn't bring it out into the open and suggest we play happy families all the time she thought I was in the dark. Okay, so I was grateful that Luke got her and the others out of Greece but he'd done precious little else for his daughter all these years so I wasn't about to forgive and forget.'

Of course you weren't.

'But I was adamant that he and his tart wouldn't be at the wedding. So I slipped downstairs a bit after her, and saw Jenny and Giles emerge from that corridor. I could tell from the look on her face that he hadn't broken things off with her. Quite the reverse.' She shuddered. 'I saw red, I won't deny it. After all we'd done for that ungrateful boy! It defied belief. Anyway, I followed Giles onto the terrace to have it out with him. The stags were drunk as skunks and weren't paying attention. When I accused him of cheating on Crystabel, he simply laughed and said that ship had sailed. He'd never really loved Crystabel. He knew that now that he had actually fallen in love as opposed to being railroaded by a woman who only wanted to protect her interests.'

'She knew about Makin?' Vickery asked.

'Of course. Anyway, Giles's attitude made something snap inside of me. I recalled that knife, thought it would be connected to Jenny and well... you know the rest.'

Alexi nodded, thinking again of Gloria's oversized bag.

'I just didn't expect Crystabel to finish her conversation with her father so quickly and discover the body. In fact, I'd assumed that for once, Luke would be of use to her and would be able to say that they'd been together at the time of the killing. The bloody man couldn't even get that right.'

Vickery shared a grim look with Alexi and Jack and then stood up. Cosmo hissed at Gloria, then jumped from Alexi's lap and re-joined Toby in his basket. He seemed to realise that his services would not be required after all.

'Gloria Hennessy, I am arresting you on suspicion of the murder of Giles Preston-Smythe. You do not have to say anything...'

Alexi and Jack watched as a subdued Gloria was led from the room by the two uniformed constables stationed directly outside the door. All the stags were in the hallway to watch her being taken away.

'She really would have let Crystabel be charged

on the assumption that she wouldn't be prosecuted,' Alexi said, shaking her head. 'Talk about motherly love.'

'It's over, darling,' Jack said, taking her in his arms and kissing her.

'What happens now?' Alexi asked.

'Well, Hopgood Hall will be exonerated, which is what counts.'

'I wonder what Crystabel will do.'

'Oh, she will exploit the situation for all its worth, I would imagine. She will cosy up to her father and go online to tell the world all about how the mother she adored had spoiled her life.'

Alexi rolled her eyes. 'I have no difficulty in believing you,' she said. 'God, I'm exhausted!'

'Then I'll take you home and tomorrow, we'll devise a strategy to exploit the publicity.'

'Jack!'

'Sorry, darling, but it has to be done. Those murder mystery weekends are a really good idea,' he said, slipping an arm round her waist and leading her from the kitchen with Cosmo following faithfully behind.

She smiled up at him and nodded, feeling safe and secure with such a competent man at her side. 'You know,' she said, 'I think that perhaps they are.'

ACKNOWLEDGMENTS

As always, my grateful thanks to the wonderful Boldwood team and to my editor, Emily Ruston, in particular for creating order out of my chaotic scribbles.

ABOUT THE AUTHOR

E.V. Hunter has written a great many successful regency romances as Wendy Soliman and revenge thrillers as Evie Hunter. She is now redirecting her talents to produce cosy murder mysteries. For the past twenty years she has lived the life of a nomad, roaming the world on interesting forms of transport, but has now settled back in the UK.

Sign up to E.V. Hunter's mailing list here for news, competitions and updates on future books.

Follow E.V. Hunter on social media:

 twitter.com/wendyswriter

 facebook.com/wendy.soliman.author

bookbub.com/authors/wendy-soliman

ALSO BY E.V. HUNTER

The Hopgood Hall Murder Mysteries

A Date To Die For

A Contest To Kill For

A Marriage To Murder For

Revenge Thrillers

The Sting

The Trap

The Chase

The Scam

The Kill

The Alibi

Poison
& Pens

POISON & PENS IS THE HOME OF
COZY MYSTERIES SO POUR YOURSELF
A CUP OF TEA & GET SLEUTHING!

DISCOVER PAGE-TURNING NOVELS FROM
YOUR FAVOURITE AUTHORS &
MEET NEW FRIENDS

JOIN OUR
FACEBOOK GROUP

BIT.LYPOISONANDPENSFB

SIGN UP TO OUR
NEWSLETTER

BIT.LY/POISONANDPENSNEWS

Boldwod

Boldwood Books is an award-winning fiction publishing company seeking out the best stories from around the world.

Find out more at www.boldwoodbooks.com

Join our reader community for brilliant books, competitions and offers!

Follow us
@BoldwoodBooks
@TheBoldBookClub

Sign up to our weekly deals newsletter

https://bit.ly/BoldwoodBNewsletter

www.ingramcontent.com/pod-product-compliance
Lightning Source LLC
Chambersburg PA
CBHW010700100726
47900CB00010B/2746